PIRATE'S GOLD

Nations of North America
Circa 1937

1 Pacifica
2 Disputed Western Territories
3 Lakota Territory
4 People's Collective
5 Industrial States of America
6 Empire State
7 Maritime Provinces

8   Atlantic Coalition
9   Columbia
10 Outer Banks (Protectorate of Dixie)
11 Appalachian Territory
12 Confederation of Dixie
13 French Louisiana
14 Republic of Texas

15 Free Colorado
16 Amio
17 Navajo Nation
18 Utah
19 Nation of Hollywood

N

PIRATE'S GOLD

BOOK 1, WINGS OF FORTUNE

BY

STEPHEN KENSON

PIRATE'S GOLD

Published by FASA Corporation
1100 West Cermak - B305
Chicago, Illinois 60608

Series Editor: Donna Ippolito
Cover: Eddie Smith

Crimson Skies™ is a Trademark of Microsoft Corporation.
Crimson Skies Pirate's Gold™ is a Trademark of FASA Corp, used under license.

Printed in the United States of America.

Any book is a shared effort, and work in a setting like Crimson Skies™ even more so. I'd like to thank all the people who helped make this book possible: Morton Weisman, Donna Ippolito, and everyone at FASA Corporation for their trust and support; Eric Trautmann and Tim O'Brien at Microsoft for their information and quick answers to often difficult questions; Eddie Rickenbacker for his engaging memoirs; and my friends and family for keeping my feet on the ground while my head was up among the clouds. I couldn't have done it without you. Thanks!

To my parents, who first showed me how to fly, then let me.

BOOK 1

THE GREAT WAR

No closer fraternity exists in the world than that of the air-fighters in this great war.

— Capt. Edward Rickenbacker, 94th Pursuit Squadron, U.S. Air Service

CHAPTER

1

THE ACE'S DREAM

I've always been lucky, although you wouldn't necessarily know it to look at me. Take now, for instance: 15,000 feet off the ground in the seat of a baby Nieuport, Archie bursting shells all around me, German Pfalz buzzing around like someone stirred up a wasps' nest, machine guns tracing lines of fire through the air. But not a single bullet hole marring the canvas of my Nieuport, much less me.

Like I said: lucky.

A Pfalz roars past, guns chattering. I pull back on the stick hard, bringing up my machine's nose and climbing after him. I roll to the side and come up right behind the Hun pilot. He doesn't even see me. With a grin I get him in my sights and hit the trigger on the paired machine guns mounted on the nose of my machine.

They yammer out 650 rounds a minute, tracers lighting the way to the Pfalz's tail. Smoke pours out in a steady stream, and the Pfalz goes into a dive, the wind fanning the flames spreading across his tail. He's finished. I don't bother watching him go down, not when there are so many other tempting targets to deal with.

I climb up to 20,000, the ceiling of my little Nieuport, and look down, spotting another Pfalz some 4,000 feet below. I bank to the left and come down in a dive, putting the Hun directly in my sights. Machine guns roar and the tracers announce my attack, but too late. The Pfalz banks one way and then the other, trying to get away, but I stay on him, my rounds ripping through canvas and cracking framework, looking for a vital spot or the pilot himself.

I find it when some rounds reach the Pfalz's engine, which starts to smoke. The machine goes into a long, slow dive, trailing smoke like a flag of surrender. Making a close pass, I give the Hun pilot an ironic salute as he starts to drop, almost close enough to imagine he can hear me, even over the roar of the wind and the crackle of the flames spouting from his crippled engine.

"When you get to ground, tell 'em Nathan Zachary sent you!"

There's no reply, and I don't wait around for one, banking and climbing toward another Hun, less than a thousand feet above. He thinks having the high ground gives him an advantage, but he hasn't had to deal with the likes of me before. You'd think even German pilots would know enough to quit when they're losing so badly, but if they want to be beaten there's no one better to do it than …

"Nathan! Nathan Zachary! Mr. Zachary?"

***

The persistent shaking of my shoulder roused me from the end of what was turning out to be a very pleasant dream. I looked up, bleary-eyed, into a face considerably less pleasant.

"Mr. Zachary," the orderly said, "it's 0500, time for you to wake up for your patrol."

I muttered something barely coherent in acknowledgment and levered myself up out of bed. I wanted more than anything else to collapse back onto my thin mattress to finish up my dream of downing German planes, but it was time for me to take the opportunity to down a few for real. Glory waits for no man, even when it forces us awake at the crack of dawn.

In fairly short order I managed to force myself out of bed, splashed some cold water on my face, and then showered and dressed. I skipped breakfast. I don't like to eat before I go up. Even though I have a pretty calm stomach, some maneuvers are best performed on an empty one. I liked to think of eating as part of the reward for a job well done, and I looked forward to a hearty breakfast upon returning to the aerodrome. As Lt. Quentin Roosevelt from the 95th once put it, "There's no sense in using up perfectly good food until you know for sure you're coming back." A bit morbid, but sound advice.

Dawn's first light was crawling up over the horizon, seeming as reluctant as I was to start the day. As I crossed the grassy field to the hangar, I was feeling considerably more ready to face whatever awaited me on the German lines. I was very young in those days and eager to improve an already impressive reputation, if I do say so myself.

It was France, in May of 1917, in the aerodrome of Lafayette Escadrille. We were a unit of American pilots fighting under the command of the French in the early days after the United States entered the Great War—the first Americans to fly planes in wartime. How I miss the old squadron some days. How I miss the old United States, for that matter. Like I said, I was young back then, and somewhat idealistic. I believed in fighting for my country, even if my country had never really done anything for me.

I was born Rom, what most folks call a gypsy. My family probably once lived not too far from where our aerodrome was located, in the north of France near Toul, although we were originally from farther east in Europe. We're a traveling people. You only have to look at me for proof of that. I've traveled a long way, and my traveling days are far from over, God willing.

I'd left my tribe behind, feeling I never fully fit in with the gypsy life. I went off, looking for a place where I felt I really belonged. In those days I kept quiet about my real heritage. With my dark coloring and olive complexion I could easily pass for any of the various Mediterranean folk that were seeking opportunities in the New World. I was also a big lad for my age, which is how I managed to lie my way into the Army at the tender age of sixteen. A pilot with the Escadrille for only a little over a month, I'd already shot down three enemy machines. Two more would see me made an Ace, the youngest in American history.

I made my way into the hangar, returning the nods and hails of the mechanics—who had been up far longer than I—working on the machines. There I spotted the real Ace of the Lafayette Escadrille, Lieutenant Edward

Rickenbacker, my commanding officer, and the man I most admired in the world.

When I'd run away from my tribe I didn't know what I was going to do with my life. I had some vague notions about settling down and becoming wealthy, a respected man about town. I was tired of living on the fringes. I wanted to feel part of something bigger. But I was only a young gypsy boy with nothing to my name but the clothes on my back and all my worldly possessions in a small satchel. Not long after I set out on my own, I happened by a rally to stir up support for the war effort. The rumors were that the United States was going to declare war on Germany and the government was drumming up enthusiasm among the people.

The man speaking at the podium was none other than Eddie Rickenbacker. The son of European immigrants, he'd already made a name for himself as a racecar driver in the States. Now he was talking about how Europe needed American support, not just money and guns, but also soldiers to help protect France and Great Britain from German aggression. His motto was "The Three M's—Men, Money, and Munitions."

I stood and listened, enraptured by his speech, and for the first time felt a surge of patriotism. Here was this man, his own family newcomers to this nation, proclaiming his intention to fight for what every American was supposed to value. It was the first time I considered myself an American rather than an outsider, and I knew then and there what I wanted to do. I went straight away to the local recruiting office and signed up. Little did I know that my desire to be a pilot would ultimately see me serve with the man whose speech inspired me in the first place.

"Morning, Nathan," Rickenbacker said, an easy, genuine smile splitting his handsome face. "Fine day for hunting, wouldn't you say?"

I returned the smile in full measure. "Yes, sir," I said. "It certainly is." A number of the other pilots called Lt. Rickenbacker "Rick" or "Eddie." He certainly wasn't a stickler for protocol. In those days the Escadrille was far less military than it was among the rank-and-file soldiers. But I was honestly in awe of Rickenbacker and his impressive string of victories, so I couldn't think of calling him anything other than "sir." I suspect he found it amusing.

"We're just waiting for Peterson and Johnson, then we'll be on our way," the lieutenant replied casually, like we were embarking on a stroll around the field rather than an assigned patrol. I nodded and started changing into my flight suit while the mechanics did the final checks on our machines, making sure everything was ready. Each machine in the Escadrille had three mechanics assigned to it, to ensure it was always in top operating condition. There are just too many things that can go wrong when you're dealing with something as complicated as an aeroplane.

"Good morning, Rick," said David Peterson, late of Honesdale, Pennsylvania. Peterson was Lt. Rickenbacker's wingman this morning, only a few years older than I, with what folks call "corn-fed" good looks and an easy-going manner. I liked Peterson a great deal—everyone in the Squad did—even the somewhat distant Rickenbacker. The two exchanged pleasantries, and I acknowledged Peterson's wave as I climbed up onto my Nieuport to check things out. Then another voice rang out in the hangar.

"Gentlemen! I'm in the mood to bag me some Huns!"

Johnny Johnson made a strong contrast to the quiet modesty of Peterson and Rickenbacker. Johnson was a loud-mouthed braggart, considered himself God's gift to womankind, and was quite proud of his record as a flyer—overly proud, in my opinion. Johnson was a good pilot, to be sure, but he wasn't an Ace. In fact, he had only one confirmed victory to his credit. He would have us believe it was many times that, but circumstances had robbed him of his rightful accounting—enemy planes fell on the wrong side of no man's land or weren't counted by the French authorities.

I could handle Johnson's good-natured exaggeration of his abilities. It was practically a sport for aviators, then as now. The thing that put me off was that beneath his pleasant and joking exterior, I sensed a man who didn't really understand what it meant to be a soldier and didn't respect or honor the code we fought by. Johnson believed in winning at all costs, without acknowledging that some costs are simply too high.

I gave Johnson a nod as well and hopped down from my machine to gather with him and Peterson around Lt. Rickenbacker as he explained our morning's mission.

"We've been getting sporadic reports of Hun spotter planes crossing the lines," Rickenbacker said, "photographing sites on our side, probably earmarking them for possible attack. There's been more activity behind their lines, so keep a sharp watch up there. I don't want any surprises, understood?" At our acknowledging nods the lieutenant smiled and clapped Peterson and me on the shoulder.

"Then let's go hunting, shall we, gentlemen?"

***

In short order, we took off from the aerodrome and climbed to 16,000 feet. The sky was brightening quite well by the time we were off, although it remained bitterly cold, especially at the heights we were flying at. One of the other pilots called Rickenbacker an "Esquimo" for his ability to fly at such heights for hours without any concern for the temperature. I was too filled with excitement and anticipation to really notice the cold as we took our places in formation and headed for the German lines.

Our patrol that morning was to take us from Pont-à-Mousson in the east, near the Moselle River, to Saint-Mihiel in the west, following the German lines and keeping a sharp eye out for any signs of Hun aircraft. Our Nieuports were quick little machines, so we reached the river in no time at all, banked, and headed west along the lines.

The trenches far below snaked across terrain that was once rich farmland, now a no man's land of barbed wire and mine fields between the German trenches and those dug by the Allies, girded with machine gun nests. I certainly didn't envy the soldiers on duty in those trenches, either the Huns or our own boys. The trenches were one of the reasons the war dragged on; one side would fire artillery bombardments at the other, but the opposing soldiers would simply retreat into their bunkers. When the shelling stopped, the enemy emerged from their trenches to charge the lines, but their opposite numbers simply manned the machine guns, cutting down anyone trying to cross no man's land. It was a long, ongoing stalemate.

The United States hoped to break that stalemate, and our presence in France was a part of that effort. If we could do that, put swift end to the war and prove the value of the aeroplane in war as well as peacetime, so much the better.

My thoughts were interrupted by a dull thump that made my little machine shake like a bucking bronco, making me look toward 6 o'clock and my plane's tail. A cloud of dark smoke spread not a hundred yards behind me, a clear sign announcing Archie's presence. Several more thumps and puffs of smoke made that quite clear.

"Archie" was our nickname for the German anti-aircraft artillery. Batteries were set up all along the German lines, much like our own anti-aircraft guns. They fired heavy shells in an attempt to down enemy aircraft; it was mostly a symbolic gesture since Archie was notoriously inaccurate. Still, at that moment, with shells bursting around my machine, I was starting to reconsider that assessment.

None of the other pilots seemed disturbed by the barking shells. In fact, Lt. Rickenbacker waggled his wings a bit, as if taunting the Archie crew below. The Huns answered with several more shells, none of which came anywhere near their mark. Still, we didn't linger long enough to let the Huns get in too much target practice. No sense in helping the enemy improve their skills. In short order, we left Archie behind and continued along the lines.

We were about halfway, I estimated, not far from Seicheprey, when Lt. Rickenbacker waggled his wings again, as if saying, "Look there, fellows." I craned my neck to look past the fuselage of my Nieuport and down some 2,000 feet, where a German Albatross was flying sedately along, on a direct heading for our lines! It looked to be just over a mile away, well within striking distance. Rickenbacker must have agreed, because he began a slow climb to higher altitude and we began to follow, maintaining formation.

The Albatross was a two-seater machine, typically used for aerial reconnaissance missions, flying over the lines to photograph vital enemy sites and to hunt for places like our aerodrome, so the Huns could plan future attacks. The photographer/lookout also doubled as the rear gunner, operating a swivel-mounted machine gun, while the pilot controlled the machine's forward-mounted guns. Compared with the Nieuport, the Albatross was large and slow, but it had a higher ceiling. If we allowed it to get high enough, the Albatross would be beyond our reach but still able to fire down at us. Lieutenant Rickenbacker clearly intended to deny them any such opportunity.

We leveled off at 18,000 feet, closing on our unsuspecting prey. The Albatross grew larger below us. With a dip of his wing, Rickenbacker turned into a dive and plunged after the target, with Peterson following in close formation. I saw Johnson waggle his wings, trying to signal that he wanted to take the lead when we followed our senior officers. I shook mine in response, like an emphatic "fat chance!" There was no way I was going to allow Johnson to take the lead on this one.

Just as we prepared to make the dive ourselves and help finish off the Albatross, I caught a glimpse of something in the glare of the late-morning sun behind us. Turning to 7 o'clock, I saw four dark shapes silhouetted as they screamed down from the clouds high above. Hun Pfalz!

It was a trap!

CHAPTER

2

THE TRAP IS SPRUNG

There was no way for me to warn Rickenbacker or Peterson about the approaching enemy machines, but I waggled my wings desperately to signal Johnson of the approaching danger and then took evasive action as the Huns opened up on us with their machine guns.

Tracer rounds lit the air around me as I banked hard to the left with a Hun closing on my tail. I could feel and hear the buzz of the rounds as they passed close by, although they apparently caught nothing but canvas. I pushed hard on the stick, taking my Nieuport into a dive and getting the Pfalz to follow. As he did, I swerved from side to side, doing my best to stay out of his sights.

Like our Nieuports, the machine guns on the German Pfalz were fixed forward-firing, so the pilot had to line up the nose of his plane exactly on target in order to score a hit. I was making that as difficult as I possibly could while more tracer rounds whipped past in streaks of phosphorescent fire, unseen bullets that could seriously damage my machine, to say nothing of what they would do to me.

I dropped some 1500 feet in the dive, with the Pfalz close on my tail the whole way. Then I pulled back hard on the stick, putting my machine into a steep climb. The world flipped upside down, with the earth above me and the endless blue sky below. Moments later, I executed a barrel roll and loop, what our French comrades called a *retournement*, putting myself squarely behind the Pfalz.

"Now the tables have turned," I said with a smile as I lined up the German machine in my sights. At just under eighty yards away I mashed my thumb onto the firing stud. My machine guns responded with a chatter, bright tracers cutting through the air toward the tail of the Pfalz. The rounds knifed through the Hun's tail as he banked off to the right, and I followed as closely as I could.

The enemy pilot did his best to shake me, I have to admit. He swerved right and then left, but I cut another line of fire across his tail, scoring what looked to me like a solid hit. Then he pulled up into a *retournement* himself, but I was expecting the maneuver and followed him into the loop, spinning and flipping myself precisely back into the same place where we started and opening up my guns on him again.

This time I saw smoke spout from the tail of the Pfalz. One of the tracers must have ignited his fuel, because flames quickly followed and the German machine went into a *vrille*, a tailspin, losing altitude and spinning out of control as it plunged down toward the lines.

"When you get to the ground," I shouted with a grin, "tell 'em Nathan Zachary sent you!"

I spotted another of our planes, which I later found out was Johnson's, engaged in a dangerous aerial dance with another of the German machines. Johnson was trying to outflank him, get out of his enemy's sights and move into a position where he could bring his own guns to bear. But the German pilot was sticking to him like glue, matching every maneuver Johnson tried.

I swooped in from above. The Hun pilot was so focused on his prey he failed to notice my approach. That gave me the chance to get the Pfalz in my sights as I dived down toward it. I waited until the very last moment before squeezing the trigger, closing to a scant few hundred yards before sending a hail of bullets into the back and tail of the German machine. I was immediately rewarded by the sight of smoke pouring from the tail section and what looked like a part of the engine breaking away, as the Pfalz went into a steep dive.

A fifth! I thought with a grin that must have gone from ear to ear. I had done it! We were so close to the lines that my victory was sure to be recorded by French or British troops, or our own boys. That made five in all, which made me an Ace! The youngest Ace in American history!

My joyful celebration was cut short, however, when I banked to take stock of the dogfight. To my horror, I spotted one of our Nieuports to the right, fleeing with a Hun close on its tail, smoke pouring from its engine. At more than 200 yards away, I couldn't make out whose machine it was, but I quickly moved to assist him.

I climbed, gaining as much altitude as I could while scanning for other Hun machines that might spring out to attack. I didn't want to fall victim to the same strategy I'd used against the Pfalz that had been dogging Johnson. When I was almost 2,000 feet above the dogfight, I banked and dove down at the German Fokker dogging my comrade. As I closed in, the Hun seemed completely unaware of me, focused entirely on what he thought was a certain kill. His mistake. I figured the tactic I'd used so effectively before would work again. But it turned out I was the one a bit too eager for the kill.

When I had closed to only a few hundred yards, I opened up with my guns, glowing tracer rounds announcing my presence, but too late for the enemy pilot to do much about it. The rounds riddled the rear of the Fokker as I swooped in, and I banked sharply to fly past him, preparing for a tight turn, a *renversement*, to swing back and finish him off.

That was when I heard a loud groaning and tearing sound that made my heart sink and my stomach fall like it had just dropped to the ground without me. I looked to my left just in time to see most of the fabric from that wing tear off and flutter away in the wind. I was a fool! My successive dives had been too steep, and the rounds from the previous Pfalz's guns must have torn my wing fabric. The stress and the furious wind were too much for the strained fabric, and it gave way altogether. I was left with nothing on my left side but a skeleton of wooden slats covered in a few tattered scraps of cloth, and my Nieuport was listing dangerously.

I fought to keep my nose up as the Fokker passed through my sights. When it did, I got a better look at its markings and saw the black crosses, edged in red, and the black and crimson "K" along the fuselage. My God! The pilot of the Fokker was not just any Hun airman, but Heinrich Kisler, the infamous "Black Ace," one of the most feared German pilots in the sky. Kisler was often said to be second only to the infamous Manfred von Richthofen, the "Red Baron" himself, in victories against Allied pilots.

Kisler seemed to take notice of me then and waggled his wings as he started to bank toward the other damaged Nieuport, like he was dismissing me as any sort of concern. I aimed to prove him wrong.

I fired a long burst from my machine guns. Kisler sideslipped smoothly out of my line of fire, but I was still rewarded with a thin stream of smoke billowing from the Hun's tail. One of my tracer rounds must have ignited some of his fabric, and the wind was fanning the flames. Kisler began banking away from the fight. I looked around but could see no sign of the wounded Nieuport he was chasing. I had problems of my own to worry about.

I was beginning to lose altitude and list to the left. I fought the stick to keep my machine from slipping over into the tailspin it wanted. There was no way I was going to accept my rightful place as America's youngest Ace posthumously! Regretfully, I turned away from the dogfight. We were only a few miles from our side of the lines, so I thought I had a chance of making it back.

Pilots these days might wonder why I didn't simply abandon my machine. There are several reasons, not the least of which is my own stubbornness and unwillingness to admit that something as simple as a lost wing could stymie me. There was also the fact that the fight had taken us inside the German lines, and I had no wish to enjoy the Huns' hospitality for the remainder of the war. Finally, in those days we didn't have parachutes. I had to either set my machine down safely or learn how to fly without it. I decided the first option was more likely, although not by much.

Keeping the nose up, I maintained speed, trying to use my forward momentum to keep me in the air just a few precious minutes longer, just long enough to make it to our side of the lines and find a reasonable place to land this beast. I continued to lose altitude; the altimeter showed me at a little less than 5,000 feet as I approached the German lines and Archie decided to offer me a warm welcome, or possibly a fond farewell.

Fortunately, the German anti-aircraft fire maintained its reputation for inaccuracy. The bursting shells were little more than a fanfare for my departure from behind the German lines, and I like to think that some of the closer bursts provided that little extra lift that helped keep me in the air a few minutes longer.

I glided over the German lines and across the barren desolation of no man's land. I was going to make it! I briefly considered trying to set down in no man's land but quickly rejected the thought. Although the area was crushed flat by the conflict, it was also riddled with mines, barbed wire, and other hazards. Plus, if I could put some additional distance between the lines and myself before I was forced to set down, so much the better.

I passed over our own lines and trenches at just over 2,000 feet and dropping rapidly. I'd reached relative safety—now all I needed to do was to land without turning my machine into a fiery wreck, or myself into a bloody and broken mess in the process. At this point, I focused on the old pilot's maxim: "Any landing you can walk away from is a good landing."

I came in steep towards a fairly open French field, fighting the stick to keep the nose up and cutting the engine to glide the remaining distance like a wounded bird. The ground rushed up to greet me, and I slammed down the flaps to slow my descent as much as possible. The wheels of the Nieuport hit the ground with a thump, bounced, and hit again and again, before rolling rapidly over the bumpy ground. I threw my weight against my seatback, trying by sheer willpower to force the tail to the ground and keep my machine from flipping forward and tumbling tail-over-head. I rolled for some distance before slowing to a stop, a scant few yards from a stately old oak tree.

I climbed from my machine to examine the damage. The fabric of the left wing was a complete loss, of course, and I saw that my machine's tail and other wing had more than a few bullet holes in the fabric. But otherwise the little Nieuport was in decent shape, and the red, white, and blue logo of the Escadrille still showed proudly on the right wing, unmarred. I looked up into the clear sky, shading my eyes with one hand, but I saw no sign of my companions. They were likely miles away, having either finished off their opponents or returned to the aerodrome.

I smiled as I recalled the two Pfalz going down in flames and what it meant for me, but my smile faded when I thought about the smoke pouring from my fellow pilot's plane. I hoped he was well.

Just then a car made its way down the dirt road a short distance from the field, and a French officer climbed out to hail me and offer a ride back to the aerodrome. I returned his greeting in French—having picked up some of the language while on liberty—and accepted. On the way back, I told him the tale of our encounter with the Huns, particularly my close brush with Heinrich Kisler, and he was most impressed. He assured me he would arrange for some soldiers to look after my Nieuport and move it back to the aerodrome for repairs.

When we arrived back at the aerodrome near Toul, a number of airmen were gathered out on the field. I spotted Rickenbacker talking to a number of them, with Lt. Johnson close at hand, a sour look on his face. As I dashed up to them, several of the men turned and saw me, smiles splitting their faces as they cheered. Several ran forward and picked me bodily off the ground, hoisting me onto their shoulders as Doug Campbell called out, "Three cheers for the newest—and youngest—American Ace!"

The squad echoed Campbell's cries of "hip-hip-hooray!" over and over. Then I was lowered to the ground, where many of my squadron mates patted me on the back, shook my hand, and offered congratulations and envious praise for my achievement, all making me promise to tell the tale of my encounter with Heinrich Kisler later that night. Gradually, most filed away, promising a party in my honor.

As the crowd began to thin out, Lieutenant Rickenbacker approached me, a somber smile on his face. He offered me his hand, and I proudly shook the hand of the man who would be America's Ace of Aces.

"Well done, Nathan," he said. "You should be proud." A twinge of sadness seemed to touch his voice and color his congratulations. At my quizzical look, Rickenbacker's expression darkened a bit.

"What is it, sir?" I asked. He shook his head sadly.

"Peterson went down," he said simply. "He hasn't returned."

CHAPTER

3

HONORED HEROES

They found David Peterson's body later that day. Apparently he'd managed to keep his burning plane aloft long enough to reach the Allied lines, much as I had done. But his plane was far worse off, and his landing considerably less graceful than mine had been. His plane flipped over and crashed, trapping Peterson inside the burning wreckage. It was a terrible way to die, and after coming so close to reaching safety. It could have been my fate, if I'd been just a bit less lucky. I imagined it over and over again and shuddered at the thought.

The body was brought back to our aerodrome, placed in a casket draped with Old Glory, and set in our small chapel where the men could pay their respects to their fallen comrade. It wasn't the first time one of the Escadrille Lafayette had been lost in combat, nor would Peterson be the last American pilot lost in the war. But it was the first time since my assignment to the Escadrille, and I swore standing before David Peterson's casket that it would be the last American life lost to the likes of Heinrich Kisler.

Peterson's death cast a pall over the festivities that followed that evening. The entire squadron gathered in the mess hall to hear me tell the story of our patrol, the ambush, my encounter with Kisler, and my narrow escape and flight back to our lines. Although I told the tale to the best of my ability, and received the applause and cheers of my comrades for it, my victory felt hollow because of Peterson's absence.

But his death didn't seem to affect anyone else's mood. Even Lt. Rickenbacker was cheerful and full of praise for my actions. And to hear Johnny Johnson talk, he was responsible for chasing off Kisler and striking fear into the hearts of Huns everywhere, despite the fact that he hadn't downed a single plane—or fired a significant shot, so far as I know—in the entire fight. The whole thing seemed somehow disrespectful. Johnson tried to make it clear on several occasions that he believed the second Pfalz I'd downed was actually his kill. I dismissed his claims and Rickenbacker backed me, so Johnson quickly backed down.

Eventually, I tired of the festivities. As soon as I could, I begged off, making vague excuses about combat fatigue and the like, and slipped away from the party.

I made my way out into the cool spring night. The sky overhead was wonderfully clear, filled with hundreds of bright stars. My hands deep in the pockets of my leather flight jacket, I wandered across the grounds of the aerodrome, my steps carrying me almost unaware toward the small chapel. It was little more than a temporary building, like most of the aerodrome; it hardly seemed a fit place to hold the body of an American hero.

A single light burned inside, casting a pale golden glow over the wooden casket with its red, white, and blue bunting and small bouquets of spring flowers. I stood and stared at it for I don't know how long before I felt a gentle touch on my shoulder.

I spun around to see the somber face of Lieutenant Rickenbacker looking back at me. I relaxed when I realized it was him and not Peterson's ghost, come to rebuke me for my failure that morning. The lieutenant smiled tightly and lifted his chin toward the silent casket.

"Hardly seems fair, does it?" he said. I just nodded in agreement, so he continued. "Although we do our best, learn all the tricks, sometimes Fortune takes a hand and we never know what she will decide. Will it be life or death? Will a crippled plane make it back to the lines or crash and burn?" His eyes left the casket to meet mine.

"Whatever Fortune decides," he said. "She does so without consulting us. There is nothing you could have done to save him, Zachary." I began to shake my head, a protest forming on my lips, and Rickenbacker put a hand on my shoulder.

"Nothing," he repeated firmly. "You did your best, and that is all anyone can ask of you. The harsh truth of the matter is, Nathan Zachary, that this is war, and in war men die. I learned that truth myself some time ago."

He lapsed into silence for a moment, looking at the coffin as I thought about its contents—only the mortal clay of a brave man. It held nothing of his courage, his spirit.

"I know that you and some of the men consider me distant," Rickenbacker said, "perhaps even a bit cold. There is a reason for that, Zachary. I've seen too many men I called friends lowered into an early grave. I've learned not to grow too close to those I serve with. If you do, then the pain of their passing can cripple you, blind you with anger. It will pass and, in time, you'll learn not to attach too much feeling to comrades who may not see the next day with you."

I didn't take my eyes off the casket. I couldn't believe what he was telling me.

"I don't want to learn anything like that," I said. "I want justice. I want to make Kisler pay." I turned to look my superior officer in the eye. "I want to volunteer for additional patrol duty, sir. I …"

"I don't think so, Zachary," Rickenbacker said, shaking his head. "You need some time, and we don't need any pilots going off half-cocked, looking to make martyrs of themselves."

"But, sir, I …"

"That is an order, Mr. Zachary," he said in a firm tone, his eyes narrowing dangerously. I realized whom I was arguing with, and all the fervor seemed to drain away, deflating me like a busted balloon.

"Yes, sir," I mumbled.

Rickenbacker sighed, patting me on the shoulder. "God willing, Heinrich

Kisler will pay for what he has done, but if you want justice for David Peterson, Zachary, then don't throw your own life away. That is the only justice we can ask for." Then he walked away, his steps echoing in the silence of the chapel, leaving me alone with my thoughts.

Sometime later, I found my way into the hangar where our machines rested, dark and silent. It was quite late and even the mechanics weren't around. I made my way over to my Nieuport, looking over the skeletal wing where the canvas had been torn away. If only I had thought about the dangers of such a steep dive, if only the fabric had held out, I might have been able to engage Kisler longer. I might have been able to do more.

"That was some pretty impressive flying, kid." The voice made me turn to see Johnny Johnson, leaning against the wing of his own Nieuport, picking his teeth with a wooden toothpick that he then flicked to the floor. He fished a cigarette from his coat pocket and struck a match, the glow casting his face into planes of light and dark as he lit up and took a long drag before blowing out a cloud of smoke.

"Want one?" he asked. I shook my head. I wasn't in the mood for a smoke, or for Johnson, for that matter. He merely shrugged.

"Yeah, pretty impressive flying," he drawled.

"Not impressive enough," I said.

"You want to get Kisler, don't you?" Johnson said. I looked up at him. His face was calm and composed, almost unreadable, but there was a certain eagerness there.

"Yes. I want him. I want him to pay."

"And you want to be the one who brings down the Black Ace of Germany, right?"

I shook my head. "I don't care about that. This isn't about getting the glory, it's about justice."

Johnson smiled sardonically. "Whatever you say."

"It doesn't matter," I said. "Rickenbacker isn't going to let me fly for a while. I'm grounded."

"So? If you really want this guy, there are ways ..."

"Like?"

"Well, I'm sure the lieutenant won't object to you honoring Peterson's memory, and that gives you a shot at Kisler, as long as you're willing to give me my fair shot at the Black Ace this time, 'kay?"

I looked Johnson in the eye for a long moment. I could tell he wasn't interested in justice or vengeance, just in the glory of bringing down a famous German Ace. But did it really matter what he wanted?

"All right," I said. "I'm listening."

***

David Peterson's funeral was held the following day, which dawned as bright and clear as anyone could ask for. The ceremony was to be held later in the morning, with all the pomp and honors due a respected American airman who gave his life for his country and the lives of others. According to Rickenbacker, I was to be awarded a medal by the French government for valor and courage in combat, and honored as America's newest and youngest Flying Ace. That hardly mattered to me, so long as Johnson's plan gave me the opportunity I craved more than anything else: another shot at Heinrich Kisler.

As part of the funeral ceremonies, befitting one of our own, two pilots from the Escadrille were scheduled to fly maneuvers overhead. It wasn't difficult to get Johnson and me assigned to the duty, since we were flying with Peterson when he went down. In fact, I suspected Lieutenant Rickenbacker would have offered it to us regardless.

So, while everyone else in the squad turned out in their dress uniforms and gathered on the field near the small cemetery plot outside the aerodrome, Johnson and I went to the hangar and put on our flight suits as the mechanics got our planes ready. My own Nieuport wasn't repaired yet, of course, so I accepted Lt. Rickenbacker's offer to use his machine, with a twinge of guilt about what I was planning.

Once we had suited up and the mechanics had finished their final checks, we climbed in and took the bundles they handed up to us. Then I checked everything, making sure the machine guns were fully loaded, even though we were only expected to fire a ceremonial salute. A mechanic spun the propeller as I opened up the engine.

"Contact!" I called, and he replied with the same. The engine caught, and the propeller roared to life. I gave the mechanics the thumbs-up, and they scurried to pull away the blocks in front of my machine's wheels, allowing it to roll forward. I guided the Nieuport out of the hangar on to the field, with Johnson not far behind me. Picking up speed, we were soon airborne, rising up above the aerodrome and circling back toward the cemetery field off to the east.

We made several circles around the aerodrome, slowly gaining altitude, although we didn't rise much higher than a few hundred feet, low enough so the men gathered on the ground could see us clearly. I could make out Lt. Rickenbacker and other officers gathered at the front of the squadron as the chaplain concluded the funeral service.

Johnson and I banked, rolled, and performed a display of aerobatics over the aerodrome. There was no applause, only the silent, somber regard of our fellow airmen. We rose up and fired a brief salute, tracer rounds sending streaks of fire toward heaven. Then we dived down toward the mourners and the casket itself, draped with the American flag and piled all around with flowers sent to honor the deceased. I thought about Peterson's family back in Pennsylvania and how they would take the news of their son's death.

Our planes passed mere tens of feet above the heads of the gathered squadron. As I flew over the grave, I tossed out my precious cargo, and a shower of spring blossoms fell over the casket. Goodbye, Peterson, I thought. Au revoir, Escadrille. I pulled up out of the swoop and started to climb again. At the top of the loop, I did a reversement, rolled over, and righted my plane at 2,000 feet. Then I headed out over the aerodrome.

Instead of banking and circling in for a landing, however, Johnson and I flew out over the aerodrome and kept climbing, headed for an altitude of 15,000 feet, which would carry us to the German lines to look for our prey. I could imagine the stunned looks of our squadron mates as they watched our machines begin to recede into the distance. Even if they should decide to pursue us, they could not get to their planes quickly enough. By the time they realized what was happening, we would already be miles away.

The aerodrome quickly fell away behind us, and I turned away from it, focusing on what lay ahead. Somewhere, out along the German lines, I was certain Heinrich Kisler, the Black Ace himself, would be out hunting fresh prey, flush from his recent victory. What Kisler did not know was that he was about to become the hunted.

CHAPTER

FLIGHT OF VENGEANCE

At an altitude of just over 15,000 feet, we made our way toward the German lines. Johnson had said the previous night that he thought we should start our search for Kisler near the area where we first encountered him, where the Huns had laid the trap that cost David Peterson his life. I disagreed, however. Kisler was as cunning as a fox, and he certainly wouldn't lay the same trap in the same place twice. No, it was more likely Kisler would try something else. Perhaps he would be emboldened enough to make some kind of sortie across the lines into our territory. If so, he was likely to do so in the morning, giving us a chance to beat him to the punch.

We began by setting a course to the Moselle River and Pont-à-Mousson, as we did before. We could cover the entire patrol route several times before lack of fuel would force us to return to the aerodrome to face whatever punishment our superiors would hand down for our insubordination. I doubted we would be drummed out of the Escadrille altogether, since capable pilots were hardly a dime a dozen, but at the least we would be severely disciplined for our violation of Lt. Rickenbacker's orders and military protocols. I suspected that Johnson thought a spectacular victory would wipe away any wrongdoing in the eyes of our superiors. Personally, I didn't care. I would willingly accept whatever punishment was coming to me, so long as I got my chance at Kisler.

When we reached Pont-à-Mousson and banked around to head along the lines, Archie greeted us with a welcoming volley of shells. Naturally, none of them came within more than fifty yards of our planes, and Johnson and I took a few moments to wheel and roll over the area where the German guns were placed, showing our contempt. More shells burst around us, but they got no closer than the first. I quickly tired of playing with them and turned to head down the lines. Johnson followed shortly behind me.

I opened up my throttle and moved at a brisk pace over no man's land, keeping a close eye on the sky on both sides of the line, searching for any signs of enemy aircraft, particularly Kisler's distinctively marked Fokker. As the miles passed beneath us, my heart began to sink as I realized the enormity of what we were attempting. There were hundreds of miles of territory to cover, and no certainty that Kisler was even flying this morning. Locating the Black Ace would be like looking for a needle in a very large haystack. Still, I was committed, and I certainly wasn't going to turn back until I had my chance.

We went all the way along the lines to Saint-Mihiel with no sign of any enemy aircraft—or any friendly aircraft sent to find us for that matter. Banking around, we set course back the way we had come. Although we encountered some Archie batteries along the way, including revisiting our friends near Pont-à-Mousson, there remained no sign of the Huns in the air—not an Albatross, a Pfalz, or particularly the distinctive Fokker I sought.

On our way back west again, I decided we should make ourselves a more tempting target for any Hun airmen who might be reluctant to put in an appearance. So I veered farther to the north and east, putting myself behind the German lines, flying in boldly and daring them to do something about it. Johnson followed me with only a moment's hesitation, and we continued on our way, certain an alert would go out to the nearest German aerodrome about our invasion and provoke a response.

We didn't have long to wait; only minutes later I spotted a pair of black dots in the distance. I dipped one wing to get Johnson's attention, and he signaled back. He'd seen them as well. I pulled back on the stick, and my Nieuport began to climb. I wanted to gain as much altitude as possible as we approached the enemy planes. Johnson followed me up to our ceiling of 20,000 feet, as high as the engines of our little machines could carry us.

It wasn't long before we could make out the profiles of the approaching planes. There was a Pfalz single-seater and ... yes! A Fokker! My heart leapt at the sight of it, and I was certain we'd found our quarry. I opened up my throttle and zeroed in on the pair of planes, now less than a mile away and some 3,000 feet below us. With a waggle of my wings, I indicated to Johnson to let me take the point. I thought he was going to ignore me for a moment, but then he fell back a bit and allowed me to take the lead.

I turned and focused my attention on the Fokker. I was still too far away to make out its markings, but something, some intuition, told me it was Kisler's machine. Perhaps it was a gypsy's gift of sight. I estimated the distance between us, carefully maneuvering to place my Nieuport between the Fokker and the morning sun.

Looking at my prey below, I thought, When you get to the ground, *Herr* Kisler, be sure to tell them Nathan Zachary sent you! Then I pushed the stick forward and put my plane into a dive, streaking down out of the sun like a hawk swooping onto its prey. I made sure not to make my dive so steep this time. Fortune and a torn wing would not rob me of my chance again.

The distance between us closed—a thousand yards, eight hundred, five hundred. I was vaguely aware of Johnson soaring down to attack the Fokker's wingman, but my attention remained focused on my target, my thumbs resting tense on the firing studs of my machine guns. Four hundred yards. I waited until the last possible moment, so as not to alert my prey until I had him solidly in my sights. At three hundred yards I hit the triggers, paired machine guns chattering and spitting fire in front of me.

Then the Fokker went into a *vrille*, a roll and a spinning dive. For a moment I thought I'd scored a hit, sending it out of control, but then I realized the *vrille* had begun the moment I'd fired my guns. It was too quick for a bullet to have struck; they had seen us! I saw the Pfalz likewise turn into a dive as Johnson's Nieuport rushed toward it. They were on to us.

I immediately scanned the skies for any signs of other planes. It could be another trap. But the sky was clear for miles around, with no signs of other aircraft, or even any clouds they might conceal themselves in. I spun to look for my opponent and found him gone. Without even looking into my 6 o'clock, I swerved my plane to the left. A maneuver that surely saved my life, as lit tracers buzzed through the space just to my right, rounds tearing small holes in the fabric of my right wings but doing no other damage I could see.

The Fokker was right behind me. His dive had carried him directly below, followed by a climb and a *retournement* to put him on my tail. His guns chattered again, bullets hailing around me as I swerved madly from side to side, trying to stay out of his sights and protect the vital areas of my machine. I pulled back on the stick and started to climb, trying to gain altitude and perhaps reverse our positions.

But the Fokker stayed with me as I looped up and hit the right pedal hard, barrel rolled, and swooped back down upright again. He matched my maneuvers perfectly, like an image in a mirror, staying on my tail a scant hundred yards away. I wished more than anything right then that my little Nieuport was a two-seater with a gunner who could fire into my six, giving me something I could use to shake my pursuer. But I had only the front-mounted machine guns, which were useless unless I could get the Fokker in front of me.

Pushing the stick forward, I dropped down and closed the throttle, slowing and hoping my pursuer would overtake me. When he slowed in response, staying close behind, I opened up the throttle and executed another *retournement*, climbing up sharply until I could see the Fokker over my head. Then I kicked the pedals, rolled over, and dropped down behind him, guns blazing.

But I wasn't fast enough. Although my sudden maneuver had caught my opponent off guard, he recovered quickly and slipped out of my sights, putting on the speed to pull away from me. I was surprised. Was he running? In the moment when the Fokker began to pull away, it dipped its wing, and I could make out the distinctive markings: the black crosses edged in red and the black and crimson "K". It was Kisler, and there was no way I was going to let him escape.

I opened up the throttle to pursue, with Kisler some four hundred yards ahead and gaining speed. As I did, the Black Ace suddenly did a barrel roll, flipping over so his machine's belly faced the sky. Then he climbed sharply, flicked his tail into the air and dove down, coming straight at me. He had not attempted to flee at all. Instead, he had lured me into chasing him so he could turn the tables once more!

The Fokker was nearly forty degrees above me. I pulled back on the stick, trying to bring my own guns up to bear on him, as Kisler's twinned machine guns opened up on me. The angle most likely saved my life, as the high-caliber rounds smashed into the front of my plane, missing my seat by mere inches. They didn't miss the Nieuport's engine, however, which sputtered and died under the hail of gunfire. Smoke began pouring from the front of the plane, and the propeller spun to a stop as I began to list into a tailspin.

As I fought the stick to keep the Nieuport steady, the Fokker passed by, almost close enough for me to reach out and grab hold of it. I caught a brief glimpse of the pilot, hidden behind his leather helmet and goggles. He offered me a salute with one gloved hand as my machine—held once more in the relentless grip of gravity—began to drop from the sky. Then the German plane banked, and the Black Ace gave no further thought to me.

I struggled with joystick and pedals, doing my level best to keep the nose of my plane up and straight, trying to turn my fall into a glide that would allow me to reach the ground safely. Flames began to crackle from the engine, fanned by a wind that howled past at nearly 14,000 feet, and dropping rapidly. I'd heard of cases where the wind would sometimes blow out the flames from a burning engine or fuselage, but it was just as likely they'd reach a fuel line and turn my machine into an inferno, like a meteor dropping from the sky.

The countryside far below was a patchwork of wooded hills and farm-land. I realized I had no idea where I was, only that I must have pursued Kisler well inside the German lines. My chances of making it back to our side of the line were nil. It was all I could do to try and find a place to land.

I picked out a likely looking field that seemed untouched by the bombing runs and trenches. It was large and flat enough that I could have landed on it easily were my plane functioning. As it was, I aimed the Nieuport at the field with careful maneuvering and sheer willpower.

The steep glide rattled the wings and rustled the hole-ridden fabric. I feared a repeat of my earlier performance; if I lost canvas now, there was no hope for me. As it was, the heat from the flames now spouting from my engine was becoming difficult to bear. Sweat poured off me, despite the chill air, and I focused on my goal, working the pedals and holding on to the stick with both hands.

The ground rushed up to meet me, and suddenly the clearing filled my entire field of vision. I was coming in too steep! I fought back on the stick and slammed down the flaps to slow my descent as I braced myself against my seat. The Nieuport hit the ground with a lurch, bounced once, and then came down hard. I heard a snap as my landing gear crumpled and felt an echoing snap in my leg as I cried out in pain and the machine slammed forward. The nose hit the ground with considerable force, flipping the plane tail over propeller. I threw up my arms to protect my head as the ground rushed at me. With a crash, the plane came to rest in a crumpled mass.

I hung suspended upside down from my seat for a moment, stunned by the impact. Then I realized I was still alive and began choking and coughing from the thick smoke spilling from the engine. The plane was in ruins; it was only a matter of moments before the flames ignited my remaining fuel. I released my harness and slipped out of my seat, dropping down onto my shoulder with a wrenching thud. Then I crawled through the mud to get out from under the wreckage.

A burning pain in my ankle caught my attention as I hauled myself across the ground. Once I was out and a few yards from the remains of my plane, I tentatively tried putting some weight on it, only to feel the burning sensation transform into flames shooting up my leg. It would not support me. It was likely that I'd broken it when the Nieuport hit the ground.

I hunted around and found a stout branch that would serve as a crutch. With it I was able to lever myself up and hobble away from the wreckage, now burning fiercely like a Roman candle. The flames would be a beacon for the Huns, should they decide to come and see whether the crash had killed me. There was no way I could get far on foot with a broken ankle, so I needed a place to hide. There was a barn at the other end of the field, and I made my way toward it.

It seemed like the barn was a hundred miles away. By the time I reached it, I was exhausted and drenched in sweat. I pushed open the door, hearing the excited braying and clucking of the animals within, and hobbled inside. I briefly considered trying to climb into the hayloft but quickly dismissed the idea. Instead I made my way to an empty stall in the back—recently cleaned, thank God—and hunkered down, covering myself with a horse blanket that smelled of age and long use. I started to examine my ankle but trying to remove my boot was so painful I nearly passed out. I leaned my head back against the wooden wall behind me and tried to catch my breath.

I must have blacked out, because the next thing I became aware of was a hand roughly slapping my face. I came awake in an instant and instinctively tried to stand. I instantly regretted it as my injured ankle sent burning pain lancing up my leg, nearly bringing tears to my eyes.

I looked up to see a knot of German soldiers at the end of the stall, with one fellow standing over me, a grim look on his face and a pistol leveled not three feet from my head. He barked something in a commanding tone in German and waved the gun at me.

I looked up at him and slowly raised my arms, hands open and palms out.

"No need to translate that for me, Hans," I said. "I take it I'm under arrest."

And so it was, at the age of 16—the youngest Ace in American history—I became a prisoner of war.

CHAPTER

5

ANGEL OF MERCY

The soldiers bundled me into an open truck; two Huns rode in back with me while the other two climbed into the cab and started up the engine. Soon enough, we were trundling along the rutted dirt roads, every bump and pothole sending shocks of pain through my leg.

The soldiers riding in the back of the truck with me—along with a few barrels, crates, and assorted other items—were hardly older than I was, but they kept a wary eye on me as I huddled in the back and did my best to prop up my injured ankle. My ankle was swelling so much, I was fairly certain they'd have to cut my boot to get it off, but I'd be damned if I was going to ask them for any help—not that I spoke enough German in any case.

The idea of escape certainly passed through my mind, but it kept on going with hardly a moment's pause. Even if my hosts weren't holding rifles trained loosely on me at all times, even if I could manage to overpower them and bring the truck to a halt, I could only hobble away. I certainly couldn't drive. No, for the time being, I was a prisoner—but only for the time being, I promised myself.

The Huns in back exchanged few words, and I could only understand about half of that. I took to keeping an eye on the surrounding countryside, trying to figure out where exactly I was and where they might be taking me. I was certain we were still in France, at best only a matter of ten to fifteen miles from the lines. From the position of the sun we were heading west, deeper into German-held territory. That certainly came as no surprise.

A particularly nasty bump made me gasp in pain. I bit my lip to stop myself from crying out further as my two German friends jumped at my sudden exclamation, weapons at the ready. I closed my eyes and clenched my fists. I didn't want them to know just how badly injured I was, didn't want to show any sign of weakness—an impulse reinforced a thousand times over by my gypsy background.

When I opened my eyes again, one of the soldiers was crouched down right in front of me. He'd left his rifle back near his companion, and he looked up at me and repeated something in German. I shook my head, gritting my teeth at the lances of pain shooting up my leg. The soldier said something in what I took to be a soothing tone and placed his hands on my ankle.

Despite my best efforts, I cried out. The pain was so intense it brought tears to my eyes. I could taste blood in my mouth where my teeth had cut my lip. The soldier said something to his companion, who moved closer. I didn't even try to follow their conversation as the pain started to recede, drawing me down into a blissful unconsciousness. I lay back against the shuddering rails of the truck and allowed darkness to claim me.

***

When I was a boy, living in the Southwest, other children often used to tease me because I was Rom. They said I was a thief and a liar, even though they didn't know anything about me. I remember it used to make me very angry, and I once got into a fight with three older boys—all of them much bigger and stronger than I was—because they said I was a filthy sneak thief. I actually did quite well for a while, but naturally they overpowered me and beat me rather soundly.

Later at our camp, my mother treated my hurts, dabbing at them with a cloth warmed with a poultice of fragrant herbs and shaking her head sadly. I asked her if what the other children said was true, that it was bad to be a gypsy.

She looked very sad for a moment then she took my hand gently in hers.

"No," she said, "it is not true. They are *gaje*—they are not of the people, and they do not understand." She gently lifted my chin so I would look into her dark eyes. "Do you think I am bad?"

I shook my head. "No, Mama," I said and she smiled. "Well I do not think you are either, my brave one. You are special, and *gaje* don't always understand special people. They want everyone to be like them. But you're not, and you should be happy for that, and proud, as I am proud of you."

Her strong, gentle finger brushed the dark hair from my forehead, and I could almost hear her voice. "Are you all right?" I felt a cooling touch again, followed by an accented voice. "Can you hear me?"

My eyes fluttered open and tried to focus in the cold light. A pale face hovered nearby. As it finally came into focus, a whisper escaped from my lips. "Beautiful ... "

For she was. Curling hair the color of gold framed a heart-shaped face with full lips that curled up naturally into a smile and high cheekbones flushed pleasantly with color. Deep blue eyes flicked down and then back up to regard me through long, lowered lashes. A silvery laugh escaped those lips.

"Well," she said, "it's nice to see you've returned to us, *Herr* Pilot."

German. The sound of her accent brought reality crashing back as I tried to sit bolt upright and instantly regretted it. My head swam, and it felt like someone was trying to pound a rail spike into my skull.

"*Nein, nein*, slowly!" the vision at my bedside said. "Slowly." She eased me back onto the pillows and I raised one hand to lightly touch the bandage covering my head.

"Where ... ? Who ... ?" I managed.

"You are safe, and being well cared for," the girl said, for she was not much older than I was, if at all. "You are in Castle Eisen, and I am Hanna. Hanna Ullen."

I'd heard of Castle Eisen. It was in Germany, an old fortress that dated back hundreds of years. It had been converted, like many old castles, into a military base for the army-in this case, a prison camp. The reality of the situation came upon me; I was a prisoner of war, deep in enemy territory.

I tried to sit up again, this time more slowly and carefully, and managed it with a minimum of pain and dizziness. I turned to the young woman sitting on the edge of the bed and saw she was wearing a simple gray dress. Although it would have looked drab and plain on most girls, on her it became an elegant gown that clung to her curves nicely. Her blond hair was mostly bound back into a long braid, with some tendrils coming loose to frame her face. I leaned back on one elbow and gave her my very best smile.

"I'm Nathan Zachary," I said. "I must say, this is the most comfortable prison I've ever been in, and you're by far the most beautiful jailer I've ever seen." She colored nicely again but didn't look away this time. I decided to take her silence as an invitation to continue. "What happened?" I asked.

Suddenly Hanna was all business. She rose from the edge of the bed and gently pressed me back down against the mattress, smoothing out the blanket. That covered me "You were shot down," she said simply. "In the crash you broke your ankle and hit your head." I didn't recall hitting my head at all, but things had happened so fast.

"You passed out shortly after you were captured," Hanna continued, "and you were brought here. We set your ankle and treated your cuts and bruises. They said you fell from a great height. You're very lucky to be alive at all."

I smiled again. "That's me, lucky. After all, if I hadn't crashed we would never have met, right?" She returned the smile in full measure. "You speak English very well, " I said. "Where did you learn?"

"My father was an ambassador," she said. "We traveled a great deal when I was young."

"You don't seem that old to me," I said.

"Neither do you," Hanna said. "You seem very young to be a pilot. How old are you?" I was suddenly very aware of my youth, probably at least two or three years younger than her.

"Old enough," I mumbled.

Hanna started to say something else, but just then the door opened and we both turned toward it. A German officer stepped in and looked at Hanna. His eyes flicked to me for a moment, and then he spoke a few words in German to her. Her strong tone surprised me; clearly they disagreed about something. The officer responded in an equally firm tone and Hanna turned back to me.

"Please excuse me," she said, bending down to brush her fingers across the bandage around my head. "I'm needed elsewhere. I'll be back shortly. If you need anything in the meantime, ask one of the other nurses." Then she rose and strode to the door, past the officer, who looked at me a final time before stepping out and pulling the door closed behind him.

As soon as they were gone, I levered myself up in bed again and began to take stock of the situation. My head ached a bit, as did my ankle, but I was feeling considerably better than after I'd crashed. I immediately began taking stock of the situation. I was wearing thin flannel pajamas; I wondered briefly if Hanna had been the one to dress me in them. There was no sign of my clothes anywhere in the room. There were several other beds, two of them taken up by unconscious men, a small writing desk, and a standing cabinet. Other than that the room was empty. Some light trickled through tall, thin, windows, so it was daytime. The windows were covered with iron grates, too small to fit through, even if they opened, which I suspected they did not.

I whipped off the covers and examined my ankle. It was expertly splinted and bandaged, covering everything but my toes and running almost halfway up my calf. I ran my fingers over it gingerly. It was sore, but the splint seemed to be supporting it well enough. I looked around and spotted a wooden cane leaning against the other bed. I swung my feet down off the bed and grabbed the cane, slowly levering myself to my feet. I might not be 100 percent but I wasn't going to just lie around.

With the cane I was able to hobble over to the door, although I wasn't going to be setting any track records for a while. I stopped at the door and tried the knob. Strange—it wasn't locked. Maybe they figured I wasn't going anywhere. Their mistake.

I eased open the door and found myself standing almost face to face with a tall, slim man with dark hair and a full, neatly trimmed beard and mustache. His face split into a wide smile when he saw me, showing white teeth that reminded me of a wolf up its prey. He was wearing a crisp German uniform with insignia identifying him as a major. Flanking him was a pair of matched soldiers, their rifles at ease, but also at the ready.

"Ah, *Herr* Zachary," he said in a deep, lightly accented voice. "So good to see you up and about. I am Heinrich Kisler. Pleased to finally meet you. Won't you join me for a moment?"

***

Kisler's men escorted us to a large sitting room in the castle, which apparently doubled as a meeting room of sorts. The walls were the same heavy gray stone as the rest of the castle, but modern amenities had been added to soften the effect. A fire burned in the large flagstone hearth, driving away the chill that seemed to linger in the stones. Several large bookcases of dark wood filled with leather-bound volumes lined the walls. Overstuffed chairs sat around the perimeter of a large Persian rug that covered most of the cool stone floor, the subdued jewel tones picking up light from the hearth and the few gas lamps along the walls. A long wooden table to one side was spread with maps covered with markings, which I took to be battle lines, trenches, and other tactical information.

I tried not to look too interested in the maps as I hobbled into the room, but I noted them for future reference. If I could get a good look, I might learn something of value to the Allies if—no, when—I escaped this place.

"Please, make yourself comfortable," Kisler said, as he shrugged out of his heavy uniform coat and passed it to one of the soldiers, who took it without a word. I hobbled over to one of the chairs and carefully lowered myself into it. The truth was, the short walk from the infirmary had been exhausting and my ankle was throbbing a bit, but I didn't want Kisler or his men to know it. I kept my face composed and completely neutral as Kisler crossed to a sideboard.

"Some wine?" he said. "I think you'll find the local vintage quite pleasant."

"Thank you," I said as he lifted a waiting bottle and filled two glasses. With a wave of his hand, he dismissed the guards. They withdrew, closing the stout door behind them. I noticed Kisler was armed with a pistol, secured in a holster at his side. But the German Ace's manner was far from threatening. In fact, he seemed as genuinely pleased to see me as he claimed to be. He came over and handed me a glass of wine, which I sipped and found to be as good as advertised. I was no stranger to wine—we drank it often with meals when I was a child—but this stuff was much better than what I was used to.

Kisler took the seat opposite me, sipping his wine and regarding me over the rim of the glass. Then he swirled the wine a bit and set it down before looking up at me again. For all his charm and the comfort of the surroundings, Kisler's eyes were cold.

"Tell me, *Herr* Zachary—may I call you Nathan?"

"If you want," I said. "It's your nickel."

"And you may call me Heinrich. There is no need for formality and titles between us. We are both pilots, both warriors of the air, part of a greater brotherhood."

"Except you're the enemy," I said coolly.

But I didn't shake Kisler's pleasant façade. He simply smiled and sighed. "A meaningless distinction," he said. "We are rivals, yes, but I find you an opponent with a great deal of potential, Nathan. I saw it in the way you handled your machine in our encounter."

"And in the way I smoked your tail before," I said with a smile.

"So that was you, then," Kisler said, returning the smile without any warmth behind it. "I thought as much. A pity you lost the canvas on your wing. You might have made more of a show of it then."

My thoughts flashed to Peterson's Nieuport, going down in flames. "You killed a good man that day."

Kisler raised one eyebrow as he regarded me. "Is that why you came after me with such fervor then? Revenge? A desire for some sort of justice?" Before I could answer, he continued, "A poor motive at best, young Zachary. A warrior must have passion and drive, but he cannot allow himself to be ruled by those feelings, or else he faces defeat, as you have learned." My cheeks burned from Kisler's rebuke. He might have beaten me once, but I wasn't going to let that happen again, if I got half the chance.

Kisler reached over to the table where his wine goblet sat, but, instead of picking it up, he plucked a rook from the chessboard that lay there. "Do you play chess, Nathan?" he asked, turning the piece over in his hands.

"Not really," I said. "I didn't have a lot of time for games like that. I was more of a cops-and-robbers type as a kid."

"You should," Kisler replied. "They call it the game of kings. Chess is a game for a true warrior. Perhaps we could play sometime."

"Maybe," I said, not understanding. Why was Kisler being so nice to me? He responded, almost as if he could hear my thoughts.

"I have no wish to treat you in anything other than an honorable manner, Nathan. You strike me as a man of honor. If you give me your word, pilot to pilot, that you will not try to escape or cause trouble, I can see to it that you're given a greater degree of freedom, and we can talk further about your future."

"About betraying my country, you mean."

Kisler shrugged noncommittally. "You're clearly a pilot with some potential. We have need of good pilots, and I'm sure there's a great deal I could teach you. I am a fine teacher, if I say so myself—my current protégé is already one of Germany's finest pilots."

No doubt, I thought, considering my options carefully. I would never take Kisler up on his offer. But it wouldn't do to alienate him either. An adage I'd heard many times as a child came back to me: Keep your enemies close. "It sounds like a good deal," I lied. "But I'll need some time to think it over. I'm not promising anything."

Kisler eyed me and then smiled, nodding slightly. "You'll be placed with the other prisoners and treated fairly. *Fräulein* Ullen will attend to your medical needs. Until we meet again, *auf Weidersehn*, *Herr* Zachary."

He called for the guards and they escorted me from the room. Kisler picked up his wine and made his way over to the table and its maps, turning his back on me. Clearly, our audience was at an end. I did my best not to limp too much as I made my way out of the room, and the guards escorted me to my cell.

(HAPTER

STRANGE BEDFELLOWS

The room the guards brought me to was good-sized, and it had to be,
since it accommodated a half-dozen men. Simple cots were arrayed in rows,
each with a small foot locker that probably held whatever personal possessions
these men were allowed. They all looked up as I entered the room, and I could
feel their eyes on me, assessing me, trying to figure out who I was and how I'd
ended up here—like them.

I caught sight of a familiar face but kept any sign of recognition from my
own as one of the guards pointed me toward an empty cot. Then the Germans
turned and left, locking the door behind them. As I dropped gratefully onto the
cot, the room suddenly burst into activity as if someone had thrown a switch,
as most of the men came over to greet me—one in particular.

"Zachary!" Johnny Johnson said with a smile. "I never thought I'd see
you alive again!" I returned Johnson's handshake and smile.

"Same here. What happened to you?" I asked.

"In a second," Johnson said, sitting down on the edge of my bunk. "First let me introduce you around. Everyone, this kid is Nathan Zachary, another pilot from the Escadrille, almost as good as me!" I decided to let that comment pass as Johnson pointed out each of the men in turn and rattled off their names and backgrounds.

Emile Dellier was a French flyer whose Nieuport crashed inside enemy territory like mine. He was a few years older and carried himself with a somewhat superior air, although he warmed to me quickly enough, no doubt as a fellow aviator.

Eddie Lancourt was an Englishman with a ready smile and a pleasant disposition, despite having been imprisoned at the castle for more than five months after his Sopwith was shot down. He had managed to land safely and hide out in the French countryside for nearly two weeks before German troops captured him.

Also from the British Isles was "Mad" Angus McMullen, a big Scotsman with little hair to speak of up top but a bristling beard and mustache of fiery red. He, too, was a Sopwith pilot, but I got the impression that he had ended up in Castle Eisen for something other than fighting with the Allies. He was one of the oldest men there—at least twice my age.

"Jack Mulligan," the fourth fellow said, taking my hand and shaking it firmly. I thought I detected a Chicago accent as he said, "It's good to have more guys from the ol' U.S. of A around here. Even if it does mean we're stuck with the lousy Krauts … oh, sorry Doc," he said to the final gentleman, who rose from his bunk in the corner and approached our little group. Despite the fact that he was clearly a man of intellect and learning, he seemed quite fit. Horn-rimmed glasses framed pale eyes that didn't miss a single detail, and short, curly white hair retreated from a high forehead lined with worry.

"No offense taken, *Herr* Mulligan," the man said with a slight German accent. He extended his hand toward me. "I am Dr. Wilhelm Fassenbiender. A pleasure to meet you, young man, despite the circumstances."

"Doctor," I said, shaking his hand. "Don't suppose you know anything about treating broken ankles, do you?"

Johnson laughed. "He's not that kind of doctor, you dope. Dr. Fassenbiender is one of Germany's greatest experts on planes and aviation gear. He worked with Wylie Post!"

I glared at Johnson before turning back to Dr. Fassenbiender; I didn't need him making me look dumb. "Sorry, doc," I began. He shook his head and chuckled.

"It's quite all right, my boy," he said. "I would hardly expect you to have heard of my humble efforts."

"But, doctor, what are you doing here?" I asked. "I mean, the rest of us are all pilots and airmen, but what about you? If you're a German scientist and aviation expert ... "

"What am I doing here?" Fassenbiender echoed. He shrugged and shook his head as if he wasn't certain himself. "As you say, Mr. Zachary, a man of my talents could be quite useful to the Kaiser, but only if I am willing to turn my abilities to the creation of better planes and more powerful weapons, to kill young men like yourself. I am a man of science, not a butcher. I refused to build the planes and armaments the Kaiser wanted for his war."

Fassenbiender slumped down on the bunk next to mine and continued. "I feared for my wife and our little girl, Ilsa, so I sent them away. Natalia is from Russia, and she has family there. They will be safe there, away from where the Kaiser might try to use them against me. I destroyed my lab and all of my notes—those that I did not send away with Natalia—to ensure they would not fall into the wrong hands. They came and arrested me shortly thereafter, and brought me here, so I could 'reconsider' my actions. Even now, I could be free, if only I am willing to compromise all I believe in."

"I think I got made a similar offer," I said, drawing all eyes in the room back to me. "I just met with one of our 'hosts,' Kisler."

"Ah yes, the Black Ace himself!" Jack said, "Yeah, he likes to talk to the prisoners, at least the pilots."

I smiled wryly. "He said he respected me, and that Germany could use good pilots."

"They sure as 'ell don't have any of their own!" Angus crowed, to the laughter of the other men.

"We all got similar offers," Johnson said. "But work for the Huns? No way!"

"I hope you told him where he could stick his offer, too!" Jack said. I shook my head.

"Nope. Didn't see any reason to close that door, not when it might be a way out of here."

"You would nae work with these Huns, wouldye?" said Mad Angus, a dangerous gleam in his eye. The other men were looking equally stormy.

"No, of course not," I said, keeping my voice low in case anyone was listening in on us. "But as long as Kisler thinks there's a chance of it, then maybe it's something I—we—can use." There were some nods.

"So you're planning an escape, are you?" Dr. Fassenbiender said, giving me an appraising look.

"Well, I'm sure as hell not planning on spending the rest of the war here!" I said.

"But how are we gonna do it?" Jack said.

"Yeah, I'd like to hear your plan, kiddo," Johnny chimed in, with a touch of sarcasm. I suddenly became acutely aware that I was the youngest person in the room, at least a couple years younger than most of my fellow pilots and decades younger than Kisler and Angus. I held up my hands to stem the tide of questions.

"Whoa! I haven't gotten all that worked out just yet, I just woke up a little while ago! My ankle's still busted and my head has to heal up some, too. Give me some time to think about it. But I'll tell you one thing I'm sure of right now."

"What's that?" Johnny asked.

"We're all in this together, and together we can find a way out of it," I said. This wouldn't be the first time a gypsy had to get out of a scrape and I'd seen enough master swindlers in my childhood to have picked up a few tricks. "There's always a way."

Just then, the door opened and the conversation stopped as Hanna Ullen stepped into the room, followed closely by a German guard, who stayed back by the door, his rifle trained warily on our little group.

"Excuse me," she said quietly, "but I have to examine Mr. Zachary's injuries and change his bandages, if you wouldn't mind." As a unit, the others all took two steps back from me, leaving me leaning up against the wall on my bunk as Hanna came over, a tray of supplies in her hands. Setting them down on the footlocker, she set to work quickly and efficiently. Her touch was gentle, but firm and certain, and there was no sign she felt nervous working in a room full of prisoners, under the watchful eye of a guard. Her eyes strayed up to meet mine from time to time as she worked, but we exchanged no words.

When she finished, she put away her instruments and packed up her tray. As she turned to go Johnny, lying back on his cot, gave her an oily leer.

"Hey, doll," he said, "any time you want to give out some more of that tender lovin' care, I could use a sponge bath."

"Too bad I don't have something to wash out your mind with," Hanna said icily, "or your mouth, for that matter." She stalked out of the room to the sound of catcalls and jeers directed at Johnson, who just laughed as he watched her go. The arrival of the evening meal quickly turned everyone's attention from Johnson's crash-and-burn to food, and soon we were sitting in small clusters chewing on the tasteless German rations.

***

At first, my injury spared me from having to deal with some of the worst aspects of life in the German prison camp. The Huns put everyone to work, doing everything from the camp laundry to digging ditches. I avoided most of the hard physical labor, at least while my ankle was healing, but I had to grapple with the boredom of prison, broken up only by occasional visits from Hanna, and evenings when my cellmates returned from their day's work, exhausted and grumbling. I noticed more than one resentful glance directed my way, but I could hardly help my position.

My being laid up also gave me time to study what went on at Castle Eisen and to learn as much as I could about the prison's routines. I questioned the others about what they saw during the day, and about the layout of the place, which included an airstrip. It seemed the place held about two hundred prisoners, held in similar cells. Of course, the Huns didn't give me too much time to consider any of this too closely. As soon as I was able to manage a limping walk, I was put to work, mostly working in the castle's laundry or the kitchens.

The Germans were harsh taskmasters, and I quickly began to understand the fatigue felt by my fellow prisoners. It seemed that the work itself was less important than ensuring we were all exhausted by the end of the day, too tired to move from our hard bunks except to have something to eat, then collapse into a dreamless sleep, only to be awakened for work the next morning.

So one day seemed to blend into the next as the weeks passed by in a dull and unending routine.

As we ate quietly one night, Angus McMullen sat down opposite me and dug into the food on his tin tray, watching me like he was trying to size me up as he chewed. I returned his look before continuing to eat. The Huns fed us rations barely suited for human consumption. The war made for dwindling supplies, and the Germans could not afford to waste good food on prisoners. This evening's fare was a thin broth with some chunks of potatoes and turnips, along with some hard, stale bread. I glanced up to see McMullen looking at me again.

"Yer a smart lad," he said in his Scots brogue. "I can see by the way ye look at things, like yer always thinkin'"

"Helps to pay attention," I said, soaking a piece of bread in broth to soften it and make it more edible. Angus leaned in closer, his voice dropping to just above a harsh whisper.

"So, ye think ye have a way out of here, do ye, lad?" he said, bushy brows lowering as he regarded me across the length of the bunk.

"Never said that," I mumbled around a mouthful of food, "only that we should be looking for one. I don't want to be the guest of the Huns for the rest of the war, do you?" He shook his head.

"That I do nae," he said, "and I've good reason to want to be away from here and back home."

"Oh?" I said. "A girl waiting for you, is there?" I tried to imagine some country lass watching and waiting for Angus McMullen to come home to her, but I found it difficult, to say the least.

The Scotsman smiled a crooked grin, as if he knew what I was thinking. "Nae fair lass awaits me, Zachary, but something far better, and somethin' that'll sure win me any lass I want."

"And what's that?" I asked. With a glance at the others, listening to some tale Johnson was spinning about a girl he met in Paris, Mad Angus leaned forward, his voice pitched low so only I could hear.

"Gold," he whispered. The way he said it made my skin tingle and Angus smiled at the look I gave him. "Aye," he said, "a fortune in gold."

"From where?" I asked. "You're not in the British Army, are you?"

He offered another crooked smile. "Nae any more, laddie. Some mates and me heard about a shipment of British gold, money going to Canada and America. We saw our chance to all be rich men, so we hijacked that gold, and hid it someplace safe, intending to come back fer it."

"I haven't heard anything about any gold robbery," I began and Angus shook his head.

"Ye wouldn't hae, lad. They covered it up all careful like, because they could nae let word of the truth out, that a small band o' flyers had pinched their gold. But it's true."

"Then what are you doing here?" I said. McMullen's face darkened.

"They got on to us sooner than we thought. We hid the gold where it'd be well watched without bein' found, but no sooner had we hid it then they came a-looking for us. McPhee and Crozier were gunned down by the constables when they tried to shoot their way out. Murphy's machine went doon trying to cross the Channel, leaving me alone to try and make it to France. I did, but ran into some gusts across the Channel and ended up off course. By the time I figured out where I was, the damned Huns were upon me. I had to surrender or let 'em shoot me doon.

"And so I ended up in this godforsaken place," he said.

"And you're the only one of your band who's still alive," I concluded.

"Aye," he whispered.

"But why tell me?" I said. "How do you know you can trust me?"

"Trust ye?" Angus said with a snort. "I didn't say that, lad, any more than ye should trust me. But I can tell from the look o' ye that yer a clever one, and that ye've got as much chance of getting out of this place as any man, surely more than this lot. So if ye do, and ye want a share of the treasure… well, then ye'll see to it that ye bring old Angus along with ye."

I smiled slowly. I'd counted on these men, and any other prisoners we could contact to help get out of this place. Knowing that Mad Angus had a strong motive for getting out himself made me certain I could rely on the old pirate's help, so long as it served both our interests.

"You can count on me," I said. Angus smiled his crooked smile and nodded. He extended me a hand and I shook it, before he stood, picked up his tray and left, looking quite pleased with himself.

"He is not a man to be trusted," said a lightly accented voice. I turned to see Dr. Fassenbiender standing nearby, looking at me over the tops of his spectacles. "May I?" he asked, gesturing toward the now empty seat across from me.

"Be my guest," I said. "What makes you think I can be trusted, doctor?"

Fassenbiender considered for a moment before answering. "First, I judge you to be a young man of some intellect. I can tell from your manner and your speech that you're clever. You told us about how Kisler attempted to sway you, and how you parlayed that offer into something that might serve us later."

"I could have been lying," I pointed out. "Maybe I actually am working for the Huns."

"True," the doctor said, "but what would you gain? If you were in league with Kisler, why would you still be here? Second, your friend Mr. Johnson told us how you went out looking for Kisler to avenge your comrade's death. I judge that the action of an honorable man, if a young and impulsive one." I returned the doctor's smile and nodded my head in acknowledgment.

"All right then, we've established my honor, intelligence, and general goodwill."

"To say nothing of your modesty," Fassenbiender said.

"That too. I'm flattered that you find me trustworthy, Doctor. I get the feeling you're looking for a trustworthy man."

"*Ja*," Fassenbiender said quietly, "I am. You spoke of wanting to escape from this place, Mr. Zachary. How badly do you want that?" I looked Fassenbiender in the eye.

"My freedom is worth everything to me, doctor."

"*Gut*, because there may be a way, but it will not be easy."

"I'm all ears," I said. "But if you have a way to get out of here, why haven't you used it yet?"

"As you said, Mr. Zachary, I am looking for a trustworthy man. Do you think any of these other men are the man I've been looking for? No, I cannot accomplish my plan alone, and I need someone else I can trust, to help organize things. I am a scientist, not a soldier, or a leader of men. The others will not follow orders from me, but I think they will follow them from you."

"What makes you so sure?"

"I have seen you in the barracks. Despite your youth, you have a commanding presence. I am a good judge of character, my boy, and I judge you to be a man of honor. Together, I believe we can reach our goal."

"All right then, what's the plan?" I asked.

"In good time," Fassenbiender said, patting me on the shoulder. "We should not discuss such things here. Also, you need rest and time to heal. I will explain everything to you at another time, when we can be alone, and you can decide the best way to include the others."

As one of the guards approached, Dr. Fassenbiender excused himself. I went back to my meal with considerably more appetite, plans already forming in my mind.

CHAPTER

GAMBIT

"Checkmate," Kisler said, moving his bishop onto a square near my king.

I looked over the board sitting between us for a few moments and was forced to agree; Kisler had beaten me yet again. Our chess games had become a regular feature of my stay at Castle Eisen over the past few months. Kisler visited the castle often, and each time he did, he would invite me into the study for a game of chess.

We would talk about various things, with Kisler subtly guiding the conversation toward matters concerning my future and with me feigning interesting in what he had to say, offering some hope that he might win me over, and expressing interest in his stories about happenings on the front. In our verbal thrust and parry I gathered—even through Kisler's bias—that our own boys were doing well, pressing the Huns hard from all sides. The summer of '17 was a difficult one for them, and the fall and winter didn't look to be any easier, with more American troops arriving all the time.

Kisler would eventually pin me down and checkmate my king, bringing our game to an end, and German soldiers would come to take me back to the prison barracks, or Hanna would appear to escort me to the infirmary to check on my recovery.

Today it was Hanna who appeared at the door, wearing her gray nurse's uniform under a white apron; her golden hair neatly coiled at the nape of her neck. I couldn't help but smile when I saw her, standing in a ray of fading sunshine coming through one of the high, thin windows. She was beautiful, and she looked at me with eyes filled with genuine concern.

"Well," I said to Kisler, "it seems you've trounced me soundly yet again, but I think I'm getting the hang of this game."

"Indeed you are, *Herr* Zachary," the German Ace acknowledged with a nod of his head. "You come closer and closer to winning each time. You're as apt a student as I expected."

"Thank you," I said, pushing away from the table. "However, it seems I have to give myself over into the care of *Fräulein* Ullen before returning to the barracks."

"It is not necessary for you to return, you know," Kisler said, picking up his winning bishop and twirling the piece in his fingers.

"Yes, it is," I said. "I'm looking forward to our next game, *Herr* Kisler." But if I had my way, our games were at an end.

"As am I," Kisler replied.

I levered myself out of my chair. Hanna quickly moved to my side to support me, but I stood on my own two feet and bowed slightly to Kisler before turning and slowly walking out of the room with Hanna at my side.

The truth was that my ankle was almost healed, and I no longer got the headaches that plagued me the first week or so at the castle. I exaggerated my limp a great deal and walked slowly to give the impression I was having more trouble than I really was. As long as the Germans thought I was injured, possibly permanently, they would tend to underestimate me. That might give me the edge I needed when the time came to put the plan into operation. We were nearly ready; only a few more pieces needed to fall into place. In fact, there was only one piece I wasn't certain of.

Hanna closed the infirmary door behind us as I made my way over to the nearest bed. I heard the key turn in the lock as I settled down on the bunk.

There was no one else in the room, since the prisoners rarely gave the Germans any trouble and we were some distance from the front lines. Hanna came over and slipped off my shoes, hands gently massaging and testing my ankle.

"How do you feel today?" she said, all business. I smiled and reached down to cup her chin with my hand turning her face up toward mine.

"I feel much better now," I said. Her smile seemed to light up the room as her hands slid up along my legs.

"Really?" she said. "I'm glad to see you're recovering so well but I'm disappointed, too. Soon you won't need my care at all."

"I don't know about that," I said. "I can always use a little more ... personal attention."

She leaned forward at that, and our lips met as we sank back onto the bed. No, there was one piece of the plan I hadn't expected, and I didn't know what to do about her yet.

***

When I got back to the barracks it was fairly late and the others had obviously already eaten dinner. Johnny Johnson gave me a crooked smile when I came in, but Jack and Emile merely looked sour.

"Where have you been, kid?" Even though he was only a couple years older than I was, Jack had "adopted" me and did his best to watch out for me. Jack was a lot smarter than he let on with his gruff manner and his Chicago street lingo, but he also tended to act, and speak, before he thought.

"Didn't know the Huns had made you barracks monitor, Jack," I said, making my way casually over to the table, pulling out a chair and turning it around so I could sit down and lean on its back. "I played another game with Kisler, and Hanna took care of my ankle."

"Bet that's not all she took care of ..." Johnson said quietly, but loud enough for everyone, including me, to hear.

"Spending time with that dame!" Jack snapped, scraping back his chair. "We should be figuring on how to get out of here, Zachary, not chasin' skirts!"

"Ach, yer just mad because ye're not the subject of the lass's affections, Jackie boy," Mad Angus said from where he sat in the corner, feet propped up on another chair.

"This ain't about me!" Jack said. "It's about what we should be doing, which is trying to get out of this stinkin' prison, and not spendin' time romancing the enemy!"

I stood up at that and stepped around my chair to stand closer to Jack.

"Listen, Mulligan, I am working on getting us out of here, and as for Hanna and me, well that's none of your damn business!" I said coldly.

"It is if it ends up getting all of us killed," he retorted. "What do you care about some German slut anyway?"

I launched myself at Mulligan, lashing out with a right hook that caught him in the face. He responded with a punch in my gut as the other guys leapt out of the way, none of them making any move to interfere. We went down in a heap, sending the chair Jack was sitting in skittering across the floor. I almost had Mulligan in a half-nelson when a hand grabbed me by the collar and yanked me up and away from him. Jack crabbed backward a few paces and got to his feet ready to resume the fight, but another hand slammed into his chest, pushing him away from me.

"That's enough!" Dr. Fassenbiender shouted at both of us. "*Mein Gott*, do you want to bring the guards in and have them separate you, perhaps put you in real cells, or in chains? How will that help us? We have to focus on our plans, not brawl like common hooligans! We are the only allies we have in this place! We cannot let ourselves be divided!"

"Well, it's his—" Mulligan started.

"Enough!" the doctor interrupted forcefully. "It doesn't matter who started it, or who did what. What matters now is what we are going to do. Now sit down!"

Jack and I sullenly reclaimed our seats, like schoolboys scolded by their teacher. The others did the same as Dr. Fassenbiender stood, his arms folded across his chest like a stern schoolmaster.

"*Gut*," he said. "Now, a situation exists, and we must decide what is to be done about it. Nathan, my boy," he said, turning his attention to me.

"I've thought about that," I said. "I think Hanna can help us. I talked to her about … "

"You didn't tell her the plan, did you?" Johnson said, jumping out of his chair. I glared back at him.

"No, of course I didn't," I said coldly. "I'm not stupid. I just talked to her.

She's no happier here than any of us. She has no family because of the war, and she doesn't have anywhere else to go. I get the feeling she's treated pretty badly by the commandant, too."

"So?" Jack said. "She's just feeding you some sob story. She's still one o' them."

"C'mon, Jack!" I said, standing myself up. "You can't blame her for being German. It's not like she had any choice in the matter. She's... "

The sound of someone at the door cut me off just before the guard admitted Hanna, wearing her gray nurse's uniform. She looked at us and flushed slightly. I wondered if she had heard any of what was said.

"Excuse me," she said quietly. "I have to give *Herr* Zachary some medication for his pain." I kept quiet as she turned to the guard and nodded, and he withdrew, closing the door behind him. No one said a word as Hanna approached. When she was close enough, I spoke quietly to her.

"You didn't say anything about any medication ... " I began and Hanna silenced me with a shake of her head and a glance toward the door.

"I know," she replied, just loud enough for everyone in the room to hear. "I only said that so I could see you. I've thought about what you said." She glanced briefly at the hard faces looking at her before turning back to me. "You are planning to escape, yes?"

When I hesitated and glanced at the others, she went on. "It's all right if you are. I want to help you." She took my hand in hers. "I want to leave this place with you, Nathan," she said. "I'll help in whatever way I can."

"And why should we trust you?" Jack said in a low voice.

"You have no idea of the risk I'm taking in coming to you now," Hanna said. "If the commandant found out ... " Her voice trailed off, and a shudder went through her slim form. She turned her blue eyes, shining with unshed tears, toward mine. "Please, Nathan."

I almost drowned in those eyes before I turned to look pleadingly toward Dr. Fassenbiender, knowing that his opinion might sway the others. The scientist looked from Hanna to me and back again before clearing his throat slightly.

"Well," he said, "perhaps the young woman can help us. We cannot simply leave her behind, and she may be able to give us the opportunity we need to accomplish part of our plan. Better to have her with us than against us, yes?"

He glanced around the room, and was met by murmurs and nods of agreement, even from Jack. He turned back toward us as Hanna dared to smile slightly. "Very well then, *Fräulein*, here is how you can help us … "

***

"Checkmate," Kisler said, dropping his rook into place and closing his trap. I looked around the board and saw there was nowhere for my king to go. Kisler had executed another expert gambit.

"Well played," I said, slowly tipping my king over on the board to acknowledge defeat. "I didn't see that particular move coming."

"That is the challenge, isn't it?" the Black Ace said, sitting back in his chair, "seeing all the possible moves an opponent can make in time to counter them. Still, you've come yet closer to being able to defeat me. That win was the closest one yet."

"I thought I had you for sure," I said, still looking at the board.

"You nearly did, but never count victory before it is won," Kisler said. "Such complacency is dangerous."

"Yes," I looked up to meet Kisler's eyes. "Yes, it is. Shall we play again?"

"No, I'm afraid not," Kisler said, stretching his arms then rising from his chair. "I have duties I must attend to, and I believe *Fräulein* Ullen is awaiting you." He nodded toward the doorway, where Hanna waited quietly, obviously not wanting to interrupt out little tête-à-tête. I rose to go but a word from Kisler made me pause.

"Tell me, *Herr* Zachary, have you considered further what your future is to be?"

I turned back to Kisler, exaggerating greatly the effort of doing so. "Yes, I have, *Herr* Kisler. I'll admit that I have no desire to spend the rest of my days here. Our games have also shown me that there may not be as much difference between the white pieces and the black as I thought," I lied.

Kisler nodded and smiled tightly. "Well, then," he said. "I look forward to our next conversation."

Taking that as a dismissal, I made my way over to Hanna and we walked, arm in arm, down to the infirmary. I'd been a "guest" of the Germans for just over four months, and my injuries were completely healed, although I still affected a slight limp and sometimes complained of aches and pains.

Everything was ready to put our plan into motion.

The Germans used the prisoners to perform some menial labor at the castle, including cleaning and similar duties under the sometimes less than watchful eyes of guards, who generally didn't expect trouble from us. After all, we were unarmed and deep in Germany, with no means of escape, so what were we going to do? They certainly didn't seem to notice when small amounts of cleaning supplies and the like disappeared from supply closets and storerooms, and were smuggled back into our barracks, where they were hidden under blankets and spare clothes at the bottom of foot lockers.

Too skilled to be wasted on menial duties, Dr. Fassenbiender busied himself with minor repair work and the like around the castle, allowing him to gather an assortment of bits of wire, springs, metal and other trinkets that seemed like nothing more than a harmless collection of junk. However, along with everything else we had gathered, the good doctor was able to construct several incendiary devices he called "crude but serviceable." The devices were concealed in places where they weren't likely to be noticed—at least not until smoke and flames began pouring out of them.

We had waited until my regular visit to the infirmary. As it happened, that night we had also received a visit from Heinrich Kisler, who invited me to the study for another game of chess. I was actually pleased Kisler had declined my offer of a second game this night; time was running short if we were to pull off our plan. I did my best not to hurry as we made our way to the infirmary.

The infirmary was quiet and empty, as Hanna had confirmed before. We bunched up some pillows under a blanket on the cot and I moved to the side of the door as Hanna called out for the guard. When he entered, I closed the door behind him and stepped forward, bringing both hands down in a strike at his back. He crumpled to the floor in a heap, and I grabbed his rifle and sidearm. I handed the pistol to Hanna, and she took it from me like it was a live snake.

"Can you use one of these?" I asked.

She nodded. "I think so."

"Good." I didn't care for the idea of Hanna being unable to defend herself, should the need arise. We quickly divested the guard of his uniform and I changed into it. It fit me closely enough, although it was a little baggy in spots.

Hanna sedated the guard and helped me lift him onto the bunk, covering him up with a blanket. If all went well, it would be some time before anyone found him.

Checking the hall and making sure there was no one in sight, we quickly made our way away from the infirmary. A few minutes later, I could hear some muffled thumps, followed by distant cries of alarm. Our incendiary bombs had done their work. In moments, the castle would be in chaos. We ducked into an alcove as a small group of guards thundered past, rushing to answer the calls for help in other parts of the castle. Making sure the coast was clear, I led Hanna on down the hall.

"Where are we going?" she asked. I hadn't filled her in on that part of the plan yet. The others thought it was best if we didn't reveal everything to Hanna. And I agreed.

"To the airfield," I said. "We're going to take some of the planes to get out of here. By now the others should also be free. We'll meet up there." We hadn't been able to spread word of our plan to all the hundreds of other prisoners; our chances of detection escalated with every person who knew. My hope was that. in the ensuing confusion, the other prisoners would escape into the surrounding countryside. We pilots would use our enemies' planes to fly away from here.

By the time we reached the airfield, Castle Eisen was in chaos. I could see black smoke pouring from several spots, and one of the wooden buildings in the courtyard was engulfed in flames. We moved quickly across the courtyard, my uniform ensuring that anyone who glanced our way would see only a soldier escorting a nurse to safety from the fire.

The airstrip sat a short distance outside the castle walls, with a small hangar building holding several German Pfalz machines and a single two-seater Albatross. Most of the mechanics and other personnel had already rushed to the castle to assist in fighting the fire, so the hangar was abandoned save for a single guard on duty. I stepped inside and leveled my rifle at the surprised guard, who took a moment to realize I was not one of his comrades. A universal gesture with my gun had his hands in the air.

I took a couple of steps closer. "Hanna," I said over my shoulder, "help me with him."

I was answered by the sound of a gun hammer cocking very close to my ear.

"I'm afraid I can't do that," Hanna said. "You cannot betray your country, Nathan, but you expect me to betray mine? What did *Herr* Kisler tell you—do not count victory before it is won?" I felt a slim hand reach around me to take the unresisting rifle from my hands. Checkmate, I thought bitterly to myself.

CHAPTER

CHECKMATE

"Hanna, I don't understand," I said. "Why are you doing this? I trusted you!"

The German guard came forward to take the rifle from Hanna's hand, and she took a couple of steps away from me, a sad smile twisting her mouth.

"You can ask that of me, after all your own talk of duty and being unable to betray your country?" she said. "Yet you expect me to do the same for what? A romantic smile, a kiss, a stolen night or two?" She shook her head. "That was all for your benefit, my dear Nathan. A chance to win over your heart where *Herr* Kisler's words failed to win over your mind."

"No," I said. "It was more than that, I know it. I felt something."

"Of course you did," she said. "Nothing more than boyish infatuation."

"Then you … then it was all an act," I said bitterly. "You were working for Kisler all along." My eyes narrowed. "You should have been an actress, not a nurse. Your performance certainly fooled me."

"More than you know," Hanna said, raising her chin proudly. "I'm not a nurse, although I make a good one. I am a pilot, like you, only better. I was taught by the very best there is."

"You? You're Kisler's protégé?" I said.

"Why so shocked, Nathan? Do you find it so hard to believe that a woman could be as good a pilot as you, let alone better?"

"No. I'm shocked because I can't believe I ever trusted you," I said.

"Then you definitely weren't paying attention to our teacher's lessons. It's not too late, Nathan," she said, her voice softening. "You could still give up on this foolishness. *Herr* Kisler is a fair man; he'll give you an opportunity to prove yourself."

"Downing American pilots, or our allies? I don't think so."

"Don't be a fool, Nathan! Do you really think you have anything to go back to? You told me how you defied orders to come after Herr Kisler. That makes you a deserter. As far as the Americans know, you have come over to our side! Do you think they'll ever trust you again?"

I smiled slowly, glad I hadn't told Hanna everything. "Who said I was planning on going back to the Allied side of the lines?" I said.

"But you said ... "

"No, you assumed. You're right—I don't have much to go back to, and getting back would probably be too dangerous, but there are other places that would welcome good pilots, and other opportunities that don't involve supporting the Kaiser. Oh, and Hanna?"

"What?"

"I have been paying attention. *Herr* Kisler is right: you shouldn't count your victories until they're won."

"So drop it, doll-face!" came a voice from the entrance of the hangar. The German guard brought his gun up and just as quickly went down as a shot rang out. Hanna, no fool, dropped her own gun to the floor before turning around slowly, her hands in the air.

Johnny Johnson and Jack Mulligan stood in the doorway, holding German rifles, their faces blackened with soot. Johnson's rifle was still smoking from the shot that had downed the guard. They moved to assist me as our fellow former prisoners entered the hangar, including Dr. Fassenbiender.

"So what should we do with her?" Jack said, jerking his chin toward

Hanna and keeping his gun trained on her. I took a coil of rope from one of the bins in the hangar and tossed it to him.

"Tie her up and leave her here, and make it quick. It won't be long before they find us." Jack handed off his gun to Emile and quickly bound Hanna's hands behind her back and tied her feet together, leaving her sitting in a chair belonging to one of the guards.

"Go and make sure the planes are ready," I said, coming up to stand next to the chair. Jack looked at me and back at Hanna, and then nodded and headed off. Hanna looked defiantly up at me.

"You won't escape," she said. "They'll shoot you down."

"They're welcome to try," I told her. "But you won't get that chance." She struggled a bit against the ropes, but they held fast.

"We're set, boss!" Jack yelled over the sound of engines revving up. "Let's get out of here!"

"Just one more thing," I said turning back to Hanna. "I want you to look me in the eye and tell me I didn't mean anything to you."

She tossed her head back angrily, strands of golden hair coming loose, and gave me an icy stare. "Nothing," she said in a flat, even tone.

I turned and walked away from her without looking back.

I climbed into the cockpit of the Albatross. Dr. Fassenbiender was already in the second seat, looking over the machine gun mounted back there.

"You know how to use one of those?" I asked.

"I have designed enough of the *verdamt* things, *ja*? I think I know how to use one, my boy."

"Good, because it sounds like we're going to have company once we get airborne." I slipped on the flight helmet and goggles I grabbed from the rack, adjusted the chinstrap, and signaled Johnson to fire up the engine. He spun the propeller hard and it caught, the engine coughing a bit before roaring to life. Johnson ran to his own Pfalz and soon we were ready to go. We'd provide a bit of cover for the remaining prisoners to escape, then get away from the area ourselves.

Just as we started to pull out of the hangar, a small group of German soldiers came rushing toward us.

"Keep your head down, Doc!" I yelled back to Fassenbiender and opened up the throttle to get us out onto the airstrip as the Huns opened fire, bullets whizzing through the air. Most of their shots went wide, but I heard several pass by too close for comfort, and saw at least a couple holes in the fabric of the plane as we rolled forward. Ricochets sounded in the air along with angry cries in German.

I heard the sound of shattering glass as a couple of rounds broke through the hangar windows. Hanna, I thought, glancing back toward the hangar where she was bound, helpless. Then the Hun soldiers started to within range of us and I kicked back the flaps to get us off the ground. I heard a dull roar and saw flames shoot out of one of the hangar windows.

"Oh, my God. Hanna!" I cried.

"There's nothing you can do for her, my boy!" Dr. Fassenbiender shouted to me and I resolutely turned away from the sight of the flaming hangar, my eyes burning behind my goggles. Soon we were in the air, Emile, Eddie, Angus, Jack, and Johnny flying Pfalz single-seaters, with Dr. Fassenbiender and me in the Albatross.

"Keep a lookout, Doc!" I shouted back over the noise of the wind as we climbed up to a few hundred feet and banked back toward the prison camp. The area was buzzing with German guards, many of them moving down toward the hangar area. We strafed the ground, machine gun rounds kicking up dust and dirt and sending the Huns scattering for cover. They were surprised to see their own planes attacking them, which confused the hell out of them.

As we pulled up and started to climb, I heard Fassenbiender call out from behind me.

"Coming out of the sun!" he yelled.

I looked left toward the setting sun and saw a small cluster of machines. They were a good several thousand feet above us and some distance away, but I could still just make out the shapes of four Pfalz, with a Fokker leading the formation. I couldn't see its colors, but it had to be Kisler.

We continued to gain altitude, heading east, as the Germans closed in. I waggled my wings to the others to make sure they saw our company, and they responded to indicate that they had. There was no cloud cover, nowhere to run, and their machines were as fast as ours. There was nothing we could do but try and stay ahead of them and be ready for the attack when it came.

I opened up the throttle, and the others did the same. We picked up speed and continued to climb up to around 15,000 feet. The Germans continued to close in. Although the Albatross' throttle was wide open, it simply wasn't as fast as the smaller, single-seater machines, especially not with two people on board. We were slowing the others down. I tried to signal that they should go ahead, that we would try to hold off the Huns while they escaped, but there was no way to tell them, and they kept in formation, pacing us as the distance between us and Kisler's formation closed.

We were several miles from the prison camp when the Germans made their move.

"Here they come!" Fassenbiender shouted, and I looked in time to see them break formation and begin diving down, with Kisler's Fokker in the lead. Our own formation broke, with the planes splitting and banking off left and right. I pushed the stick of the Albatross forward and began heading down, giving the doc a better field of fire. I could hear him working the machine gun, and then a loud chatter sounded as the gun fired at the incoming planes.

Tracer rounds ripped past as one of the Hun machines got on our tail. The doc's gunfire helped keep the German pilot at bay, but he was still closing in on us, counting on his machine's greater maneuverability to let him pick us off at his leisure. Fortunately, I'd fought enough Albatrosses to know something about their capabilities, even if I'd never been behind the stick of one. I pulled back on the stick and started climbing, with the Pfalz close on our tail. Fassenbiender opened up again with the machine gun, but the German plane slewed from one side to the other, avoiding the worst of it.

We kept climbing higher and higher, and I kept my eye on the altimeter. The Pfalz was faster than the Albatross, but our plane had a higher ceiling. A Pfalz would be lucky to reach 20,000 feet, while an Albatross could operate well over two thousand feet higher than that.

The Pfalz pilot realized it as we passed 20,000. His machine's engine was fighting to go higher, but it just didn't have the horsepower. I leveled us off, and the Hun wasn't able to get a shot at us. He needed to angle his plane upward to bring us into his arc of fire, and to do that, he needed to drop down. In a moment, he started doing just that.

"Hang on, Doc!" I yelled. Then I pulled back hard on the stick, kicked down on the pedals and flipped the Albatross into a loop and into a shallow dive at the end of it, bringing us down behind the Pfalz, with an almost perfect view of his tail. I bumped the stick to the right, got him in my sights, and hit the trigger on the plane's front-mounted machine gun.

Bullets ripped into the tail of the German machine, and I pulled back on the stick to rake the fire along the Pfalz's length. I must have hit the pilot because the plane immediately went into a tailspin, dropping like a stone toward the ground thousands of feet below.

"And when you get there," I said quietly, "tell 'em Nathan Zachary sent you."

I banked and looked all around us to appraise how the fight was going. I could make out several other planes engaged in a dogfight a few thousand feet below us. That's when I realized one of the other problems we faced. From this distance, I had no idea which side was which! With both sides piloting German machines, the only distinctive planes were the Albatross I sat in and Kisler's Fokker. I looked for the lead machine and spotted it engaging a Pfalz a short distance away. I immediately veered in that direction.

The Fokker was close on the tail of the other plane. Even as we closed in I couldn't tell who was flying it, but he was making a valiant effort at evading Kisler's attacks. I dropped us lower to get behind the Fokker, trying to use the setting sun for some cover and hoping Kisler would be too focused on the target in front of him to notice the possibility of any danger from behind.

"Keep an eye on our six, Doc!" I yelled back to Kisler. I didn't want to make the same mistake and allow someone to sneak up on us. I got us into position and headed down after the Fokker. As I did so, I saw a burst of smoke and some flames from the tail of the Pfalz, which began to lose altitude, although it looked like the pilot was still in control.

Kisler must have seen us, because immediately after hitting the Pfalz, the Fokker banked hard to the right. I had to level out our dive and fight the stick to match his maneuver, trying to keep him ahead of and below us. I lined up for another attack, giving a parting glance toward the burning Pfalz as it dropped lower and lower. Kisler was nearly in my sights. I loosed a burst from the forward machine gun, glowing tracers cutting through the darkening sky and showing I was still off the mark.

Then the Fokker pulled up and went into a loop, so suddenly that for a moment it was as if it had simply disappeared into thin air. When I recovered from my surprise, I called back to Dr. Fassenbiender.

"Watch out to our six at 10 o'clock high!"

"He's coming in!" he answered, and I heard the chatter of machine gun fire. We had the advantage of having guns both forward and aft, while Kisler's machine had paired machine guns facing forward only. Still, his shots whizzed dangerously close; I could hear their angry hum and almost feel the heat of the tracers as they flared past.

I banked sharply to the right to bring the Albatross into a long loop, rather than looping upward, as Kisler might have expected. It was a slower maneuver, but I gambled it would buy us the opportunity we needed. Unfortunately, Kisler remained on our tail the entire time, although his guns fell silent as he matched our maneuver.

"I don't know if I can shake him!" I said. We leveled out and Kisler's guns barked again, rounds flying around us. I saw several rents in our left wing. Even if a round failed to hit me, Fassenbiender or our gas tank, Kisler would eventually take us apart piece by piece.

"Get us some altitude!" Fassenbiender yelled to me. I pulled back on the stick and started to climb again, with the doc firing back down at Kisler as he followed us. As we climbed, an idea started to form. I hoped Kisler thought we were trying to use the Albatross' superior ceiling to climb to safety. I kept our climb steep and watched the altimeter, knowing the Black Ace would stay close on our tail.

As we neared the Fokker's ceiling, I jammed the flaps and pushed the stick, flipping our tail up into the air and pointing the nose down. Our speed fell off, and for a moment we hovered suspended before we began to drop. Kisler's Fokker shot up past us, exposing its underside to Fassenbiender's gun. The doctor immediately understood my plan, and his machine gun roared, bullets chewing into the fuselage of Kisler's machine. He was too steep to easily maneuver away without stalling his engine or, worse yet, ripping his canvas. He went into a *renversement* and looped away, but he lost us in the maneuver.

I looked over to see smoke trailing from the Fokker as it leveled out some distance to the left and below us. I thought for a moment it was going to come around for another pass, but then the machine banked slowly and began dropping downward as it headed back toward the west and Castle Eisen's aerodrome. Watching Kisler recede in the distance, I leveled out the Albatross and smiled to myself.

"Checkmate," I murmured.

"What did you say?" Fassenbiender called from behind me.

"Nothing, Doc," I replied. "Let's get out of here."

It wasn't too difficult to find the others, since Kisler's men followed their leader's example and withdrew. We found four of our appropriated German machines, but of the fifth there was no sign. We circled a bit looking for it, then regretfully set our course westward. We still had a long trip ahead of us before we reached the Russian border. Dr. Fassenbiender's family was there, and he told us the Russians would appreciate some good pilots and some captured German machines without asking too many questions.

I gave a silent salute to the pilot we left behind and headed off to face the future.

BOOK

2

THE GLORIOUS REVOLUTION

It is necessary to prepare men who devote to the revolution not only their free evenings, but their entire lives.
— Vladimir Lenin

CHAPTER

9

IN THE LAND OF THE BEAR

After four months in a German prison camp, the days it took us to reach the Russian border seemed short by comparison. We made our way into Russian-controlled Poland, where Dr. Fassenbiender was able to get in touch with his brother-in-law. Grigori Yuloff was a colonel in the Russian army fighting along the Eastern Front. When he received word of Fassenbiender's presence in Russian territory, he arranged for us to fly our machines farther behind the lines, making our way from Warsaw to Petrograd. There we would meet with Alexander Kerensky, the Russian prime minister and former minister of war.

We quickly discovered that a great deal had changed in Russia during Dr. Fassenbiender's incarceration in the German prison camp. Several of us already knew of the February revolution that displaced the Tsar and his family, resulting in their exile to some distant region of the country. A provisional government was in control of Russia now, and Kerensky was one of the most powerful and influential men in it.

News of the revolution only made Dr. Fassenbiender more concerned about his wife and daughter's safety, and more certain that he wished to go to Russia. Since the Russians had no real air forces—indeed, no real aeroplanes to speak of—I figured we could strike a deal with Kerensky and his government. We could offer our assistance in exchange for political asylum and a chance to contact our respective homelands and clear up any misunderstandings-and maybe even get back home someday.

I wasn't sure how I felt about "going back home." I never really had much of a home growing up, and I left it behind to join the army. I considered the Escadrille Lafayette a home of sorts for a while, but I left it behind as well to pursue what I considered justice. I didn't really have a home to go back to.

For the time being, I concerned myself with my fellow escapees, especially Dr. Fassenbiender. The good doctor was so happy it was as if he could have flown from Poland to Petrograd under his own power. When we finally reached the outskirts of the Russian seaport in the early days of July 1917, Fassenbiender's excitement could barely be contained.

We landed on an unused field outside the city, a small farm dotted with tiny cottages and farmhouses, with Russian peasants going about their business in their simple, often-patched clothes. A small crowd turned out to watch our machines touch down in the field, but no one approached too close as several cars pulled up along the road, doors opening to release a number of Russian soldiers led by a broad-shouldered man with pale hair and a full beard. With him were a woman and a young girl who launched herself across the field on full throttle, hurling herself into Fassenbiender's arms.

"Papa! Papa!" she cried, throwing her arms around the doctor's neck and kissing him as he lifted her off the ground and twirled her around. Fassenbiender laughed, lifting his daughter up into the air before setting her down and turning to the woman who stood nearby, smiling at the sight of them, tears gathering in the corners of her eyes.

"Natalia," he said, holding out his arms, and she came to him joyfully, hugging him and speaking to him quietly, in Russian or German I couldn't be sure. I busied myself making sure the Albatross was in good shape before I climbed down to the ground. Fassenbiender turned toward me as the commander of the soldiers approached.

"Nathan Zachary," he said, "this is my wife Natalia, and my daughter Ilsa.

This is Nathan Zachary, the young man who helped engineer our escape from Germany."

Mrs. Fassenbiender directed a smile at me that made the effort well worth it. She was a beautiful woman, of "White Russian" stock, with pale hair and eyes. She wore her hair long, pulled back into a braid that extended almost halfway down her back. Her clothing was slightly outdated, but firmly middle-class, far better than the stuff the local peasants wore, and on her it looked like finery.

"Thank you," she said in heavily accented English, "for helping bring Wilhelm home to us."

"My pleasure, ma'am," I said. I felt a tug on my pantleg and looked down to see little Ilsa looking up at me with big blue eyes the color of a lake in springtime. She wore a pretty little dress and had her blond hair, like her mother's, done up in braids.

"Are you a pilot?" she asked shyly in an accent as heavy as her mother's. I was taken aback for a moment that she spoke any of my language at all. I knew right then that she took after her papa in the smarts department. Dropping down on my haunches, I gave her my best smile.

"Yes, I am a pilot," I said. She smiled back and looked adoringly at her father.

"I'm going to be a scientist, like papa," she declared firmly. Fassenbiender came forward to gather her up in his arms again.

"That's my girl," he beamed. "She's already as smart as a whip."

"I can see that," I said. "She already speaks English?"

"And German and Russian, too!" Fassenbiender said proudly.

The deep rumble of someone clearing his throat caught our attention, and Fassenbiender turned toward the burly man in charge of the Russian soldiers, who were currently keeping curious onlookers back from our machines.

"Nathan, may I present to you my brother-in-law, Colonel Grigori Yuloff. Grigori, this is Nathan Zachary, the pilot I told you about."

Colonel Yuloff and I took each other's measure. The colonel was darker than his sister but still quite fair by Russian standards, his dark blond hair cropped fairly short and slicked back from a high forehead, his full beard neatly trimmed. He wore a crisp, colorful military uniform with golden epaulettes and braid, and the sword and spurs of a cavalry officer. He was clearly a man with considerable experience in the field; it showed in his movements and his manner. I'd seen similar features in commanding officers in the French and American armies. Apparently some things were universal.

The colonel extended his hand and I shook it firmly. "It is a pleasure to meet you, Mr. Zachary," he said. His English was more strongly accented than even Ilsa's, but I understood him clearly enough.

"The pleasure is mine, Colonel. I appreciate all you've done for us." Yuloff smiled broadly, showing an expanse of white teeth through his beard.

"I am sure we will give you an opportunity to show your thanks," he said with a chuckle. He looked over the planes sitting in the field. "Interesting machines, I hope they can be of some help to us."

"I'm sure they can," I said. "Compliments of the German army."

That brought a booming laugh from Yuloff, and he slapped his thigh. "I will tell my men to look after them," he said. "Come, we will get you something to eat and drink; then you can meet with Minister Kerensky."

***

A short while later, having eaten, rested a bit, and gotten cleaned up and dressed in new clothes provided by the Russian army, Dr. Fassenbiender and I accompanied Col. Yuloff to the Winter Palace in Petrograd to meet with Prime Minister Alexander Kerensky. The Winter Palace, along the shore of the Neva River, was one of the homes of the Romanov family, now spending the summer against their will in Siberia. Tsar Nikolas had abdicated as leader of the Russian government several months before, leading to the formation of the provisional government and Kerensky's eventual appointment as prime minister. Yuloff told us Kerensky was active in the Tsarist government, and considered a moderate for the most part.

He occupied a large office in the palace, and he rose from behind his desk to greet us as we entered. I was immediately struck by Kerensky's resemblance to portraits of Napoleon I'd seen in France. He was a slight man, with thin, almost pinched features, heavy-lidded eyes, and a thin-lipped mouth that curled up naturally into a smile. His hair was dark and neatly combed, and he wore a dark suit over a high-collared white shirt and tie. He was also a good deal younger than I was expecting, probably only in his mid-30s. I had assumed he would be an old man.

The prime minister welcomed us to Russia and, after asking if we wanted any refreshment, invited us to be seated in front of his wide desk so we could get down to business. Kerensky assumed his former place behind the desk, which almost dwarfed him.

"Gentlemen," he said, his English reasonably clear, although he spoke slowly, carefully choosing his words. "We are pleased to have you here in Russia. Dr. Fassenbiender's reputation as a scientist precedes him, of course, and we are pleased to welcome an American Ace like you, Mr. Zachary. Colonel Yuloff has told me that you and your men intend to remain in Russia for the time being and wish to assist us in our war efforts. Is this correct?"

"Yes, sir, it is," I said. Dr. Fassenbiender nodded his agreement. "With some resources we can maintain the German aeroplanes we brought with us and maybe even improve on them, or build some new machines and train your own people to use them."

"We understand your troops are having difficulties along the Eastern Front," Fassenbiender added. That was an understatement, to say the least. From what we'd heard from Yuloff, Russian morale was as low as it had ever been, and troops were surrendering to the Huns almost on sight. The Russians were low on guns, ammunition, supplies and, worst of all, spirit. "An effective aerial force might make all the difference," the doctor continued. "With some skilled pilots and a few machines, you can better anticipate enemy movements and perhaps even conduct some strafing and bombing runs into German-held territory."

Fassenbiender went on to outline what we would need in terms of supplies and personnel for the project. Kerensky listened with a look of interest. He was clearly considering the possibilities. I'm sure he was also considering what a turn in the war situation could mean for his political aspirations. He nodded firmly when Dr. Fassenbiender finished.

"Very well, Doctor, Mr. Zachary," he said. "You make a strong case, and we are in need of whatever weapons we can use against our enemy. I will see to it that you receive what you need to carry out your project and create a small air force to assist our soldiers in the field. Colonel Yuloff, I am appointing you to work with these men and be their liaison with the army."

"Sir," Yuloff said by way of acknowledgment.

"I look forward to seeing your work, gentlemen," Kerensky said. "Good luck to us all."

***

Our first order of business after getting Kerensky's approval was putting something—or rather someone—to rest. On the small field outside Petrograd the Russian army had provided for us to use as an aerodrome, those of us who had escaped from Germany held a brief ceremony to honor Angus McMullen. Mad Angus was the one member of our little group who didn't make it out of Germany—another victim of the Black Ace, Heinrich Kisler.

Each of us said a few words about Angus and agreed that he would have wanted to go out in a fight the way he did—in a fight in the skies. Then we drank a toast to his memory and I had to fight back a coughing fit as the Russian vodka burned its way down my throat, nearly bringing tears to my eyes. I didn't mention Angus' story about stolen British gold, and I wondered briefly about where it might be hidden, but such thoughts quickly gave way to the work that lay ahead of us.

Although we were all pilots, only Dr. Fassenbiender was skilled in the mechanics of aeroplane design. In the Escadrille, and in most other Air Squadrons throughout the war, pilots had a number of mechanics to care for their machines on the ground. I knew the essentials of how an aeroplane functioned, enough to understand the machine's abilities and limitations. But I was more familiar with the inner workings of a machine gun than a plane, since I was more often called upon to fix a jammed gun in midair.

Under Dr. Fassenbiender's guidance, we all became aeroplane mechanics, studying the design and construction of our purloined German machines—even taking one of them apart and putting it back together several times to see how the engine and various other moving parts functioned. The good doctor almost constantly pointed out ways he thought the German machines could be improved, once we had the proper equipment to do the job.

It didn't take too long to acquire them, either. Although the Russian factories seemed always to be behind in producing enough rifles, ammunition and artillery shells for the army, the influence of Minister Kerensky and Colonel Yuloff was enough to secure whatever Dr. Fassenbiender needed, if it was available at all. We were sometimes forced to improvise with the tools at hand, since Russia had next to nothing in the way of aircraft herself. In effect, we had to create a new aircraft industry from scratch.

We designed and built planes almost entirely by hand, like constructing giant models that actually flew. Tractor and automotive parts and equipment were retooled to serve our needs, and canvas meant for sails became the covering for wings. Stout wood from the Russian forests was planed and shaped into frameworks. Jack Mulligan even displayed a flair for art and took to painting insignia on the tail and wings of our new craft, while painting over the black crosses of the German machines.

There was some debate at first over what our insignia should be. We were a rag-tag group of three Americans, a German, an Englishman, and a Frenchman in service to Russia's provisional government, which was not more than a year old. We finally settled on a white star edged in red, echoing the colors of our homelands and honoring the colors of our patrons.

Once our German machines were retooled, several of us, myself included, were eager to begin flying some missions along the Eastern Front, where the Russian army was waging a difficult struggle against the Germans and Prussians, with the Germans fortunately still tied up in France for the most part. However, Colonel Yuloff pointed out that the Russians did not want to play their hand too quickly; nor did they want to lose their newest weapon, should we be shot down or fall into enemy hands. Although I didn't much care for the colonel's estimation of our abilities, I agreed we should keep our sorties to a minimum while we also trained new Russian pilots to handle the machines and Dr. Fassenbiender oversaw the design of new aeroplanes.

I was quite surprised when Yuloff himself volunteered to be trained as a pilot. In fact, he insisted, saying he could not endorse any training program he was not willing to undertake himself. I suspected from the beginning that Yuloff felt the call of the skies in his blood, like many pilots, and would have wanted to learn regardless of whether he was in command. He proved an able student, better than many of the dozen or so Russian soldiers chosen to train with us.

The training was painstakingly slow because of the limitations under which we operated. We had few enough machines as it was, and Dr. Fassenbiender estimated it would be well over a month before any of the new ones were finished. So we spent a great deal of time on the ground, showing our would-be pilots the ropes of operating the machine before we even lifted off. We used the Albatross as a training vehicle, since it was the only two-seater, allowing an experienced pilot to ride along with the student. Even with our preparations, we nearly lost the Albatross on several occasions, and we spent considerable time fixing up the results of minor bang-ups and botched landings.

On a few occasions, some of us were able to fly to a staging area near the front lines, refuel, and head out over the lines for a look-see. What we saw was not encouraging at all. The Russians outnumbered the Prussians and the Germans, but in nearly all other areas the enemy army was superior. They were better equipped and better organized, and they had far better morale. Even machines flying overhead boosted Russian morale only slightly, and I heard that some of the front-line troops actually considered our small Air Squadron a waste of time and money. For a soldier who had to wait until one of his comrades died to acquire a rifle, I can see how that might be. We had little or no word from the Western Front, but I sincerely hoped things were going better there than they were here.

So my mood was already somewhat somber when Grigori Yuloff appeared at the aerodrome early one August morning for his flying lesson. Yuloff looked as saddened and angry as I had ever seen him. As I dropped down from the wing of the plane I was inspecting, he shook his head and looked at me.

"We may have a problem," he said. "Prime Minister Kerensky has removed General Kornilov as commander in chief of the army. He says Kornilov is plotting a coup against the provisional government. His army units may be moving on the city as we speak."

CHAPTER

10

CHOOSING SIDES

"What?" I said, looking at Yuloff in disbelief. "How can that be?"

The Russian soldier shook his head sadly. "I do not know, but I have just received word from Petrograd. The prime minister has evidence that General Kornilov is planning a coup to depose him and the provisional government. Kerensky has removed him from office and ordered him to appear in Petrograd, but the general refuses to obey the order, and rumors say he will come to Petrograd only with an army at his back."

I knew General Kornilov only by reputation. He was a Cossack and spent most of his time at the front. Kerensky had appointed him commander in chief of the Russian army only a month before, in hopes he could restore order and discipline to the dispirited Russian troops. I recalled that Kornilov had made certain demands of the prime minister, things he needed in order to get the job done, like harsher disciplinary measures for desertion and mutiny and increased production from the Russian factories. On most counts, Kerensky hadn't delivered.

I also knew Kornilov was a popular military leader, both with the general populace and with a lot of the politicians in the provisional government. Even if he was something of a tyrant, the general had a reputation for getting the job done, and that carried a lot of weight with people.

"What does the prime minister want us to do?" I asked.

"For the time being, nothing," Yuloff said. "Kerensky has ordered soldiers in Petrograd to guard and reinforce government buildings like the Winter Palace. He wants you and your aeroplanes to stay out of the situation. If Kornilov does attempt to take the city, you will have to be prepared to leave at once. Perhaps you can carry some of the government officials to safety."

"Yeah, and leave behind their families and subordinates to face a coup?"

Yuloff gave an expressive shrug. "What else can we do?" he said. "The orders are given."

"Well, I'm not part of the Russian army," I said. "I gave up following orders when I left my squadron to hunt for Kisler, and I don't know that I'm too crazy about following them now."

Yuloff's brows drew closer together and his eyes narrowed dangerously. I was concerned for a moment he would try to ensure that I did exactly what the prime minister wanted, but then he nodded and clapped me on the arm with one massive hand.

"Nor am I," he said. He looked like he wanted to say something further, but instead he turned to look over the machine I'd just climbed down from.

"I think we should dispense with our lesson for today," he said. "I have other matters to attend to."

"All right, then. It's not like you need a lot more training," I said. "You're becoming a good pilot."

A smile split Yuloff's face. "Thank you," he said, clapping my shoulder again before turning and walking out of the hangar. I was left alone with the machines to contemplate what was happening, and I had a lot to think about.

***

Kornilov's anticipated coup never did happen. The general did order troops into the area of Petrograd and did promise the Russian people that he would throw back the Germans and convene a constituent assembly to address problems with the provisional government. We only learned later that the entire affair was the result of a huge misunderstanding between Kerensky and Kornilov, worsened by Kerensky's paranoia and fear of a coup.

Kerensky contacted the commander of the Cavalry Corps approaching Petrograd, General Alexander Krymov, and invited him to the Winter Palace under a promise of safe conduct to talk over the matter. Yuloff told me that when Krymov arrived, Kerensky ordered him to report to the Military-Naval Court for discipline for following a traitor. Instead, Krymov went to a friend's apartment and put a bullet through his own heart, ending the conflict between his commander in chief and his prime minister.

But the situation in Russia was becoming steadily worse. The army was in shambles, unable to defeat the Germans even with huge odds in their favor. Kerensky was descending into paranoia, seeing threats to his power in every shadow, while the provisional government was paralyzed with political infighting and the uppermost ranks of the military were either too busy politicking or out of favor with Kerensky to accomplish anything. Any leader that did take the initiative, like Kornilov, was seen as a potential threat to those already in power.

That's when I started to wonder about the little air squadron I was helping to put together. How long would it be before Kerensky decided we were a threat to his power and influence? How many of the supply delays and problems we had were because the provisional government didn't want us becoming too useful in the war effort? Already we had no lack of people who wanted to be pilots, and a lot of Russians saw us as a slim sign of hope in the desperation of the war. Those qualities had to be threatening to a man like Kerensky.

I finally turned to Dr. Fassenbiender. I had never really had the chance to get to know my own father; he left us when I was only a child. I'd begun to think of Fassenbiender as the father I never knew. The doctor remained quiet while I explained my rambling thoughts to him and then stood and made his way to the window of the small office he kept in the hangar, littered with drawings and plans for new machines and improvements on existing ones. Small machine parts and tools held the papers in place. Somehow Fassenbiender still knew where every single thing in the room was. Looking out the window onto the field outside, Fassenbiender sighed deeply.

"You want to know what I think, my boy?" he said, not looking back at me. "I think I am happy to see my family and to be doing the work that I love, and that happiness has made me blind to things that are going on around me. You're right: a man like Kerensky is going to consider you … us … a threat to him, sooner or later. And when that happens … " He left the thought unfinished, but his meaning was clear. If Kerensky decided we'd outlived our usefulness or, worse yet, were a threat to him, then he would do whatever was necessary to ensure we weren't a problem anymore.

"I didn't want to involve you in this, Nathan," Fassenbiender said, turning away from the window, "but perhaps you're already involved, and you have a right to know."

"To know what?" I asked. The doctor shook his head.

"*Nein*, not here, and not now. Meet me back here tonight at eleven, and I will explain everything. Then we can talk about what is happening, and what our options are."

I was burning with curiosity but I withheld my questions and agreed to do as he asked. I left the hangar with more questions than I'd come in with, but an assurance that I would have some answers soon.

I moved through the rest of the day like a dream, barely paying attention to what was going on. Reports from the front were as bad as ever, but fortunately the Germans were still focusing most of their attention on the Western Front. Many had feared they would press the attack all the way to Petrograd and Moscow, but they seemed content with the status quo for the time being.

At dinner there was a lot of talk about the new planes we were supposed to be getting, planes I knew were the focus of some hostility from Russian soldiers who didn't even have decent equipment, while the provisional government devoted resources to new planes. Johnson talked about some Russian girl he had met, in enough detail to keep everyone but me riveted. I excused myself early and tried to get some rest, since I had no idea how long my conversation with Dr. Fassenbiender would last. But sleep didn't come, no matter how hard I tried. So I just lay in my bunk and thought about how a gypsy kid from America had ended up at the age of nearly 17 in a foreign land far from home. I was probably considered a traitor to my country, working with the Russian army on the far side of a war, and I was responsible for the lives of so many people.

When the time finally came, I threw on my flight jacket and made my way quietly out to the hangar, sliding open the door just enough to slip inside. It was dark, lit only by faint shafts of moonlight coming in through the dirty windows. I could see the light in Dr. Fassenbiender's office leaking under his door, and I made my way toward it, opening the door quietly.

He was waiting behind his desk, dressed in his usual rumpled suit, his face thrown into deep shadow by the single light on his desk.

"Mr. Zachary," he said, "please, sit down." I moved some things off the nearest chair and pulled it up to the desk to sit across from him. Fassenbiender cleared his throat and glanced down, collecting his thoughts.

"My boy, how much do you know about politics?" he began.

"As little as possible, Doc," I said with a smile. "I'm just a pilot."

"Yes, but a pilot in the middle of a war, in a country that's in political turmoil," Fassenbiender added. "I think it would benefit you to know a little something about the situation—not the war, but Russia, and what's happening here."

He leaned back a bit from his desk, with the air of a schoolteacher about to deliver a lecture. "Do you know anything about a man named Karl Marx?" he asked.

"I think so. He was a philosopher, wasn't he? And German?"

"*Ja*," the doctor said. "He said, 'The empirical world must be arranged so that in it man experiences and gets used to what is human. If man is shaped by his surroundings, his surroundings must be made human.' He is trying to make some sense out of the oftentimes mad world that we live in."

"Sounds like an idea Russia could use," I said, and Fassenbiender smiled broadly.

"Exactly, my boy, exactly. That is why I wanted to talk to you, to make you aware of the other options and of what we're doing."

"We?" I asked. Dr. Fassenbiender rose from behind his desk and made his way over to the door. He put on his long coat and opened the door.

"Come," he said, "and I'll show you."

Behind the hangar a dark motorcar was waiting with a shadowy figure leaning against it, difficult to distinguish in the dark.

"So," rumbled a deep voice, "you think he's ready, then?" I recognized it immediately.

"Grigori?" I asked, finally making out the Russian colonel's features. He nodded.

"Let's be on our way," Fassenbiender said.

"One moment," Yuloff interrupted and turned toward me. "Do you know that what we do now is very dangerous, and that some might consider it treason? Think carefully before you decide to come along with us."

I glanced over at Dr. Fassenbiender, his expression lost in the shadows, then back at Col. Yuloff. "If you both feel it's important, then I'm going with you. I don't care what anyone else thinks—I'd rather make up my own mind about things."

Yuloff nodded. "Very well, then," he said. "Get in."

We climbed into the car with Yuloff at the wheel, and he drove us into a part of Petrograd I was unfamiliar with, at least from the ground. I'd flown over it several times, but that didn't convey the feel of the darkened, maze-like streets at night, with only a few lonely lights burning. We were some distance from the river and the Winter Palace. I tried to take note of any landmarks, but there were none I recognized. I suspected Yuloff was deliberately taking a roundabout route, just so I would have difficulty finding my way back.

Eventually we made our way out of the city to a secluded villa a short distance away. It must have been after midnight when we arrived. While it was no match for the Winter Palace, the villa was still an impressive building, far more so than the crowded houses of Petrograd.

"It belongs to Madame Mishesinskaia," Dr. Fassenbiender said quietly, "the ballerina. It is said she was the mistress of the Tsarevich Nicholas in her youth. A fitting place for us to meet, eh?" When I shot him a confused look he only smiled and said, "You will see. Come along now, my boy."

We entered the fine villa, shedding our coats in the spacious foyer before a grim-faced young Russian led us into the library. The fireplace was cold, but the room was lit by a number of small lamps. Tall shelves lined with books covered one wall, while a beautiful portrait of a woman I could only assume was Mme. Mshesinskaia hung on one wall. Two men sat in the room, engaged in deep conversation; they rose to greet us when we entered. The scents of tobacco and liquor hung heavy in the air.

Both men had dark hair and wore dark suits. One was balding, with a neatly trimmed goatee and piercing eyes that seemed to take in every detail. The other had a thatch of dark hair, a full mustache, and a small, pointed beard. He wore small, wire-rimmed spectacles that made him look bookish, like Dr. Fassenbiender, but did nothing to conceal the glint of keen intellect and what I suspected was a powerful personality. Both men were quite animated and seemed pleased to see us. They greeted Fassenbiender and Yuloff warmly but were a bit more guarded when they turned their attention toward me.

"Gentlemen," Yuloff said in English (purely for my benefit, I'm sure), "may I present to you Mr. Nathan Zachary, late of Escadrille Lafayette, and a capable pilot and teacher." He turned to me, gesturing to the men.

"Nathan, these are our hosts: Leon Trotsky," the man with the spectacles nodded slightly in acknowledgment, "and Vladimir Lenin, the architects of a new Russia!"

CHAPTER

11

COLD OCTOBER

Whatever history might come to think of him, Vladimir Lenin was a very persuasive, charismatic man. I found my discussion with him and Trotsky that evening compelling. The two men outlined their philosophy of socialism, based on the works of Marx and other thinkers, and described the revolutions that had taken place thus far in Russia as only a prelude to the one that was coming. A revolution to sweep away the provisional government and put a new one in its place, a government that met the needs of the Russian people first, the peasants and farmers that suffered first under the rule of the Tsars, then under ministers like Kerensky.

The infighting between Kerensky and Kornilov was merely a symptom of the greater disease they called Imperialism, with powerful politicians and generals fighting for the reins of power while the common people suffered. They wanted to put an end to that, something I saw as an admirable goal. In hindsight, perhaps it wasn't the best decision I'd ever made. But, by the end of the night, as the hours stretched on toward morning, I agreed to help in whatever way I could, if it would put an end to the conflict and help ensure the safety of the people I felt responsible for. We parted with handshakes and mutual good-will, with Trotsky informing me that it wouldn't be long before the Bolsheviks would make their move.

We talked little as we drove back to the aerodrome. I was alone with my thoughts and I considered what I was going to do next. I'd offered the Bolsheviks my personal support, for whatever that was worth, but implicit in that was the support of my small squadron. Before I could be comfortable with that, however, there was something I had to do.

"You did what?" Johnny Johnson said the next day. I'd gathered my men around Dr. Fassenbiender's desk in his office. It was a little bit crowded, but what I had to tell them wasn't for anyone else's ears. Johnson, Jack Mulligan, Emile Dellier, and Eddie Lancourt were there, along with Dr. Fassenbiender. I didn't invite Colonel Yuloff, partly because I thought his presence would make matters more difficult and because I wanted everyone to feel they could speak freely. The close quarters made it easy for Johnson to get right in my face, which was what he was doing.

"I met with the leaders of the Bolsheviks and told them I supported their goals," I repeated, keeping control of my temper. I didn't much care for Johnson's tone, although his reaction was understandable, and not entirely unexpected. "Still, I can't speak for the rest of this squadron, especially about something as important as this, which is why I'm telling you this. I want to know what you think and what you want to do."

"Sure, but you already told your Russian buddies that you'd help them out!" Johnson continued unabated. Jack Mulligan put a hand on his shoulder.

"Ease off, Johnny," he said. "He just did what he thought was right, and he said he wasn't speaking for any of us." He turned to me, "Nate, you know me, I'm no politician or anything, just a pilot. What do you think of these guys and their plans? What makes you think they can pull this off?"

I silently thanked Jack for his support and leaned back against the desk. "Russia is falling apart," I said. "The provisional government can't get anything done, the army is a mess, and there are protests and near riots in cities like Petrograd and Moscow. The little people are the ones caught in the middle of it all, just like the farmers and villagers in France where all the trenches are getting dug. If things fall apart, what's going to happen to them? I know this isn't our country, but they've helped us out and, the way I see it, we should help them out."

"Whether they want it or not?" Lancourt spoke up.

"I think they do want it," I said. "You just have to look at some of the protests in Petrograd to see that. People aren't happy with the way things are being run around here, they want a change, and the Bolsheviks are going to make their move, with or without us."

"Then why bother?" Johnson said. "If there's going to be a revolution, let's get out of here and back to the Allied lines. If we get to France or England, or even Finland, we can start over again or even get back home."

Home. That was what it was all about for them, I realized, and not for me. Yuloff was involved with the Bolsheviks because he felt it was the best thing for his homeland, and Dr. Fassenbiender because of his wife and daughter. The others wanted to get back to wherever they called home to pick up lives they put on hold to join the war effort. But me, I didn't have a home to go back to. Because my tribe was always on the move, I wasn't even sure where my mom was anymore. I hoped one day to be able to find her again. In the meantime, was I just doing this because I wanted to find some way to make myself a home, a place where I felt I belonged? Maybe. And was that so bad a thing?

"I can't keep anyone from leaving," I said slowly. "If that's what you want to do, then do it. But I'm staying here, and I'm going to try and help make things right, whatever it takes. We've gotten a lot of help here … "

"From the provisional government!" Johnson interjected.

"We've gotten a lot of help here," I continued, shooting him a look, "and, provisional government or not, it's the Russian people who ultimately paid for it. I aim to pay them back, if I can. Now, who's with me on this?"

Jack Mulligan was the first to step forward. "I am, boss. If you and Dr. Fassenbiender think it's the right thing, then I'm in. 'Sides, it doesn't seem right to run out now that things are startin' to happen."

"You can count me in as well, old fellow," Lancourt said. "I never cared for Kerensky myself, and it certainly couldn't hurt to have the new government owe us a favor."

"Oui," Emile said, "perhaps we can get more planes and more men and get this war over with all the sooner, no? I am with you, also."

I turned to Johnny, who straightened up and lifted his hands from the desk he'd been leaning on.

"Johnson, what about you?" He glowered at everyone for a moment.

"All right," he said, "count me in. I'm not going to run off in the middle of a fight. Besides, you bums would probably mess it up if I weren't around. If we're gonna do this, we might as well do it right."

"Glad to have you along," I said, extending a hand. Johnson gave a wry smile and shook it, our differences settled for the time being.

"All right, then," I said, "here's what we're going to do."

***

The next few weeks were tense, as we continued to go about our normal routines as much as possible, while keeping alert for the moment when the Bolsheviks decided to make their move. In many ways, Kerensky played right into their hands. He'd called on the Bolshevik faction to support him when he believed Kornilov was planning to invade Petrograd, handing over thousands of Russian-made rifles and other supplies to Bolshevik troops in preparation. Those supplies quietly disappeared into the background until they were needed.

Our small air squadron continued its training and preparation for war missions that would never come. Although we still sometimes flew patrols, there was little to see along the front lines except more of the status quo and the disheartened Russian troops. Their morale remained at an all-time low, and the military higher-ups were split among the various factions supporting one side or another in Russia.

In mid-September, the Bolsheviks gained a majority in elections in the workers sections of Petrograd and Moscow. The movement was clearly gaining in strength and popularity, particularly in the cities where so many workers toiled in factories to produce the equipment the military desperately needed. All the Party needed was an opportunity. In early October, they got one.

A German naval operation in the Gulf of Riga seized three strategic islands, perilously close to Petrograd, one of Russia's only seaports and the only one near the front lines of the war. The Russian General Staff recommended to Kerensky that they prepare to move the seat of the government to Moscow in case the Germans tried to take Petrograd. Kerensky probably didn't see the loss of Petrograd as that great, considering it was also a hotbed of revolution, but the provisional government rejected the plan. Instead, they proposed the formation of a committee to assume charge of the city's security against not only the Germans, but also any "domestic revolutionaries" that might cause trouble.

The Bolsheviks supported the proposal since the new Military-Revolutionary Committee (or Milrevcom) was backed almost entirely by Bolshevik troops. In effect, Kerensky handed responsibility for the protection of Petrograd into the hands of those who wanted to depose him. The time for the revolution had come.

"Are you ready?" Yuloff asked me as I picked up my flight jacket. I paused for a moment before shrugging into the well-worn leather that was my constant companion.

"As ready as I'm gonna be," I said. "I'd still like to be doing more than causing trouble for the German navy."

"It will be enough," the Russian colonel replied. "With your squadron working with Milrevcom and showing the people that we are accomplishing things, as well as providing a spectacle to keep all eyes focused on the harbor, things will go more smoothly when the Committee announces its plans to the people."

I picked up my flight gear from where it sat on the wing of my new machine. Dr. Fassenbiender based it off the Spad, which was seeing use along the Eastern Front these days, although he assured me it was a better build machine than most of the Spads in service. We called them "Firebirds" after a creature from Russian mythology Natalia Fassenbiender told me about. It certainly had it all over the German Pfalz I flew into Russia, and even my old Nieuport that got shot down by the Black Ace. I'd spent plenty of hours flying it and it was a fine machine. I'd just finished going over it one last time to make sure everything was in order.

"We'll put on a good show," I said, "you can count on that."

"We are, *tovarich*," Yuloff said gravely, "we are."

"Are we ready?" Jack Mulligan asked, coming into the hangar. He was immediately followed by Johnny Johnson, then Lancourt and Dellier, who all began suiting up.

"Finally," Johnson said, "a chance to take down some Huns, even if they are just floating targets." Jack smiled and chuckled as the other two pilots exchanged glances and grins. I couldn't help but echo them, knowing that shooting fish in a barrel was Johnson's idea of a fair fight. No doubt if he did any damage we'd be hearing tales about it for months to come.

In short order, we were ready. I'd asked Yuloff if he wanted to come with us on this flight, but he declined, saying his presence was more important on the ground with the troops of the Bolshevik cause. From what I'd picked up on, it sounded like the Milrevcom commanded the loyalty of only a fraction of the troops, but it was still greater than the loyalty commanded by Kerensky and the provisional government following the Kornilov incident. The Committee simply hoped the majority of the remaining troops would choose to remain neutral and stay out of the way. It was a gamble, but Lenin, in particular, felt swift and decisive action was required in order to succeed.

Yuloff still assisted in getting the planes fired up and soon we taxied out onto the field and took to the air. As soon as my Firebird left the ground I felt as if I'd left all my doubts and concerns behind. Soaring through the air and climbing to greater and greater heights, I knew there was nothing we could not accomplish, including paving the way for a new and better Russia, or dealing with a few German ships. We circled the field, dropping into formation with my plane in the lead, then set course for the Baltic Sea and our German quarry.

The mission was a fairly simple one: we were to strafe the German ships holding territory near Petrograd. It would send a clear message to the Germans that rumors of a Russian air squadron were true, and show the people in Petrograd, Moscow and on the front that the Milrevcom was getting things done, that they were the best hope for Russia. Trotsky called it a "propaganda victory" and I suppose that it was. Still, it wasn't a cakewalk, since we were attacking near sunset and would have to make our way back to the aerodrome before it got too dark to navigate. Although the Germans didn't have any air-power of their own with them, their ships still had guns more than capable of smashing our machines, and the Baltic Sea was no place to attempt any sort of landing, particularly in the end of October.

We stayed on course and in a short while left the land behind to soar out over the choppy waters of the sea at an altitude of some 15,000 feet. The sea air was cold and a stiff wind made level flying difficult. My machine swayed and jumped, making me fight to keep her on course from time to time. Still we stayed in formation and I was proud of how my comrades handled the weather.

Emile waggled the wings of his machine and I looked down at the darkly gleaming waters. The sharp-eyed Frenchman had spotted our quarry! Three German ships lay at anchor near an island not far from St. Petersburg. The provisional government feared they might move close enough to shore to launch a bombardment, although they were too far away to attempt anything like that now. I dipped my wings in response and signaled everyone to prepare for our attack. Then I banked my machine and started into a dive.

The Firebird handled beautifully, and was capable of a much steeper dive than the Nieuport with less risk of losing fabric, something I would not want to see out here. The German ships grew larger and larger below as we raced down to meet them. By the time I could make out sailors scurrying along the deck, I was certain they had spotted us. They were likely trying to bring their big guns to bear, but they were moving at a snail's pace compared to us.

I plunged straight at the deck of one of the ships and pressed the triggers for the twinned machine guns mounted on my machine's prow. Tracer rounds lit the air as bullets showered down on the ship, striking sparks from her rails and deck plates and sending sailors scattering for cover. At only a few hundred feet from the deck, I pulled my Firebird out of the dive and swooped a scant few dozen feet over the sailor's heads, starting to climb again and banking to the left so I could come around for another pass.

I could hear the chatter of gunfire behind and to my side as my compatriots made similar strafing runs against the ships, two of us for each. Jack was my wingman, and I could see him staying in close formation as I banked away from the ship.

A booming report caught my attention, followed by the whistle and dull "whump" as a shell from one of the ships streaked through the air, exploding some thirty yards away from my machine. The force of the blast made my Firebird buck a little, but no worse than the wind had done, and the flak didn't do any serious damage. I was reminded of dodging old Archie back along the German lines, although I couldn't assume that these sailors were poor shots like the Hun anti-air artillery.

I looped around to come at the German ship from the aft and Jack followed along, smooth as silk. We swept in, guns blazing, and sailors scattered like field mice confronted by a diving hawk. I saw several of them literally dive overboard into the chilly waters to avoid being hit. Several others were not so lucky. This time, instead of pulling up right away, I put my machine into a roll, flying sideways and practically skimming the rail of the ship before righting myself on the other side of its stacks and letting loose with another volley of fire along the foredeck. Jack matched me the whole way and I knew this was one encounter the Germans were certain to remember!

As I soared over the end of the ship and started to climb again, as the guns boomed once more. I banked hard to the left, just in time to see another Firebird that was sweeping down toward one of the other ships burst into flames. The plane's right wing fell in flaming shards. The machine continued to drop down like a comet, crashing into the deck of the ship and scattering burning debris across it. I saw several sailors leap out of the way, some of them over the rail into the drink, but no sign of the pilot jumping clear of the crash. The plane's fuel tank caught with a boom, sending a thick pillar of black smoke roiling up into the sky. Another shell burst close to my machine, too close, tearing me away from the spectacle of the burning wreckage.

I pulled my machine up and waggled my wings to indicate that the others should do the same. We fell back into formation as best we could and began gaining altitude as the German guns continued to boom, although no other shot came even close to us. We circled once around the area with the black column of smoke in the center before I turned and led the flight away from the ships, saying a silent prayer for whoever it was we left behind.

It was these moments in combat that I hated the most, knowing that a friend and comrade was lost but not knowing who. It was as if I had to mourn all my friends on the flight back to the aerodrome before I could discover the identity of the unfortunate one. I could see why Rickenbacker had advised me against getting too close to the men I flew with. Anger and sorrow wrestled inside me. I'd led them into this, and now one of them was gone. Even if he'd somehow survived the crash—which I seriously doubted—he would be the prisoner of the Germans once more, and probably not treated as well as we were the first time.

It seemed an eternity before we reached the aerodrome once more, low on fuel and the sky growing darker with each passing moment. Lanterns lit the landing field, allowing us to set down with no further problems. When my machine rolled to a stop, I leapt out and removed my headgear, looking at the faces of each of the other men that disembarked their machines. Jack, Johnny, Eddie Lancourt, but no sign of Emile, the clever Frenchman whose sharp eyes spotted our quarry. The man who hoped our involvement with the Bolsheviks might end the war that much sooner.

We drank to Emile's memory that night, and I hoped his sacrifice would at least allow his hope to come true, to put an end to the senseless violence. Little did I know then that it was only just beginning.

CHAPTER

UP IN SMOKE

My wake up call about the "glorious revolution" came literally one night while I was sleeping off another long day of meetings and working at the aerodrome to further the training of the Russian pilots. The Committee remained interested in the opportunities offered by having air power on their side, despite the problems with our assault on the Germans in the Baltic.

"Nathan," said a German-accented voice as a hand shook my shoulder. "Nathan, wake up, my boy."

"Hrrmm?" I managed as I opened bleary eyes to see Dr. Fassenbiender standing over me, a stricken look on his face. "What is it, doctor?" I asked, "What time is it?" He shook his head sadly.

"They're dead," he said and I became instantly awake.

"Who's dead?"

"The Tsar," he began. That wasn't unexpected. Tsar Nicolas had been in exile for months, even before the October Revolution secured power for the Bolsheviks. Most believed it was only a matter of time before the Committee had him tried and executed. But I didn't recall hearing anything about a trial.

"But it's more than that," Fassenbiender went on to say. "They didn't just kill the Tsar. They had the entire royal family butchered, along with several of their servants. All the Romanovs, women and children included. They had Duke Michael killed a nearly a week ago."

"But the trial …" I began and Fassenbiender's grip on my shoulder tightened.

"Don't you understand, my boy? There was no trial! No public hearing, no sentencing, just soldiers going in the night to take the royal family down into the cellar and shoot them dead, then cart their bodies away where no one will ever find them! They feared the possibility of a counter-revolution too much."

"But … how? How did you find out about it?" I said still reeling from the news.

"I overhead a Bolshevik soldier talking about it," Fassenbiender said. "He was drinking rather heavily and said he was one of the men sent to carry out the orders."

"Maybe he was just making it up …" I began, but the doctor shook his head grimly.

"No, he knew too many details," he said. "I saw it in his eyes. No, he saw what he said he saw."

I was stunned by the implications. For the most part, the communist revolution that seized control of Russia was relatively peaceful, as such things went. The Provisional Government had offered practically no resistance to the October Revolution. To hear it told, the Bolshevik revolutionaries simply walked into military headquarters and other key places, the soldiers of the Provisional Government got up and walked out, and the Red Army moved in and sat down. Kerensky fled to the front, but otherwise the remaining government officials were quietly taken into custody and made no trouble for the new regime.

Of greater concern to me and to the rest of the squadron was the speed with which the Bolsheviks turned to Imperial Germany for aid and assistance in consolidating their new government. They ratified the Brest-Litovsk Treaty not long after seizing power, signing an armistice with the Germans and ending Russian involvement in the Great War. Although that was a concern it was nothing to match the troubles that followed, as the new Communist government slowly began to gain greater and greater control over the nation, despite resistance from the White Russian Army.

In March of 1918, the Soviets transferred their capitol from Petrograd to Moscow, much as Kerensky had been asked to do months before. They declared that all property belonged to the state and encountered resistance from the Russian peasant farmers, understandably reluctant to give up their entire grain harvests to a government they scarcely knew, even if it claimed to be fighting for their rights. The summer saw the beginning of civil war in Russia, as Red Army troops sought to pacify and control peasant uprisings, along with defections within the army, like the rebellion of the Czechoslovak Legion.

But this was the final straw, the beginning of the purge of "seditious elements" starting with the Tsar and his family. A few hours after Dr. Fassenbiender woke me I burst into the office occupied by Grigori Yuloff in Petrograd. Col. Yuloff represented the Bolshevik government in the city and was in charge of ensuring a "peaceful transfer of power." I also suspected he was in charge of keeping an eye on my air squadron and Dr. Fassenbiender, along with the progress of our work. I ignored the protests from the guard outside as I stalked up to the office door and threw it open.

"Yuloff! I want words with you!"

The colonel and another man, wearing a military uniform, looked up from their conversation when I burst into the room. Yuloff's look of surprise went away quickly and he nodded to the expectant guard behind me, who backed off a few paces. I didn't even consider how thin the ice was that I was walking on. I rarely did when something motivated me to act from the heart. I suppose that was always my greatest strength, and my greatest failing.

"We need to talk," I said.

Without missing a beat, Yuloff turned to the other man and said, "We will conclude this business later, Captain." The soldier got up, saluted, and walked past me as he headed for the door. Our eyes met for a moment and I thought I saw a flicker of recognition. No surprise there, considering my picture had appeared alongside Fassenbiender and the rest of the squadron in Pravda and several of the other government-allowed publications.

When the door closed behind the departing soldier, Yuloff leaned back in his chair, resting his hands on the edge of the antique desk. I took several steps closer. If he felt threatened by my presence, the colonel certainly didn't show it.

"Now then," he said, "what can I do for you Comrade Zachary?"

"Is it true?" I asked. "Were the Tsar and his family murdered?"

Yuloff's eyes narrowed and he covered his surprise well. "How do you know about that?"

"Is it true?" I repeated

"Were they murdered?" Yuloff said in a patronizing tone. "Of course not. They were executed, as enemies of the state."

"Executed without a trial," I interjected. "And not just Nicholas, but his entire family!" Yuloff didn't even flinch.

"We can hardly make our nation safe from Imperialism if we allow the greatest imperialists to continue to exist as a focus for counter-revolution." I could practically heard Lenin or Trotsky speaking when he said it, like he was quoting something from one of their tracts on rule by the proletariat.

"Then you knew about this," I said. It wasn't a question and Yuloff's expression showed it wasn't in error, either.

"Certain sacrifices had to be made," he said flatly.

"So long as you don't have to be the one to make them, right?"

Yuloff's face darkened. "We have all made sacrifices, Nathan," he said. "We have all done what was needed to bring this nation, our nation, into the 20th century and out of the dark ages of Imperialism."

"Even if that's not what her people want?" I remembered what Eddie Lancourt had said when I talked the rest of the Squadron into going along with this. Now it seemed like he was right.

"The people," Yuloff said, almost with a note of contempt. "The people do not understand the nature of government as we do. All they understand is that the harvest has been poor and the revolution asks much of them, for the benefit of everyone. In time …"

"In time what? You'll bring them to heel? They're not dogs, Yuloff, they're people! And I think they understand a great deal more than you think. They certainly understand a lot more than I did."

Without giving Yuloff time for an answer, I turned and stormed out of the office, slamming the door behind me. I was a good distance down the hall before I noticed the officer Yuloff had been talking to following me. I stopped and turned toward him, raising my guard as I appraised him carefully. He didn't seem hostile, so I allowed him to approach.

"Your pardon, but I could not help but notice you are upset, Comrade Zachary," he said in heavily accented English. His tone dropped a bit pitched only for my ears. "And I regret to say you are not the only one displeased with the current turn of events. Is there somewhere we can speak privately?"

"I think so, Captain … ?"

"Rostov, Mikhail Rostov. There are several things I would like to speak to you about, including your future within the new regime."

"Or lack thereof?" I said. Rostov didn't smile but his expression showed that I'd hit the mark before he nodded slightly.

"Meet me at the aerodrome," I said, "I look forward to what you have to say."

***

Capt. Mikhail Rostov was a young officer in the army, one of many won over by Bolshevik propaganda and rhetoric, not unlike me in many ways. Like many military men, he was seeking an end to the war, or at least a government that supported the needs of the military more than the Provisional Government had done. But now he found himself in the position of waging a way against his own people. Having come from peasant stock himself, Rostov found the civil war a moral dilemma of the first order. The government that claimed to have the concerns of the proletariat at heart was in the position of forcing them to accept its help and guidance. Rostov explained as much to Dr. Fassenbiender and me in the tiny office at the aerodrome.

"And now the purges of Imperialists and those loyal to the old order," he said with a sigh. "It is too much. Now that they have won, the Bolsheviks are turning against their own people like maddened dogs. It seems like the killing will never end. But it must, if Russia is to survive."

"You said you knew something about my future in the new regime, or a lack of one," I said and Rostov nodded.

"*Da*, the Central Committee thinks your aeroplanes and the new machines designed by Dr. Fassenbiender may be important, both in putting down any resistance to the new regime and to safeguarding the security of Mother Russia against foreign invaders. The Germans are reluctant to share their aerial technology, but some believe if Russia can demonstrate similar machinery the Germans will be more willing to sell machines to us, so we can train more pilots and build our own aerial force."

Dr. Fassenbiender's face went white while Rostov spoke and I felt my stomach do a long, slow turn, like feeling the bottom drop out at 15,000 feet.

"*Mein Gott,*" Fassenbiender said softly. "You mean they would use these machines against civilian targets? Against peasants armed with nothing more than pitchforks and a few hunting rifles? That's madness!"

"That is the madness that grips Russia, Doctor," Rostov said. "The Bolsheviks have achieved their Glorious Revolution and they mean to ensure that it succeeds, no matter what it takes. If that means signing an armistice with Germany, murdering the Romanovs in cold blood, shooting down peasants, burning farms, selling their own souls to the Devil, then that is what they will do. They've felt what it's like to be in control, and they intend to keep it."

The slow burn I felt growing for the past several weeks was quickly being fanned into a powerful flame. "If they think they're going to use my planes to ..."

Rostov shook his head. "Not your planes, Comrade Zachary. These machines belong to the state, like everything else here and everywhere else in Russia. The Central Committee has not been oblivious to your objections or your reluctance to fully support the Revolution. They've known that from the very beginning. Now that you've trained enough pilots and Dr. Fassenbiender has helped provide the designs for enough machines, your usefulness to the party and the state are coming to an end. You're being considered a liability."

I couldn't believe I didn't see it coming. Yuloff was more and more involved in overseeing the operation of the aerodrome, the production of the new machines and the training of new pilots. He was a fair pilot himself. The Russian pilots already outnumbered us foreigners several times over, and some of them were more than competent. Dr. Fassenbiender's shoulders sagged as he leaned against the desk.

"I'm sorry, my boy," he said. "I got you involved in this, I..."

"It doesn't matter," I said. "You were just doing what you felt was right, and I was doing the same. We were won over by an ideal and men who never really intended to make it a reality, at least not in any honorable or decent way.

We made a mistake supporting them because all we could see was how bad men like Kerensky and the Provisional Government were for the country and not how dangerous men like Lenin and Trotsky were. Captain Rostov is right, now that they've got what they want, they don't have any further use for me, and I'll be damned if I'm going to let them use the machines and the skills we brought here against innocent people."

"I don't think there is much you can do about it," Rostov said.

"That's where you're wrong, Captain," I said. "There's a great deal I can do about it, starting right now."

***

Later that afternoon, the day's training was over and most of the pilots headed off to the mess hall for their daily rations (which were still far better than soldiers in the field were eating, to say nothing of the peasants). Capt. Rostov told the Russian guards at the hangar that Col. Yuloff had arrived and wanted them to report to the office immediately. When they stepped inside, they found themselves face to face with Jack Mulligan and Eddie Lancourt, armed with Russian-made rifles. We quickly relived the guards of their weapons and tied and gagged them to ensure they wouldn't cause any trouble. Jack dumped then into the back of the truck and drove it around to the other side of the aerodrome. I wanted to ensure they were well away from the hangar.

Then we gathered in the hangar, Johnny Johnson, Mulligan, Lancourt, Rostov, Dr. Fassenbiender, Natalia, little Ilsa, and me. Of the seven of us who escaped from Germany there were now only five, and I wanted to make sure that number didn't get any lower. We quickly suited up, checking the machines while Rostov, Natalia, and even Ilsa helped with the other preparations. We had to work quickly, and Jack helped keep a lookout to let us know if anyone was coming.

When we were ready, we moved our machines out onto the field, four Russian Firebirds and a medium-sized plane Dr. Fassenbiender called a Sokolov or "falcon," intended for carrying cargo or a small number of passengers. Fassenbiender designed it himself and oversaw its construction. It was intended to be the first of many, but now she would probably be the only one of her kind. The doctor was primarily an engineer, but he was a good enough pilot to fly her, especially with Natalia's help. She was no slouch as a pilot herself. We started firing up the engines and I looked back at the hangar that housed the rest of the planes.

It would only be a few moments before all the activity, or the powerful smell of petrol, would draw some of the other Russians out to investigate. I revved up the engine on my Firebird and struck a match along the metal edge of the cockpit. Pulling my goggles down, I flicked the match over the side into the small puddle of fuel on the ground, giving the machine her head and pulling away from the hangar as quickly as possible.

The others were already taxiing to the end of the runway, the first of the Firebirds launched into the air as I pulled forward and the gasoline caught, sending a streamer of fire rushing along the ground toward the hangar. I spotted one of the Russian mechanics emerging from the latrine, zipping up his pants. He looked up and took in the whole scene in an instant: four smaller planes escorting the new prototype down the runaway, taking off without authorization or fanfare, the fire rushing toward the hangar. I have to give him credit, he rushed forward rather than away, somehow thinking he could stop us, but it was too late.

I heard him yell "*Nyet!*" over the roar of the engine as I shot down the runway. As I pulled back on the stick, I heard the gasoline-soaked hangar explode into flames, sending an orange ball of fire and a thick cloud of black smoke billowing into the air. We climbed up above the aerodrome and I looked down to see the rest of the planes we'd built for the Russians, along with all of Dr. Fassenbiender's plans, notes, and designs, going up in a cloud of smoke. Russians poured from the other buildings to vainly put out the fire that was quickly reducing it all to ashes. They'd be lucky if they could save the other few buildings of the aerodrome. Those machines would never be used against innocent civilians in a civil war they never asked for, and the Bolsheviks would have a difficult time scraping together the resources to build any others, much less convincing Germany to share her technology.

As we set course for our destination, my mind was full of plans. I made a mistake, but I was going to do everything in my power to help set things to rights. If the Central Committee thought the revolution was over, they were dead wrong. I was just getting warmed up.

CHAPTER 13

THE RUSSIAN TREASURE

The dim light gleamed off the gold and jewels of the necklace as the old woman added it to the small pile already in the middle of the table. I picked it up and held it in my hand, turning it slightly to allow the shafts of sunlight coming into the tent to play over its many facets, diamonds and emeralds winking from the delicate web of gold that held them.

"Beautiful," I said quietly.

"Is it enough?" the woman asked in Russian. I looked from the necklace to the small pile of coins and other jewelry, some of which I'm sure had been in her family for generations. I nodded.

"Yes, it will be enough," I replied in Russian. Although I wasn't completely fluent, Natalia Fassenbiender's tutoring had assisted me in becoming at least proficient in the language. We could sell most of the jewelry and such to pay for fuel and supplies on the black market, use some to pay the necessary bribes so that our actions would go unnoticed (or at least undisturbed) and put the rest aside for when we needed it.

The old woman breathed a sigh of relief. I thought for a moment she was going to cry, but she held her head up high and kept her composure, as if she were merely haggling in a marketplace over the price of bread and not bargaining with dangerous outlaws for her family's life.

I put the necklace back on top of the small pile. "Gather everyone and bring them here," I said to her in Russian. "Bring only those things you absolutely need, no more than a small case or bag each. Anything more you must leave behind. Do you understand?" More than likely she and her family had little or nothing to bring with them already. All their valuables were laid out on the table between us. She nodded and reached for the items on the table. I picked up the necklace again before she could touch them.

"We'll keep this," I said, "as a guarantee that you will come, or in case you are caught." She paused for a moment, regarding me with her dark eyes. I thought she might object, but she merely nodded slightly and resumed gathering her belongings, putting them into a dark bag that disappeared under her shawl. She rose stiffly and made her way out of the tent with Rostov at her elbow, although she refused to lean on him in the slightest.

Once the tent flap fell back into place, I let my folding camp chair tip forward, setting all four feet back on the ground and let out an explosive sigh. "Damn, but I hate having to do that," I said, looking at the necklace again.

"We don't have any choice," Jack said from where he sat nearby. "We need the money to keep things going, and we don't get anything if they get caught."

"I know, I know," I said, "but it still seems unfair."

"More unfair than being imprisoned or executed as an 'enemy of the state' so the communists can take everything you own and divide it up?"

"Or just shovel it all into the coffers they're building up at the Kremlin," I concluded. "No, I guess not." I held the necklace out to Jack and he took it, wrapping it up in a handkerchief and tucking it inside his jacket.

"Take it and see what you can get for it," I said. "But be careful."

"Hey, ain't I always?" he said with a grin that tended to belie the truth. Jack was a lot smarter than most people realized and he had the kind of smarts you get growing up on the streets of Chicago. Or as a gypsy thief, I thought to myself. He could take care of himself, but the situation in Russia was deteriorating, and I didn't know how long any of us were safe.

At first I simply wanted to leave Russia and leave all the memories of the people suffering here behind, but I couldn't do that. The Civil War between the Communist Red Army and the Russian White Army continued, with the common people caught in the middle. The Bolsheviks were arresting and executing people as enemies of the state and confiscating property to continue to fuel the war effort and fatten the coffers of the new government in Moscow. Worse yet, my grand gesture at the aerodrome near Petrograd hadn't destroyed all the planes the Russians built, and their engineers eventually managed to reverse engineer things from what was left, so the Bolsheviks would soon have more planes of their own to help settle the war even more quickly.

After the destroying the aerodrome, we flew a fairly short distance to the west, along the Baltic Sea, putting us only a short flight from Finland and a slightly longer one to Sweden. Then Captain Rostov quietly put the word out that passage across the Baltic could be had, for a reasonable price. A trickle of former Russian nobles and wealthy-middle class soon began making contact, seeking to buy passage out of the country, away from the Bolsheviks and the Cossacks working for the new government.

I wished it could have been more people, but our cargo space was limited almost entirely to the Sokolov. Sometimes we would stuff people into the narrow cargo spaces in the tails of the Firebirds, but that made flying across the Baltic tricky, so we tried to avoid it. Slowly, in the few short weeks since we'd been running our operation, we'd been getting the most threatened people out of Russia, one family at a time.

It cost them, often dearly, and I made no bones about that. Although I wanted to aid the people I'd helped to harm, our little "flying railroad" (as Jack jokingly called it) had a lot of expenses, not the least of which was fuel for our machines, spare parts and tools, and supplies to maintain our little camp. We had tents to sleep in and camouflage netting to cover the planes and keep them from being spotted easily. We also needed food, clothing, and money to bribe the people we bought from, to help ensure they didn't sell us out to the first commissar who happened to question them, and to bribe guards and commissars to look the other way from time to time.

A few moments after Jack left the tent, Johnny Johnson came bursting in, a Russian-made rifle cradled in his arms.

"Hey, Zach," he said, "you'd better get out here. Looks like we've got company!"

Automatically slapping at my side to make sure my pistol was in place, I jumped up and followed Johnson out of the tent. As soon as I was outside I could hear the familiar buzz of a plane engine and looked up into the sky. A machine was flying low over our camp, silhouetted by the sun. It passed overhead and began to bank around some distance away. I wasn't sure whether it was planning a strafing run or coming in for a landing.

"Everybody take cover!" I said, moving to duck down behind the beat-up motorcar we used to carry supplies to and from the camp. I briefly thought of trying to get to my Firebird, only a short distance away, but it was entirely open field between me and the plane, making me a perfect target for the intruder's guns. Even if I did reach my machine, there was no way I would get her into the air before the enemy plane could shoot us both full of holes. No, it was their move for the moment.

As it turned out, the plane did not open fire on us. Instead, it dipped down and gracefully landed on the grassy field we used for our own airstrip, taxiing toward us. Once it landed, I could make out the colors on her wings and see that it was an American two-seater, with both positions occupied. As it slowed to a halt, we came out from behind cover and approached from the sides, well away from the plane's forward mounted machine guns. It had no sign of any other weapons, so we felt safe enough as we covered the pilots with our own weapons.

The pilot killed the engine and raised his hands, showing they were empty, before slowly climbing out of the cockpit and hopping down to the ground. He immediately helped the other person down from the back seat. Both were wearing flight suits and headgear.

"Keep them covered," I said quietly, as I approached and the two figures went to remove their headgear. I immediately noticed the pilot was an American, or at least he was wearing American military fatigues, complete with Lieutenant's bars on his collar. I didn't recognize him, but the patch on his flight suit proclaimed him a member of the 95th Air Squadron. His hair was short and dark and his eyes moved slowly from side to side, taking everyone in, before settling on me.

His companion's headgear came off to reveal a cascade of dark hair that fell about her shoulders. She was a girl—only ten or eleven years old—and Russian, unless I missed my guess. Her hair was as black as midnight and her skin was pale and flawless. She was dressed in flight gear, but there was no way she could pass for a simple peasant girl. The way she carried herself, the proud carriage, the uplifted chin, and the defiant gaze all spoke of a noble upbringing.

The man spoke first. "Are you the renegade Nathan Zachary?" he asked. I took a step closer and gave him my best smile.

"Is that what the Bolsheviks are call me," I asked, "or the Americans?"

"Both," he answered bluntly. "Then you are Zachary?"

I nodded. "I'm Zachary, and who are you?"

"I'm Lieutenant Finn, 95th Air Squadron," he said, placing one hand protectively on the girl's shoulder. "This is Natalia. I understand that you help to get Russian nationals out of the country, to someplace safe."

"As safe as any place in this world," I said, looking at Natalia and not Finn. "But if you're with the 95th, why don't you just make arrangements to get her out through them." Or take her yourself, I thought, although I didn't ask that question yet.

Finn paused a moment and glanced down at the ground before speaking. I'd heard that America had sent an Air Squadron into Russia to assist the White Army against the Bolshevik Red Army in the civil war, but we hadn't really encountered them thus far, most of the action was going on further south and west. Still, it was only a matter of time before we did encounter American flyers, and it was best to know everything we could about the situation.

"I'd rather this didn't go through normal channels," he said. "For reasons ..."

"For reasons that are mine, and mine alone," the girl said fiercely, tossing her mane of dark hair back from her face. She spoke English remarkably well, with only a slight trace of a Russian accent, and she was quite well spoken for someone who was still little more than a child. "We've heard that you bring people out of Russia," she continued. "Is this true, or are we wasting our time?"

I smiled at her bravado. This girl definitely had guts, considering she was surrounded by men with guns. "It's true," I said. "For a price."

The girl nodded and lifted the shapeless bag she carried from her shoulder. She glanced my way, clearly loath to ask permission but also aware of the guns trained on her and her companion. I nodded slightly, and she reached slowly into the bag to pull out a cloth-wrapped parcel. Holding it in one hand, she carefully unwrapped the cloth and held its contents out for me to see.

"Does this meet your price?" she asked.

I couldn't help but let out a low whistle. Sitting amidst the black velvet gathered in the girl's hand was a golden egg about the size of my fist. It was covered with delicate scroll- and latticework. Gemstones studded its surface, which was covered with fine enamel and a web of thin golden ribbons. The entire thing gleamed in the light, like a treasure from a fairy story. I smiled broadly.

"Yes, I think that will do nicely," I said. "We're making preparations to leave shortly, and there's room for one more. You're welcome to stay here until then, if you want." I pointedly glanced at Finn when I said that. I was curious if the girl had family to bring with her or if Finn was planning to desert his post and come along for the ride. He glanced at her and I had no doubt that he would have if she asked him to, but she didn't. Instead she quietly folded the golden egg back inside its covering.

"Very well," she said, tucking the bauble away inside her bag once more.

Dr. Fassenbiender and his wife had approached during our exchange without my noticing. Natalia Fassenbiender approached the girl and paused, looking her over. It seemed as if she recognized her for a moment, but she didn't say anything if she did. I made a mental note to ask her about it later. She gently placed a hand on her namesake's shoulder and began guiding her towards the mess tent.

"Come," she said. "Let's get you something to eat and let you rest. You look exhausted." Now that I had time to notice, the girl was clearly tired and had probably been through an ordeal in the past few weeks, or even months. She turned away from Mrs. Fassenbiender for a moment to embrace Capt. Finn, who looked somewhat embarrassed at the show of emotion. He gently stroked her hair as she looked up at him with eyes that fought back tears.

"Thank you, Finn," she said.

"It's all right," he replied. "Go ahead. You'll be safe now." She then allowed Mrs. Fassenbiender to lead her away toward the mess tent. Finn watched her go silently for a while before turning his attention back toward me.

"I expect you to take good care of her," he said.

"We will."

"You'd better," he replied, "or I'll come looking for you."

"Just see to it no one knows you came here," I told him. We watched as Capt. Finn climbed back into his plane, turned the engine over, and slowly pulled out of our camp. The plane picked up speed heading down the field and lifted off, soaring upward. Finn circled our camp once, gaining altitude, before veering off and heading south and east, no doubt back toward his Squadron. I glanced over at the mess tent and saw the girl standing just outside, looking wistfully toward the slowly vanishing plane before turning and going into the tent, with Natalia Fassenbiender close behind.

We busied ourselves with preparations to get underway. It was early in the afternoon and we had a fair distance to fly. Flying (and particularly landing) a plane at night in those days was dangerous, so we wanted to ensure we could drop our passengers off in Finland and return to our camp before it got too dark to navigate. Our other passengers arrived shortly thereafter in a beat-up motorcar, which they left for us to do with as we wished. As we began putting them on board the Sokolov, I heard a faint buzzing noise coming from overhead. I wondered for only a moment if Lt. Finn was returning to the area, then I spotted familiar silhouettes in the distance.

"Zachary!" Lancourt called out to me.

"I see them!" I said. Russian Firebirds, similar to our own, were closing in on our camp. "Get everyone to the planes!" I shouted and we scrambled for our places. Dr. Fassenbiender picked up little Ilsa and led his wife to the Sokolov while the rest of us ran for our own Firebirds, parked on the field. If the enemy planes caught us on the ground, we were doomed.

Before we could reach our machines, however, a pair of trucks came rumbling over the field, carrying a number of Red Army troops that leapt from them to train rifles on us. The officer in charge of them called for us to surrender in the name of the state. Jack Mulligan, Rostov, Lancourt, and Johnson looked to me for guidance, and I looked toward the plane filled with innocent people, along with Dr. Fassenbiender's wife and young daughter. The engines on the Sokolov were running, but there was no way they could take off.

"Don't shoot!" I called out in Russian. "We surrender."

The Firebirds circled the encampment once. Then one of them began to drop down toward the field. It coasted in for a smooth landing, taxiing up almost alongside my own machine, where I stood with hands raised as the Russian troops moved closer. The pilot of the Firebird stepped up from the cockpit and removed his headgear, looking down on me in triumph.

"So, Comrade Zachary," Colonel Grigori Yuloff said. "It seems now we will finish our conversation about how Russia deals with traitors and Imperialists."

CHAPTER

14

FLIGHT OF THE FALCON

"You disappoint me, Comrade Zachary," Yuloff said as he stepped down from his plane, one hand on the pistol that rested at his belt.

"I could say the same for you, Comrade Yuloff. I thought you were a man of honor."

"Honor?" Yuloff said, moustaches bristling. "You talk about honor after you have abandoned your own unit, come to us, accepted our aid and pledged yourself to our cause, only to betray us as well when it became convenient to you? You have no right to talk to me about honor, American!"

"I don't have to explain myself to you, Yuloff."

"No, you will explain yourself before the Committee," he said flatly. "Before you are pronounced a traitor to Mother Russia and executed as an enemy of the state, you and all those who follow you." He paused and turned toward the Sokolov, where Natalia Fassenbiender stood next to her husband as he held the trembling Ilsa and did his best to soothe and calm her.

"Natalia," he said, his voice softening. "Dear sister, come with me. There is no need for you to suffer along with them. I have already explained how you were duped by this German traitor," he jerked his chin toward Fassenbiender. "You and your daughter will be safe with me." Fassenbiender looked like he was about to speak for a moment, but his wife turned to him and silenced him with a look before she turned back toward her brother.

"No, Grigori," she said firmly. "These people have done nothing wrong, except try to protect innocent people from being hunted and killed like animals. I will not go with you because I am with them of my own free will. If you consider them criminals and enemies of the state, then you must consider me such as well, because I would rather die than let another drop of innocent blood be shed.

"But," she said, choking back tears, "I beg you, if you are the man of honor you claim to be, at least let my daughter and her father go. She is truly innocent, and she needs at least one parent to care for her."

Yuloff was taken aback for a moment. He looked truly shocked that his own sister would even think him capable of harming a child. Dr. Fassenbiender stepped forward.

"Natalia, no," he said. She laid on hand on his cheek, tears running down her face.

"Wilhelm, please, for my sake…" she began, then Yuloff interrupted.

"Natalia, you and your daughter will be safe," he said. "On that you have my word. But your husband and the rest will answer to the state." He nodded toward the soldiers and several of them moved forward toward the Fassenbienders.

"Wilhelm, no!" Natalia cried out as the soldiers pulled her away from her husband and child. Fassenbiender was knocked to the ground as a Russian soldier dragged his daughter from his hands.

"Papa!" Ilsa cried as the soldier started carrying her away, kicking and screaming.

The sound of the girl's cries almost covered up another sound I heard in the distance, a buzzing noise that grew louder by the moment. Soon everyone in the clearing could hear it, and looked up to see a plane with American colors diving toward us. The plane opened up with its twinned machine guns, bullets stitching along the ground, kicking up tiny clouds of dust and dirt before they intersected with the Russian soldiers in and around the trucks, sending several of them tumbling to the ground.

Seizing the distraction, I stepped forward and planted a right cross on Yuloff's jaw, sending the big Russia staggering back as mayhem broke out around the camp.

"Go!" I shouted to the rest of my men. "Get as many people out of here as you can!" Then I ducked a right hook from Yuloff and responded with a jab at his chin that he avoided, moving in to try and grab me in a bear hug and crush the life out of me. I ducked down and scooted to the side to avoid his grip, sweeping a leg out to kick his own legs out from under him, aided by the momentum of his charge. Yuloff did manage to get one massive paw on my flight jacket, pulling me to the ground with him.

Jack Mulligan knocked down the Russian soldier nearest to him with a devastating punch. Grabbing the man's rifle, he fired several shots that forced some other soldiers to scatter for cover as he headed for the Sokolov. Lancourt and Johnson were already climbing into the cockpits of their machines as he did so.

Dr. Fassenbiender knocked down one soldier nearest to him as another rushed up from behind to try and grab him. He twisted, swinging the man over his shoulder to slam him into his comrade on the ground, knocking the wind out of both of them and grabbing the top man's sidearm from its holster.

The soldier holding the struggling Ilsa tried to fumble for his weapon to bring it to bear on Fassenbiender, but the doctor moved too quickly for him, planting the butt of his pistol in the man's face and pulling the sobbing Ilsa from his arms as he stumbled back. Fassenbiender shot him once, and the soldier went down, clutching the wound in his leg.

Yuloff rolled, trying to pin me beneath his superior weight as I tried to reach for the pistol at my side. A massive hand grabbed my wrist in an iron grip as Yuloff pinned me to the ground, bearded face twisted in a snarl of rage, Russian curses on his lips. I kicked him, but it seemed only to madden the Russian colonel as he slammed me hard against the ground, then cuffed me with his free hand. I saw stars and tasted blood in my mouth, but I slammed my fist into his side, causing Yuloff to roll off me somewhat.

The American plane was climbing and banking around for another pass above the camp, but the pilot now had troubles of his own. After his initial surprise attack, the two Russian planes still circling above were closing in on him, trying to pin him down from either side and possible catch him in a deadly crossfire. The pilot began to gain altitude as he sought to avoid the Russian net. A small object fell from the cockpit to land squarely in the back of one of the Russian trucks. It exploded in a cloud of black smoke and deadly flak, sending several of the closest Russians flying through the air to land on the ground with the thud, and scatting the others, who dived for cover as best they could.

The soldier holding Natalia Fassenbiender thought to use her as a hostage, or possibly a shield, but she had other ideas. She brought one foot down hard on the man's instep with a loud crunch, followed by an elbow planted in his solar plexus, doubling the soldier over in pain as she pulled away from him.

I tried to use Yuloff's momentum to roll him off me and barely succeeded, scrambling backward to try and regain my feet. The enraged Russian rose and began charging forward, intent on pounding me into the ground, when someone struck him a blow from behind. He stumbled and spun to see the girl, the other Natalia, standing behind him, wielding a large rock she'd picked up. I leapt to my feet and smashed both fists into Yuloff's back as hard as I could, sending the colonel to the ground like a massive oak. The Russian girl smiled briefly at me before hopping over Yuloff's prone form to run for the Sokolov.

As Dr. Fassenbiender moved toward his wife, I saw one of the soldiers picking himself up off the ground and aiming his rifle at the doctor.

"Doctor!" I yelled, "look out!" I reached for my own pistol, but I was moving too slow, still shaken by Yuloff's blows. Everything seemed to be happening slowly, but there was nothing I could do about it.

Natalia Fassenbiender saw the danger at the same moment I did. She cried out, "No!" and leapt to protect her husband and child. The soldier fired, and Natalia fell to the ground, clutching her side.

"Natalia!" Fassenbiender cried out, rushing to his wife's side. My pistol cleared its holster and I shot the soldier, catching him in the shoulder and spinning him to the side, causing him to drop his rifle. I ran to help Dr. Fassenbiender, who was crouched over his wife, trying vainly to stop the bleeding from her side. I could see at a glance that the wound was serious. Rostov joined us. He took one look at the wound, glanced up at me, and our eyes met. I could tell he thought the same thing I did.

"Nathan, help me!" Fassenbiender said.

"We've got to get her to the Sokolov," I said. "Get her arms."

Fassenbiender numbly moved to obey as I grabbed Natalia's legs and we carried her toward the plane. Ilsa ran alongside us, trying to hold her mother's hand.

"Mama," she sobbed, "Mama, please be all right."

Rostov covered us, firing at the Russian soldiers and forcing them to seek cover as we made our way to the plane and lifted Natalia Fassenbiender's still form inside. I put Ilsa into the cabin along with her mother and father, then yelled to Jack, sitting in the cockpit.

"Take off!" I said, giving him a thumbs-up to emphasize the order. He immediately revved the engines and the Sokolov began to taxi down the field as Fassenbiender secured the cabin door.

Rostov approached. "Get to your machine," he said grimly.

"What about you?"

"Don't worry about me, go!" he said, firing off a few more rounds at the Russians. The soldiers were beginning to recover their composure somewhat, although a good deal of the fight had gone out of them. The other truck was still functional and the soldiers were regrouping around it.

I followed Rostov's advice and ran for my Firebird, hopping up into the cockpit and firing up the engine. Rostov spun the propeller and the engine sputtered and caught, roaring to life. The Russian kicked away the blocks as I struggled to pull my headgear on and slip my goggles into place. The Firebird lurched forward and Rostov gave me a parting salute before turning back toward the Russian truck. He drew a grenade from his belt and hefted it with a grim smile. With a yell he rushed at the truck, firing his rifle one-handed. As the Russia soldiers fired back, he yanked the pin on the grenade with his teeth and flung it toward them. Bullets slammed into his body as the explosive arced through the air and I caught a glimpse of Rostov crumpling to the ground just before the grenade went off with the dull "wumph" scattering men and machinery alike in front of the truck.

I trundled down the field, picking up speed, then pulled back on the stick, lifting the Firebird into the air. I began to bank around and I could see the Sokolov and two other Firebirds climbing slowly into the sky, as well as the American biplane, still engaged with the Russian Firebirds. I flew a close pass by the Russians, firing a steady burst from my machine guns across the side of one, tracer rounds whistling through the air in streaks of fire.

That got the Russians' attention and they could see their quarry was escaping. I headed for the rest of the squad and the Russians began to give chase. I looked back to see Lt. Finn, for surely it had to be him, dip his wings, bank around and begin to give chase to the Russians in turn.

We continued climbing up and away from the carnage on the ground, headed north and east out toward the Baltic Sea. The Russian planes followed closely, and Finn and I wanted to make sure they didn't get any closer to the Sokolov or her escort ahead of us.

The Russian pilots opened fire on me. Their tracers cut through the air around my Firebird, but no closer than a few dozen yards from me at most. As they drew in closer they were beginning to draw a bead on my position. I swerved my machine from side to side to make it more difficult for them to get me in their sights, all the while climbing toward the ceiling of my plane's capabilities, which was also, unfortunately, the same for my rivals.

By the time we reached 15,000 feet, the Russians were starting to close in. I was deliberately holding back a bit, since opening up my throttle to full speed would have caused me to overtake the slower Sokolov and I wanted to keep the Russians back from the people on board the larger plane. I hoped the prospect of downing "the rogue Nathan Zachary" would be too great a temptation for the Russian pilots to resist and it seemed I was right.

I let the Russian Firebirds draw a bit closer, almost feeling their crosshairs on my back as they lined up for a shot at me. Then I pushed the stick forward and threw my own machine into a dive, working the pedals to throw the Firebird completely head over tail and a reverse loop underneath the Russians. Sea and sky reversed themselves for a moment, the dark waters of the Baltic beneath me and the wide blue sky above, then I climbed sharply and came up behind the Russians, albeit slightly below them. I opened up with my own machine guns and was rewarded to see the Russians bank to the sides to avoid my gunfire. Lt. Finn's machine came up close by my right hand side and added to my fire.

We split and each banked after a Russian machine, now the hunters in this chase. My quarry did his best to get me off his tail, including going into a *renversement* loop of his own, but I stuck to him like glue, following him through the loop and back out again, staying with him the entire time. Then I loosed another volley of machine gun fire at him, raking along the tail of his machine. I watched his tail rudder disintegrate from the impact of the heavy-caliber rounds and his course began to falter.

I followed it up by dropping into a slow, long turn that brought me around toward the front of the Russian machine. The pilot was fighting to control her and clearly losing the battle, no longer able to focus on whatever it was I was doing. I almost leisurely lined up the Firebird in my sights and squeezed the triggers on my guns. They roared, stitching fire along the length of the Russian, finally hitting a fuel line or even the gas tank toward the rear and igniting a plume of fire from her as she buzzed past. The Firebird went into a tailspin, plunging down toward the waters below.

As I turned my attention back toward Lt. Finn and his adversary, I was surprised to see his biplane engaged with not one but two Russian machines! Finn had a second Firebird on his tail and, as I watched, it fired a volley of bullets that left the American with a trail of smoke pouring from his machine. With a dip of his wings, Finn turned regretfully and headed back toward Russia. I silently wished him luck and turned my own machine to catch up with the rest of my squadron, but the Russians saw and resumed their pursuit.

The newcomer had to be Yuloff, recovered from his knock on the head and out for blood. Yuloff was a good pilot, as were many of the Russians I we had trained over the past year or so but my squadron still taught them everything they knew. That was something in my favor.

I could just make out the rest of the squad off in the distance, headed for safety on the other side of the sea. The Russians were closing in, with Yuloff's plane in the lead, the other pilot acting as his wingman. Most likely, they would try and catch me between them in some way, try and box me in and catch my plane in a crossfire, and then they could go after the others. I wasn't about to let that happen.

I pushed forward on the stick and threw my plane into a *vrille*, a spiraling dive down toward the water below. I did my best to make it look like I'd lost control of the machine, that perhaps the earlier attack had done more damage than it appeared or that I'd even lost consciousness at the controls. As I hoped, they chose to follow me down, trying to ascertain my situation and see if I would crash, or get close enough to finish me off. The question of whether or not I was already disabled caused Yuloff and his wingman to hold their fire and draw closer than they otherwise would have. I carefully bided my time, waiting for them to get closer, watching the waters of the Baltic Sea spiraling up to meet me. Down past 10,000 feet, past 8,000. They were coming in.

At 6,000 feet, I pulled back hard on the stick and kicked the Firebird over into a looping barrel roll. I flipped up and over the Russians, coming in almost squarely behind them. As soon as I lined the wingman up in my sights, I jammed down on the triggers of my guns. They roared and spat fire that stitched along the body of the enemy Firebird, causing it to give off a thin trail of smoke, suggesting one of the incendiaries caught on the fabric, or possibly some fuel. The wingman went into a spiraling dive, except I was fairly sure his was genuine.

Yuloff tried to execute a *renversement* much like I had done to get around behind me. Rather than trying to follow him up through the loop, I banked my machine around hard, kicking the pedals to perform a short flip in the air. So when the Russian came out of his loop, diving downward, he saw my machine in his sights, but coming straight up at him, guns blazing.

We flew straight at each other, guns chattering, and bullets whizzed all around me, some of them tearing up canvas but none scoring a fatal hit on the Firebird or me. I felt one high-caliber round thud home into the pilot's seat mere inches from my right arm and was thankful it wasn't a tracer round. We flew closer and closer, both heedless of the danger until we were less than a hundred yards and a few seconds apart. When he saw I didn't mean to turn, Yuloff finally tried to bank his machine away from me, turning as hard as he could. But he started too late and turned too hard for the wing structure of the Firebird to take. With a terrible groaning and cracking, the left upper and lower wings gave way, fabric shredding as support spars snapped.

The Firebird started to drop like a stone and I pulled gently back on the stick, guiding my machine scant feet above Yuloff's falling plane. The moment we passed each other in the air, I could make out the Colonel's face behind his goggles. He wasn't wearing a helmet, his hair was windblown and disheveled, his beard bristling and his features contorted with impotent rage. The instant I passed by, I shouted out to him, the man I once called "comrade" and considered an ally and even a friend.

"When you get to hell, Yuloff, tell the Devil that Nathan Zachary sent you!"

Then I veered off and watched the Firebird go down. I circled until I saw a small splash far below, then I banked and opened up my throttle to catch up with the rest of the squadron. The time had come to leave Russia behind.

CHAPTER

A PARTING OF THE WINGS

Natalia Fassenbiender was laid to rest outside a small church in southern Finland, mourned only by her husband, daughter, the small group of men who'd come to know and respect her, and the few Russian refugees she'd given her life to help. The service was small and fairly brief, and nobody had much to say afterward, just drifting away from the gravesite in small groups, or alone, leaving Dr. Fassenbiender and Ilsa alone with the woman who was wife and mother one last time.

I found I felt very different about Natalia's funeral compared to how I felt about David Peterson's funeral more than a year before. Peterson's death at the hands of Heinrich Kisler made me burn for revenge, to see justice done. It led me to leave my Squadron behind to do what I thought was right, which ended up with me in prison, meeting Dr. Fassenbiender, and escaping to Russia. Trying to do what I felt was right there led to the October Revolution and helping Russians escape their own country. In some ways, I blamed myself for Natalia Fassenbiender's death. If I hadn't been so headstrong, so certain about what I felt was the right thing to do, so willing to charge ahead without considering the risk to everyone, then perhaps she wouldn't have died fighting for a cause I led her and her family into.

Apart from feelings of guilt, I felt nothing about her death. There was sadness, yes, but not the outrage or desire for justice I felt when Peterson died. Natalia's killer was likely dead already and, if he wasn't, it was likely he would die before the civil war in Russia ran its course. Her brother, who felt more loyalty to his country and his cause than his own flesh and blood, had found a grave at the bottom of the Baltic Sea. And what difference did it all make? A good woman was still dead and her family would have to get along without her. So many good people had died, in the war in Europe or in Russia: Peterson, Angus McMullen, Emile, Rostov, and now Natalia, and even her brother, Grigori, whom I once considered a friend.

I sat down on the hillside as a gentle breeze blew through the grass, making it whisper and rustle. I reached into the small cloth bag that sat on my lap and pulled out the golden and gem-encrusted egg the Russian girl, the other Natalia, had given me before she left to "meet with friends", as good as her word. I was no great judge of such things, but I was sure it was worth a small fortune, certainly enough to set us up somewhere quite comfortably for a while, once it was sold and we divided the proceeds. Was it really worth everything it had cost? I wondered briefly where Natalia had gotten it, and whether or not it meant anything to her. Was it just a way for her to get out of Russia, or did she have to trade a priceless family heirloom for her ticket out?

A shadow fell across me as I sat looking at it and I glanced up to see Dr. Fassenbiender standing nearby, with Ilsa close at hand. I slipped the egg back into the back almost guiltily, like I'd been caught with my hand in the cookie jar.

"It was a good service," the doctor said quietly. I never thought of Fassenbiender as a religious man—he was so devoted to the ideals of science—but he seemed to take a great deal of comfort from the simple service, perhaps because Natalia had been a woman of strong faith.

"Doctor," I began, "I'm so very…"

"*Ach*, enough of that," he said gruffly, "it was not your fault, my boy, not your fault at all. It is one of the terrible and senseless truths about war." For a moment I was reminded of Eddie Rickenbacker telling me much the same thing, in a small chapel outside of our aerodrome in France. "Whatever Fortune decides," he'd said, "She does so without consulting us."

Fassenbiender sat down beside me, holding Ilsa on his lap. She fidgeted a bit, but mostly sat looking at me with her big blue eyes, having cried all her tears, for now at least.

"So," Fassenbiender began slowly. "What are your plans now?"

I shrugged a bit. "I was thinking of taking the money and going to England. Eddie knows people there. I thought maybe I would go to school for a while." That evoked a small smile from the doctor. I'd never had much use for school when I was growing up, it always seemed like there were more important things to do than sit around a classroom all day. But the time I spent with Dr. Fassenbiender and the things he'd taught me over the past year or so showed I had a real talent for learning, and that I was pretty smart. It sparked a hunger in me to learn more about what I might be missing.

"What about you?" I asked.

"I will continue my work, of course," Fassenbiender said. "In France, or England, perhaps even in America. There are any number of companies that would be interested in some of the things we developed working in Russia, I'm sure. And there's this one to take care of," he said, smiling at Ilsa and brushing a finger along her cheek, making her smile a bit. She turned serious when she looked back at me.

"Nathan?" she asked, serious in a way only a child can be. "Why do you have to leave?" I looked into those deep blue eyes, no longer quite so innocent as when I first saw them, and thought about the answer myself. As it happened, Dr. Fassenbiender answered for me, hugging Ilsa close to him.

"Because everyone has to make their own way in life, *liebchen*."

I smiled and leaned toward Ilsa. "Sometimes, kiddo, Fortune decides things for us and, when she does, she often does it without consulting us."

"Will we ever see you again?" she asked.

"Oh, I think you can count on it," I said. "The world hasn't heard the last of Nathan Zachary. Not by a long shot."

BOOK 2

GREAT DEPRESSION

Regardless of the root cause, the result is the same: the United States of America, that great experiment in Democracy, crumbled in the late 1920s.
— Professor Warren Gilmont, Harvard University, 1938

CHAPTER 16

END OF AN ERA

The lights of the Manhattan skyline glittered brightly, seen from the windows of the ballroom at the Savoy Hotel. But they were no brighter than the glitter and whirl of the crowd inside the Hotel. People dining and dancing and drinking the night away, all in hopes that a large enough party would let them forget what was going on in the rest of the world, would let us all forget.

It was 1929, and the Roaring '20s were coming to an end, although even I didn't know what sort of an end then. After the Great War, America settled into a state of isolationism. The war left a bad taste in everyone's mouth, and the idea of so many of her boys dying in the trenches and on the fields of a foreign war made American turn inward, away from Europe and the rest of the world. After all, people said, we had our own problems, right? There were epidemics of influenza and polio, debates over Prohibition, political struggles between the Federal government and the increasingly independent states of the Union.

Still, in the midst of it all, people found time to get together and have a good time. Although Prohibition prohibited the production and distribution of alcohol, it wasn't illegal to own it, or to drink it, so the well to do of Manhattan's night-scene still had their champagne and wine, taken from dusty cellars and private reserves, enough to keep the city in booze for years. As for what would happen afterward, well, why worry about something that many years away, right?

All these thoughts crossed my mind as I stepped into the ballroom and adjusted the sleeves of my dinner jacket, checking my tie to make sure it was straight as I casually made my way down the steps, scanning the room for my dinner companion for the evening. She wasn't my usual sort of company these days, but when I got a call from her employer, I could hardly refuse.

I spotted her at a table near the dance floor. She was a bit younger than I expected, close to my age. Her dark hair was cut short in a popular style for the new, forceful young woman of the modern world. She wore a blue dress held up by spaghetti straps that hugged her slim form, showing curves in all the right places and a great deal of leg as she crossed one over the other, turning to glance in my direction. Our eyes met and I smiled, making my way over to the table.

"Miss Jennifer Talbot, I presume?" I asked. She smiled and nodded.

"Mr. Zachary, thank you for joining me," she said with genuine warmth.

"The pleasure is all mine, I assure you. It's not every day that a humble businessman has the opportunity to entertain a rising star from the Times." I took the seat opposite Miss Talbot and asked the waiter to bring me a martini, very dry, and gave her a glance to ask if she wanted anything. She rested her hand on the tumbler sitting in front of her and shook her head, so the waiter moved on.

"You're very modest," Miss Talbot observed, sipping from her drink and regarding me over the rim of the glass. "Not many 'humble businessmen' have achieved your kind of success before even reaching the age of 30. To say nothing of being considered one of the most eligible bachelors in New York."

I smiled in what I hoped was a self-depreciating way. "Well, I have had some success in the stock market and various investments, although I can't claim to have been quite lucky enough to correct the matter of my bachelorhood."

"Oh come now, Mr. Zachary," she replied, leaning forward a bit and giving me a pleasant view of what that blue dress sheltered. "It doesn't seem you've been suffering in monastic isolation in that house of yours on Long

Island. In fact, you're very well known as a playboy and man about town, isn't that true?"

"I suppose so," I shrugged, as the waiter brought my drink and set it in front of me. "I can't really speak to what is said about me, since I tend not to pay any attention to such things. I certainly won't deny that I enjoy the company of attractive and interesting woman, such as yourself, Miss Talbot." A flush of color darkened her cheeks pleasantly and she sat back a bit. I smiled and raised my glass.

"To a most entertaining evening," I said. We clinked glasses and drank, then Miss Talbot put down her glass and produced a small pad and pen from her purse, and her manner became all business.

"Tell me, then," she said, "what is the secret to your success, Mr. Zachary?"

"Please, call me Nathan," I replied. "The secret of my success? Well, that's a difficult question. I suppose if there was a secret, I'd hardly be inclined to give it away, now would I? Fortunately, I don't really think there is any 'secret' to being successful in life. It's a matter of hard work and being willing to do what you need to do in order to make the most of your opportunities."

"That does explain how a man appears, seemingly from nowhere, and goes on to become one of the wealthiest men in New York. Do you come from a family with money, Mr. Zach … Nathan?"

"Hardly," I said. "In fact, my family was quite poor. I served as a pilot during the War and it gave me an opportunity to appreciate life and all that it has to offer. When I was a boy I hardly had any interest in school but, after my time in Europe, I became very interested in education."

"Yes, you attended Oxford University in England," Talbot said, glancing at her notes, "and graduated with honors with a degree in law. Why did you choose to study abroad?"

"I suppose partly because I enjoyed seeing the world after my taste of European culture, and because a friend of mine lived in England and invited me to visit him and his family after the war." I didn't bother to mention that I'd bought my way into school with a substantial "donation", wealth I'd collected during my time in Russia, enough to open doors that would otherwise remain closed to someone like me.

"Speaking of the war," she said, "isn't it true that you deserted your Squadron in France in order to travel to Russia, and that you became involved with the Communist Revolution there?"

I kept my smile pleasant and my features composed. Miss Jennifer Talbot certainly earned her reputation for getting at the truth, no matter what stood in her way.

"Not entirely," I said. "I went on a patrol looking for Heinrich Kisler, the German pilot who downed the plane of a friend of mine."

"A patrol that was not authorized by your superior officers, is that correct?"

"Yes. I was quite … impulsive in those days," I said. "I wanted to see justice done." Talbot seemed taken aback by my answer, no doubt she believed I'd sought out Kisler solely for the glory of bringing down the Black Ace myself. When she didn't interrupt with more questions, I continued. "But my impulses got the better of me and I was shot down behind enemy lines and taken prisoner by the Germans. I spent some time in a German prison camp before escaping and making my way to Russia, as you said."

"Where you became involved in that country's civil war?"

"Peripherally," I said, downplaying events that still evoked unpleasant memories. "Once the civil war was underway and Russia was out of the conflict in Europe, I chose to resign my commission in the Army, go to England and attend school there. My experiences during the war gave me an interest in the law, so it seemed a natural course of study for me."

"Yes," Talbot said slowly, scribbling and consulting her notes. "You returned to the United States six years ago and began making a killing in the stock market, making quite a reputation for yourself on Wall Street. I understand that you began with a small initial investment and parlayed it into a small fortune. May I ask where a former Army Airman who spend several years as a University student with no apparent means procured that initial investment?"

I smiled again. She was fishing, but she didn't really have the answers or else she would have been a bit more eager with the questions. "I earned the confidence of several clients and investors," I said, "based on my record at Oxford. I proved their faith in me by being successful, in both choosing investments and in negotiating business arrangements for them." I mentioned nothing about how I procured my first business loans using the "collateral" I'd earned in my last months in Russia, the remainder of a small fortune spend on years of education and study.

"I'm surprised a man as interested in justice as you have said didn't go into criminal law," Talbot said, looking up from her notes at me.

"My experiences have taught me that justice and the law are often only passing acquaintances," I said.

"That's a rather cynical observation for a man your age, Nathan," she said.

"One that's been won through hard experience, Miss Talbot."

"Please," she said, "If you expect me to call you Nathan, then you should call me Jennifer."

I smiled, pleased she'd decided not to pry too much into my "hard experiences".

"I would be delighted, Jennifer."

She blushed a bit and returned her attention to the notes in front of her. "So then, as a veteran of the war, what do you think about the growing Regionalist movement in the country?"

"I think it's unfortunate that the freedoms we fought so hard to protect during the war are being used as an excuse for power-mongers and people looking only the further their own political agendas," I said. "The sort of region-alism we're seeing in America is very much like the same factionalism that led to trouble in Europe and in Russia. I'm not eager to see it repeated here."

"Then do you consider yourself a Unionist?"

"I don't consider myself affiliated with any political faction or ideology," I said. "I believe each person must choose as his or her conscience dictates, and I'm pleased that our nation still permits us to follow the dictates of our conscience."

"And where does your conscience lead you, Nathan?" she asked. The question took me aback somewhat. Where did my conscience lead me these days? Nowhere except, perhaps, to new business deals and away from some of the dirtier dealings available to a businessman in New York, willing to do any-thing to make money. Perhaps that was why the Regionalist movement grew so strong: it was so much easier to follow along with the trends of what was going on in your own state or town, rather than standing up and following the dic-tates of your conscience.

I gave Jennifer Talbot a wan smile. "Right now my conscience leads me to make a confession to you, Jennifer," I said.

"Oh? And what might that be?" she asked, her curiosity clearly piqued.

"I didn't agree to this interview entirely out of my belief in a free press," I said. "A good part of the reason was an opportunity to meet a particularly talented and lovely reporter." Jennifer blushed, bringing a stunning color to her cheeks, and glanced away for a moment before turning her dark eyes back upon me again.

"Nathan," she began, "Mr. Zachary, I don't think…"

"Would you care to dance?" I asked, rising from my chair and taking her slim hand in mine. She gave me a confused laugh ,then rose from the table and glided out onto the dance floor with me. The band played a slow, pleasant melody, and we slipped into a steady waltz. Miss Talbot proved to be an excellent dancer, and we moved along the floor for a few minutes, speaking only with our movements and steps.

"Tell me," she said, her lips close enough that I could feel her breath on my ear. "Do you always conduct interviews like this?"

"Only with reporters as accomplished on the dance floor as you," I replied. "Do you have any other questions for me?" She considered for a moment as we slid into a slower song, the trumpet and trombone low and mournful.

"I understand you're still quite the pilot," she said. She had clearly done her research.

"It's little more than a hobby these days. I do own a few small planes I fly on my own, simply for enjoyment. Have you ever flown?" I asked.

"Once, on business," she replied, "but never for pleasure."

"It's quite an experience," I said. "Like nothing else in the world. It is perhaps the greatest feeling one can hope to experience, soaring aloft; a feeling of complete freedom."

"You feel very passionately about it," she said. "It must be very important to you."

"My favorite thing in the world," I said. Then I looked down into those dark eyes and the sly smile as Jennifer's body pressed against mine and was swayed and spun on the dance floor. "Well," I continued with a smile, "perhaps my second favorite thing."

***

The jangling of the phone jarred me awake the following morning, or perhaps it was almost afternoon from the sunlight that slanted in through the partially-drawn drapes in the bedroom of my Long Island mansion. I fumbled for the receiver and lifted it from its cradle, all the while cursing Alexander Bell and his descendants for the creation of the infernal device.

"Hello," I mumbled into it, levering myself up against the pillows and running a hand through my short-cropped hair.

"Nathan, you've picked a fine day to take a holiday," said the tart voice on the other end of the line. "I need you to come to my office as soon as possible." The speaker was Hiram Winslow, the senior partner in the firm of Winslow, Stromwell, and Heard, a friend and something of mentor to me in my early days in the New York financial world.

"What is it, Hiram?" I asked.

"I'd rather explain in person, Nathan," he said curtly. "Please come in as soon as you can." I agreed to do so immediately and hung up the receiver. Only then did I turn and notice that I was alone in the large four-poster bed, except for a note torn from a small reporter's pad, left atop the opposite pillow.

It read "Dear Nathan, Thank you for a wonderful evening. Perhaps sometime we can enjoy your second favorite thing in the world together." It was signed "Jennifer" along with a phone number in Manhattan. I sighed and left the note on the bedside table, then quickly went about getting showered and dressed so I could go into the city and meet Hiram at his office.

I found the senior partner in his office about an hour or so later. Hiram Winslow was a grandfatherly gentleman, with a fair and full moustache gone iron gray and blue eyes looking out from behind wire-rimmed spectacles, giving him a penetrating stare. He wore a dark suit with a gold watch chain and fob stretched across a waistcoat, covering a full belly that some described as making him look "jolly," although Hiram was far from jolly today. In fact, he looked positively grim.

"Hiram, you look like you've just lost your best friend," I said by way of greeting. My faint attempt at humor did nothing to lighten the broker's dark mood.

"Nathan, where have you been?" he said. "Haven't you heard the news?"

I almost blushed a bit when I realized how late in the day it was. "Um, no I was rather... occupied last night," I said. "I only just woke up when you called."

"Well, I hope, whoever she was, that you enjoyed yourself," Hiram said, making his way over to the stock-ticker in the corner of his office. He lifted a length of tape and held it out to me. "Take a look," he said.

I glanced over the figures for the stock market and my heart dropped almost as fast and almost as far as the stock index itself. "My god," I said, looking up at Hiram in horror, "is this true?"

He shook his head sadly. "I wish it weren't, lad," he said, "but it's true. The Stock Market went through its worst crash ever. You're ruined, Nathan, completely broke."

CHAPTER 17

MAN WITHOUT A COUNTRY

A heavy blow of the axe split the log cleanly into two, the pieces falling to either side of the chopping block and the axe made a pleasing "thunk" sound as it bit into the block itself. I picked up the next log and set it upright on the block, getting into pleasant rhythm with the swinging and thunking of the axe, letting my mind wander. I left my heavier outer shirt draped over part of the woodpile, wearing just my lighter T-shirt. Although the nights in Arizona got cold enough to need plenty of firewood, the days were still quite warm, especially when you're doing manual labor.

Arixo, I reminded myself, bringing the axe down on the log and sending the halves flying. It's Arixo, not Arizona. It hadn't been Arizona for over a year. Still, whatever it was called, it was home to me, at least for the time being. I'd grown up in the Southwest, when I first got used to the feeling of being an outsider. Then it was because I was Rom, a gypsy. My father was nowhere to be seen. I never even knew him. All I knew was my mother, doing her best to take care of me. I had the other adults of our tribe looking out for me, of course—we look after our own. Still, it was just my mother and me for as long as I could recall.

I'd gotten tired of being an outsider, of the other kids calling me names and telling me gypsies were thieves and cheats. The truth was, I didn't want to be a gypsy any more. I wanted something more than that life. I wanted to be an American. Technically, I already was, but I wanted to be an American like in the movies, a real American. That's why I left to join the army and fight in the war—for all the good it had done me—or anyone for that matter. We fought to protect our country, only to see it torn apart by greed and selfishness.

I remembered the last couple years, after I lost my fortune, along with lots of other people. The stock market crash sent the American economy into a tail-spin it just couldn't pull out of. The states-rights people in both parties blamed the federal government for the Depression and decided to handle things their own way, and the government had little choice but to stand back and watch them. It had been coming for a while, but the start of the Depression opened the gates to a flood of isolationism.

A few months after the stock market bottomed out, Texas declared inde-pendence from the United States. They'd gone it alone before, after all, so they probably figured they could do it again without the rest of the Union to weigh them down. That sparked off a series of secessions with California, the Carolinas, Utah, and New York all following suit within ten months of the Texan declaration. The secessions proved the federal government was powerless, and only embold-ened the power-mongers in the new nations and among the remaining states. They started to fall on the United States like a pack of hungry coyotes, everyone eager to get a piece of the country's corpse.

New countries sprang up across the continent like weeds: The Industrial States of America around the Great Lakes, the Maritime Provinces in the north-east, Dixie in the deep south, and the People's Collective in the midwest. They carved up the land between them, but not without more than a few disputes about who was going to get what, which led to little brushfire wars and oppor-tunities for people looking to take advantage of them.

The railway system and roads were no longer a cohesive web linking a vast country since they now crossed many hostile borders. Airplanes were now the lifeline that connected allied countries.

Another log bit the dust. Me, I didn't know what to do after the crash at first. I'd lost almost everything I'd worked so hard to get, my house, my cars, my planes, money, clothes, everything. I also quickly found out I'd lost most of the people I thought were my friends. It was as if destitution was a communicable disease and people could catch it by associating with you. The old money types that managed to hold on to their wealth wouldn't even look my way and most of my contemporaries, who'd made their money in business or investment, were in the same leaking boat as I was.

Then I got the letter from a friend of my mother's. She'd seen my picture in the paper from some charity function or another and thought she recognized me, so she wrote to ask if I was who she thought I was. I couldn't believe it. I had been trying to locate my mother for years. I'd even hired a detective to track her down, but no go. Unfortunately, my mother's friend was writing tell me that my mother was quite ill. She'd never been especially robust; I could remember her always being tired when I was young, like she carried the weight of the world on her shoulders. I used to think it was the effort of caring for a rambunctious young son without a husband around, but I realized it was more than that. That day, I left to come back home to see her.

"Nathan!" came the voice from the house. My mother was uncomfortable calling my by my chosen name at first, but she did because that was what I wanted. For better or for worse, Nathan Zachary was who I was. I jammed the axe into the chopping block and picked up my shirt, using it to mop some of the sweat off my brow as I turned and walked back toward the house.

My mother was never a big woman, always quite petite. Nowadays she looked even thinner, like you could almost see through her. She couldn't really travel any more with the tribe, which was why she settled down and I came out to help look after her. She tired out easily and had trouble breathing sometimes. Although I suggested it on numerous occasions, she didn't want to see a doctor, preferring her own herbal remedies passed down from her mother and grandmother. Her dark hair, streaked with gray, was done up at the nape of her neck and she wore a simple housecoat and slippers.

"Mama," I said, "what are you doing up? You should be resting?"

"Nonsense," she said tartly, "I've been resting all day, it seems. How long have you been up?"

"A few hours. I wanted to get some chores done."

She gave me a wan smile. "Wish it had been this easy to get you to do your chores when you were little," she said and I smiled in return. I had been a handful for her back then.

"Were you planning on going into town?" she asked and I nodded. "Good, there are some things I'd like you to pick up for me. I've made you a list." I took it from her and glanced over it.

"No problem," I said. "I'll just get cleaned up a bit and head out. When I get back I can make us some lunch. 'Til then, why don't you get back to bed?" I bent down and kissed her on the cheek and saw her back off to bed before I splashed some water on my face to make myself a bit more presentably. Drying off with a terrycloth towel in the bathroom of our small cabin I stopped to look at myself in the mirror.

My mother was quite ill, you see, and I had been denying the truth about it to myself, but it was getting to the point where they was no denying it any more. Even though she did her best to put on a brave front for me, she wasn't getting any better, and we both knew it. The worst thing of all was there wasn't a damn thing I could do about it.

I tossed the towel into the hamper and buttoned my shirt back on before climbing into the beaten-up truck we used and driving down to the small collection of buildings we called a town. New Hope was technically part of a Hopi Indian reservation that we lived just outside of. I've always felt for the Indians even when I was a kid. We gypsies knew what it was like being outsiders, but we never really owned land to understand being driven off of it. The Hopis and the other tribes had to watch as the land they had got smaller and smaller as more and more governments got interested in taking it for themselves.

With the federal government gone in all but name, the tribes didn't have any real place to turn for solace from pirates and gangs. Or from so-called governments that decided they were no longer bound by treaties signed by the United States of America, and so could move in and take whatever land they wanted. Things hadn't gotten that bad in Arixo, yet, although I'd heard pirate nests were springing up and there was plenty of trouble with the Navajo and Lakota tribes nearby.

I pulled up in front of the general store and stepped inside out of the dust kicked up by my truck and the faint wind blowing out of the desert. Tom Cloud waved at me from behind the counter where he was talking with another customer, an older Indian woman. After he helped bundle up her purchase for her, he turned his attention to me.

"Nathan," he said, "what can I do for you today?"

I slid my mother's list across the counter. "Just a few things," I said, "and I'm going to look around a bit. How's business?"

"Could be better," Tom said, picking up the list and scanning it. "Hmmm, I think I've got most of this. Let me check a couple things in the back. You know where everything else is." He wandered off through the colorful blanket that served as a door between the shop and its back room, so I scanned the shelves for items of interest. I noticed a copy of Air Action Weekly among the small selection of magazines and newspapers and immediately picked it up.

The cover story was about increasing pirate activity in both the Midwest and Appalachia. Jonathan "Ghengis" Khan, a former businessman from Chicago and leader of the infamous Red Skulls Gang, had pulled off the heist of a military zeppelin in Utah, nearly touching off a war between Utah and the People's Collective. Apparently Khan's men posed as Collective militia. Interesting trick. I flipped through the pages and stopped when I noticed a familiar face. I quickly scanned over the headline that read: "JOHNSON BECOMES CHIEF TEST PILOT." Johnny Johnson's smug face smiled out from the pages of the magazine. The article went on to say how Johnson, now living in California, had wrangled his way into Hughes Aviation and was working as one of their chief test pilots for new machines. Well, didn't that just beat all?

When Johnson and I parted after leaving Russia, I figured for sure he'd end up on the skids or dead at the hands of some jealous boyfriend or husband. I never figured he'd go far, but I guess I underestimated his ability to spin a story and make himself look good, and just how far that'd go out in Hollywood. Out there, looking good was all that mattered. Looking over the magazine made me think about piloting again.

The sound of raised voices back near the counter caught my attention. I put down the magazine and looked around the corner to see Tom Cloud standing and arguing with a tall, broad-shouldered fellow with a face that looked like it could have been modeled after an armadillo. It was kind of snout-like, with small, piggish eyes currently under lowered brows and glaring at the Indian shop-owner.

"I told you before, Rosetti," Tom said. "You come in here, you pay just like everyone else."

"Yeah, but we're not like everyone else, see?" the other man replied. "We're doin' you a favor."

"You're doing me a favor?"

A slow smile spread across Rosetti's face. "Sure, you're helpin' us out and, in return, we're not bustin' up this place, or doin' a little fly-over some night."

I'd heard enough. I stepped up behind Rosetti and tapped him on the shoulder.

"Excuse me," I said. "I think you should either pay for your purchases or leave Mr. Cloud's store."

Rosetti turned slowly toward me. "Oh yeah?" he said. "And who the hell are you?"

"I'm Mr. Cloud's lawyer," I said with a smile. "And I advise you to be on your way."

"You just made a mistake, buddy," Rosetti said. But when his ham-hock fist came in, it met nothing but empty air as I stepped to the side. I brought my own fist up into Rosetti's ample gut, sending the wind out of him with a "whoof" and doubling him over. I grabbed his collar and his belt and gave him the bum's rush for the door. He tripped over the threshold and sprawled out on the wooden porch outside, scrambling to get to his feet. I followed right behind him, standing in the doorway.

"Now get out of here!" I said, emphasizing my statement by planting one foot against Rosetti's ample bottom and giving him a shove. He picked himself up out of the dust and stalked toward a car parked out front, pausing to turn and glare back at me.

"You ain't heard the last of this!" he said. "You just made the worst mistake of your life!" He climbed into the car and sprayed dust as he peeled out from in front of the store.

"He may be right, you know," Tom said from behind me. "I appreciate the thought, Nathan, but you don't want to mess with men like that."

"Who is he?" I asked. "A gangster?"

"No, a pirate. He's part of some new gang that's operating north of here. They call themselves the Tombstone Gang. I guess they've been causing trouble for shipping going through the area, and running a little protection racket on the side, shaking down all the local towns and such."

"Pay up or we'll do a fly-over, complete with twenty-one gun salute," I finished. Tom just nodded.

"He came in here before to get supplies and I told him I wasn't paying any tribute to his gang."

"Have you talked to the authorities about this?" I asked. Tom only looked at me incredulously and gave a snort.

"Which authorities, Nathan?" he asked bitterly. "The Arixo government is scared of its own shadow, the Feds don't come out here any more—not that they were much help even when they did—and the Tribal Council can't do anything. There's no one to report it to." He sighed. "You'd think these pirates would have enough to do with taking cargoes from big airships without bothering us."

He picked up a paper sack on the counter. "Here's everything you asked for," he said. I pulled out my wallet and Tom shook his head. "It's on the house." Then it was my turn to shake my head.

"No way, Tom. I'm not taking the deal you wouldn't give that guy. Like you said, you've got enough problems, and I believe in paying my way."

"Thanks, Nathan," he said, "for everything."

***

That night I told my mother about the incident at Tom's store, and about Rosetti's threats to Tom, and to me.

"Do you think he's serious?" she asked gravely as she sipped from a steaming cup of herbal tea that filled the kitchen with a sweet aroma.

"Yes," I said. "From what Tom said, this Tombstone Gang means business."

"It's too bad, really," she said, looking sort of distant.

"What do you mean?"

"These pirates," she said. "It makes me sad to think that they're anything like us." By "us" I knew she meant gypsies. "Seems like these days, with the country coming apart, that a lot of people are learning what it means to be gypsies. Haven't you read about the bands of folk driving across the country to try and find a better home, a better life? And these air pirates like tribes with planes. I wouldn't be surprised if some of them didn't find they liked living the gypsy life. They just don't have a code to live by, like we have."

I sprang up from the table with a wide grin on my face.

"New gypsies!" I said. "Mama, you're brilliant!" I bent down and kissed her on the cheek. "I have to go out for a while, will you be all right?"

"Of … of course!" she said. "Where are you going?"

"Back into town to get a few things, then out to the barn. I have a lot of work to do to get ready for tomorrow," I said. "Mr. Rosetti was right about one thing: this isn't over, not by a long shot."

(HAPTER 18

ARIXO HIGH NOON

The following day dawned bright and clear, with hardly a cloud in the sky. Everyone in New Hope went about their business, but there was a certain tension in the air, expectant, like everyone knew something was going to happen. Certainly, Tom Cloud knew. I'd called him up the previous night to tell him my plan, and he agreed to let me know at the first sign of trouble from the Tombstone Gang.

That sign came just before noontime, when a friend of Tom's spotted a trio of planes coming in from the north and headed for the center of town. She called Tom, he called me, and I headed out to the barn where I'd spent half the night working. I swung open the barn doors to reveal a canvas-draped form that took up most of the floor space. Pulling away the protective cloth revealed the sleek shape of a Hughes Dragonfly, painted fire engine red with black trim. She was the sole remaining part of my lost fortune, the only thing I couldn't bear to part with. I'd flown her down to Arixo with all my worldly possessions in the tiny hold. I'd stowed her away in the barn for the past two years, not wanting to think about the life that she represented: the life I used to have. But now we were needed.

I put on my flight jacket and climbed into the Dragonfly's cockpit, pulling it closed and locking it down. Then I fired up the engine, my work from the previous night ensuring it started without any problem. The propeller roared to life as I checked the flaps and all of the systems. Everything was ready, including the surplus machine gun I had installed onto the Dragonfly's nose. I didn't have as much ammo as I would have liked. I just had to be careful not to miss. Every shot had to count.

I opened up the throttle and eased off the brakes, and the Dragonfly lurched forward and started gently rolling out of the barn. I took her into a smooth turn and headed down the empty field, bumping a bit along the dry ruts in the ground, picking up speed. As I neared the end of the field I pulled back on the stick and the Dragonfly's nose lifted up into the air and we soared. How alive I felt at that moment! This was where I was meant to be, not stuck on the ground but flying up in the sky. The sense of freedom was dizzying and I knew right then and there that I wanted go out behind the stick of a plane, in a blaze of glory. Of course, if I wasn't careful, I was going to get my wish.

I climbed up above our little plot of farmland, getting my bearings and heading off toward town for a rendezvous with the Tombstone Gang. If they thought New Hope was defenseless, they had another thing coming to them.

My Dragonfly was a bit faster than their machines. Even a few years out of date, she was still a fine racing plane. I was also closer to town than they were, so I arrived just moments ahead of the air pirates. I started circling the small town below, scanning the sky for any sign of the gang. It didn't take me long to spot them. They were flying in formation (more discipline than I gave them credit for, honestly). One plane took the point, with the other two flanking it, forming a triangle pattern. They were a good 15,000 feet up, I guessed, but looked to be dropping. No doubt they were planning on making a strafing run down the main street, something to show the townsfolk they meant business.

I circled around toward them, gaining some altitude and trying to use the high noontime sun as a shield to keep them from seeing me as long as possible. The sky was clear, so visibility was excellent. There were no cloudbanks to hide behind, no cover. They'd spot me soon enough; it was just a matter of delaying the inevitable as long as possible. As I approached, I got a better look at their machines.

They were flying monoplanes, which had become pretty much the standard type these days. I think they were originally Curtis-Wright Ascenders, but it was difficult to be certain. They were single prop machines and showed signs of both age and being pieced and patched together, probably from spare parts with a fair amount of spit and bailing wire. The gang went in for a gray and black color scheme, with what looked like a tombstone painted on the nose each machine. They carried paired machine guns forward, probably War surplus, but still good enough to do plenty of damage. I wondered briefly which plane Rosetti was flying, if any, as I moved into position.

They didn't seem to have noticed me so far. They clearly weren't expecting any opposition; Arixo didn't have any real Air Militia to speak of, and rumors said the President was actually courting some of the large pirate gangs for protection against the militias of the People's Collective and Texas. Little wonder men like Rosetti acted like they owned the place and felt they could do as they pleased. Given enough time, the politicos would see to it that they did. I aimed to prove them wrong.

At just under 20,000 feet, I dropped into position, then pushed the stick forward, and put the Dragonfly into a steep dive, heading right for the lead plane. I waited as the Tombstone raiders grew closer and closer, settling my sights on the leader. I couldn't afford to waste a shot, so I needed to be as close as possible. My finger tensed on the trigger as the lead plane filled my sights.

At about 1,000 feet away, the whine of my dive alerted the pirates and they spotted me, but too late to really do much of anything about it. I squeezed the trigger and my machine gun rattled off a burst, the rounds tearing through the tail of the lead Ascender before it veered off to get out of the line of fire. I pulled up out of my dive as the pirates scattered, their formation breaking up as each of them tried to maneuver into a position to get a better look at what they were facing and, perhaps, get a shot at me. Perhaps they weren't so disciplined after all.

I stayed on the tail of the leader as he veered off to the side, trying to shake me. I didn't see any smoke or other signs of critical damage from my shots to his tail, so I had to assume I didn't hit anything vital. Watching for signs of trouble from the other pirates, I stuck close to the leader as he moved to try and stay out of my sights. He wasn't bad, but I'd faced better in my days flying patrols over France during the War. I might have been a couple years out of practice, but I still had what it took to stay on his tail. I sent another volley of .30-caliber rounds into his machine. This time I was rewarded by a thin plume of black smoke pouring out of his tail as his speed slowly slightly.

The sound of machine guns chattering somewhere behind me made me recall the presence of the other two machines. I veered off to port just as a bright swarm of tracers shot through the area where I was. I put my machine into a rolling dive, keeping the other two off my tail for the moment and keeping the leader almost directly in front of me as I dived down toward him.

The enemy plane spun around and around in my sights as I jammed down on the triggers and sent a hail of bullets along much of its length, sparking off the wings and the cockpit. At least one of those rounds must have hit home, because the machine started to roll, then went into an out of control dive, smoke and flames streaming from the engine and the tail section. I saw no sign of the pilot attempting to bail out, so he was either unable or already dead.

"When you get to the ground, tell 'em Nathan Zachary sent you," I said. Then my radio started to crackle, set to the frequency used by local Arixo pilots.

"Whoever you are," a familiar voice growled, "you're dead meat."

I banked around, leveling out from my dive and grabbed the mike. "I wouldn't count on that, Mr. Rosetti," I said. "As a matter of fact, why don't you just give up and leave these people alone before I have to start getting rough with you?" I released the switch, but there was no reply, at least not over the radio. But the two Ascenders were closing in, trying to catch me in some sort of crossfire.

I climbed steeply to avoid them, one of the planes getting on my tail and following me, sending .30-caliber rounds flying around me. A few of them caught my wings and tail, but the damage didn't look serious. I veered off to starboard and banked sharply, trying to come around to the side of the pursing plane, but the pilot stayed with me.

Pretty good, I thought, but let's see if you know all the tricks. I leveled out, then threw my Dragonfly into a loop. Earth and sky reversed themselves for a moment, and the enemy plane was directly "over" my head as I looked "up" toward it and the ground. Then things righted themselves and I dropped down behind the other plane, getting it in my sights before the pilot realized what happened. I grinned and squeezed the trigger.

There was a metallic "KA-CHUNK" as my gun jammed. Damn! The other pilot veered away as I kept flying straight and level as possible, trying to figure out a way to clear the jam while still staying out of the line of fire. I didn't have a wingman to keep my opponents busy while I went about doing repair work, so I had a real problem.

I veered off to the side as one of the Ascenders got on my tail and started peppering it with bullets. It looked like they were going to try and catch me in a crossfire again. Not terribly original but, given my current situation, it wasn't a bad strategy either. I needed to come up with my own strategy, and fast.

I eased off on the throttle a bit, maneuvering so it looked like I was in trouble and moving right into their sights. One machine was on my tail and closing in, while the other was rising up to meet us. I figured they'd open up on me when the second plane got close enough, so I had to time things just right. We came closer, four-hundred yardss, three-hundred, two-hundred. At just under a hundred yards, I threw my plane into a steep nose-dive, flipping the left wing up into the air and dipping the nose down, going into a tailspin just as the pirates opened fire.

A few bullets tore through my wing before my plane dropped out of the line of life. However, my pursuer wasn't quite so fast at getting out of the way. He tried to pull up, realized he didn't have the clearance to managed it, then tried to dive down out of the path of his partner, but a few seconds too late. I heard, rather than saw, the two planes collide, the left wing of the diving plane clipping the left wing of the oncoming machine, sheering off one and crippling the other in a shriek of metal.

As I pulled my machine out of its dive, I saw both pirate planes start to tumble out of the air, the one with the missing wing spinning madly. Then I saw the canopies of both fly off as the pilots hit the silk, chutes opening in the air and carrying them slowly down to earth as their machines plunged down to hit the ground and burst into black-orange balls of fire and smoke. I circled the falling pirates a couple times, letting them wonder if I was cold-blooded enough to gun them down in the sky, before I turned my machine back toward the area just outside of town.

As I came in for a landing, a small crowd of people rushed out to greet me. Tom Cloud was at the head of the group as they cheered and waved. I hopped down from the cockpit of the Dragonfly to shake Tom's hand and accept the congratulations of the townsfolk. A few of the kids were looking up at me all starry-eyed and staring at my place, maybe future pilots someday. Tom assured me that the local sheriff would be waiting to pick up the pirates when they finally reached the ground, and they wouldn't be bothering anyone else for a good, long time.

After promising to attend a little party later that night, I took the Dragonfly and headed back to where my mother waited. She was pleased to see me return in one piece, a wan smile lighting up her face she came out of the house to greet me. I gave her a hug and pulled back to look her in the face. She smiled again.

"You're looking better than you have since you got here," she said.

"That's because I figured a few things out."

"I know, I thought you would, if I just gave you time."

"I have to leave soon," I said.

"I know. It's all right, Nathan. You were meant for something other than this life. You were meant to be up there, doing what you do best. Fighting for what you believe in. Making a new home, a new family, a new life for yourself."

I hugged her close for a long while after that, then we went into the house together and I got her to agree to rest while I made a few calls, then we could both go into town and enjoy the evening. Once I made sure she was in bed and drifting off to sleep, I quietly closed the door and made my way out to the phone in the front hall. I rang up the operator and got her to call a number in Chicago for me.

It rang a couple times before someone picked up and a gruff voice said, "Yello."

"Hey, Jack," I said. "It's Nathan, Nathan Zachary. Yeah. You said if I ever needed a favor to call you. Well, pal, I've got an idea, and I wanted you to be the first one to hear about it."

CHAPTER 19

THE HUNTERS GATHER

I arrived back in New York in the late Fall of 1931, a few days before the maiden voyage of the zeppelin Hermes. I figured it wouldn't be too hard to sign on with its crew, but I had a few other things to do first.

"Max's" was a seedy little bar in Brooklyn, the kind of place I'd seen repeated all over the world, from France to Russia to Arixo and everywhere in between. A haze of blue-gray smoke hung near the ceiling, barely disturbed by the slow-moving fans. The place sounded with the click of pool balls, the crack of cues, the clatter of shot glasses, murmuring conversation, and the occasional loud laugh or belch. I let the door swing closed on the cool New York evening behind me and let my eyes adjust for a moment to the dim light inside.

I didn't have any trouble picking out the man I was looking for, a burly figure over near one of the pool tables, lining up a shot. He was tall and broad-shouldered, his rolled-up sleeves revealing an old Navy tattoo on his left forearm. He held a cigar clutched between his teeth, and a half-finished mug of beer rested on the edge of the table. His brown hair was thinning a bit, but his forehead was dry under the yellow overhead lights. From what I heard, not much made this lug sweat.

The bartender wiped down the bar in front of me with a damp rag that he tossed over his shoulder. He quickly looked me over, taking in my flight jacket. There were more than a couple flyboys in the bar, so I didn't look too out of place, even if he'd never seen me in here before. As long as I knew the password to get in, and didn't look like a cop, there was nothing to worry about. Since New York, like most of the country, was officially "dry", places like Max's had to watch their step. The cops might ignore private parties at the Biltmore, but they came down hard on speakeasies, at least the ones that weren't paying hefty bribes to keep the long arm of the law at bay.

"What'll it be?" the bartender asked me. I ordered a beer, paid the man, and watched the game for a few minutes, drinking and doing my best to look inconspicuous. It wasn't much of a match. In a few minutes the guy I was looking for had it all wrapped up. He lined up for another shot.

"Eight-ball in da corner," he said. With a gentle tap of his stick on the cue he made it so, the eight ball dropping into the corner pocket. "Dat's game," he said to his dismayed opponent. "Pay up, Sal." The disgruntled Sal angrily slapped a fin down on the side of the table, which was picked up and snapped a couple times before disappearing into a pocket as Sal stalked off, muttering to himself. I decided to make my move.

"Nice game," I said, sauntering up to the table. He shrugged, collecting the balls and racking them up on the table again.

"You play?" he asked.

"I've been known to from time to time," I replied. "Are you Charlie Stankowitz?"

"Who wants to know?"

"My name's Zachary, Nathan Zachary. I'm looking for a cargomaster and a mechanic, somebody who knows his way around some machines and knows one end of a wrench from another. I heard you were good and that you might be interested in some work."

Stankowitz eyed me suspiciously. "What kind of work are we talkin' about here?"

"A new venture," I said casually, "but something with a lot of growth potential. Why don't I buy you a drink and tell you all about it."

A slow smile spread across Stankowitz's face. He took the cigar from his mouth and gestured with it. "All right, Mr. Zachary, we can talk over a game, if you're up for it."

"Rack 'em up," I said.

By the time I left Max's an hour or so later, I had won two out of three games of eight-ball and secured Mr. Charlie Stankowitz's services. As I headed to where I'd parked, I noticed a group of kids, teenagers, clustered around my car. As I got closer and got a better look I broke into a run.

"Hey!" I shouted, and the young punks scattered, startled. It looked like they were stealing hubcaps and there was no way I was going to get ripped off by a bunch of dead-end kids!

I ran after them as they headed down the street and ducked into an alleyway. I could hear the clatter of garbage cans being overturned and a yowl from a stray tomcat whose dinner was interrupted. As I rounded the alley I saw the kids swarming up over the fence at the end of the alley. I ran over as the last kid was trying to make it up and over, grabbed a handful of his sweater and shirt and yanked him down. He struggled and kicked, but he was kind of scrawny and no real match for me.

"Hey, let me go!" he yelled, squirming in my grip. I shoved him up against the wall, pinning his shoulders, and go my face right up near his.

"What did you think you were doing, kid?" I asked. The kid was young, couldn't have been more than fifteen or sixteen, fresh-faced under a layer of dirt with light curly hair covered with a cap.

"Nothin', mister," he said as he struggled, finding it more difficult than he thought to get out of my grip. "Let me go!"

"I don't think so," I said. "If you don't want to talk to me, maybe I should call the cops and you can tell it to them." I was bluffing, actually, since I didn't want an extended chat with the local constabulary at that point. Getting the police asking questions about who I was and what I was doing in town was the last thing I needed. But, as much as I wanted to avoid the cops, the kid wanted to more. He practically broke down at the mention of the police, tears forming in his eyes.

"Please no, mister, don't call the cops!" he said. "We were just trying to make some money, you know?" I looked again at the kid and realized just how young he was. I was about the same age when I ran away from home. I'd been lucky enough to join up with the Army, but what did this kid have? I looked him hard in his eyes, brimming over with tears and clearly terrified.

"Okay, kid, come with me," I said.

"Where are we going?" he asked.

"To get you something to eat, then we'll talk."

A short while later we were sitting in a booth at a local diner, with the kid wolfing down a burger and fries like he hadn't eaten in a week, which could be true, I thought as I sat and watched him for a while.

"So, what's your name?" I asked him. He paused in shoveling food into his mouth for a moment and looked up at me guiltily.

"Simon, Simon Conroy," he said.

"Well, Simon, I'm Nathan Zachary. You want to tell me now why you were trying to rip off my car?"

Simon shrugged a bit. "Like I said, for the money."

"Where are your parents, Simon?"

"Dead, in the border war," he said flatly. When the Union broke under the weight of the Depression and the events that followed and the states decided to go their separate ways, everyone didn't always agree on how to divvy things up. There were some disputes between the new nations that started to come together, and some of them turned pretty bloody before they were settled. Some were still going on, in fact, mostly blamed on pirates and raiders.

"The bank took the farm," Simon continued, "and they wanted to put me in an orphanage, but I ran away. I came to the city looking to make my fortune."

"Oh?" I said, "and how were you planning to do that?"

"I'm a pretty good mechanic," he said looking up at me fiercely for a moment, before casting his eyes back down at his plate. "But I didn't have any money to pay for stuff and nobody would hire me for a job, so I had to find another way to get money."

"So you joined up with those other kids and started ripping off cars and such," I concluded.

"I didn't have much choice. I needed the money," he concluded lamely.

We lapsed into silence for a few minutes after that, Simon renewing the attack on his food and quickly polishing off the remainder, then gulping down his glass of milk and setting it down on the table with a "clunk." He eyed me suspiciously after that.

"So, how come you're being so nice to me?" he asked. I paused for a moment to consider.

"Are you really a good mechanic?" I asked by way of answering the question.

"Yeah."

"Are you willing to work?"

"Sure."

"Then how would you like a job, Simon?" I asked.

***

Mr. Reynolds, the cigar-smoking middle manager who handled hiring for Imperial Air, shuffled through the papers on his desk as I entered his office.

"Siddown," he said, gesturing toward the chair parked in front of his desk with his cigar as he renewed his attack on the sea of paper threatening to drown him. Organization was clearly not one of his strong suits. I wondered if Reynolds ever managed to start fires in his office, with his combination of stogies and loose paper.

I settled into the chair and glanced around the office, which was good sized for a man of Reynolds' position. On the walls hung photos of some of Imperial Air's zeppelins, which were making the company famous as a shipping and cruise line throughout North America. The room reeked of cigar smoke, which even the open window and small fan sitting on top of the filing cabinet did little to alleviate.

Reynolds finally found the manila folder he was looking for and dropped it on the desk, flipping it open.

"Now then, Mr ..."

"Ross," I supplied helpfully, "Jordan Ross."

"Yes, Mr. Ross," he said, glancing up from the papers a moment. "I see here you were a pilot during the War."

"That's right," I said, "with the 95th Squadron. We mostly saw action in France, although we were assigned to assist the Russian White Army for..."

Reynolds ended my prepared narrative with a wave of his cigar. A pity, I'd put a fair amount of work into my story to make it plausible. Now I wasn't even going to get to use it.

"So you know how to handle a plane?" he said. I nodded.

"I'm one of the best. I got into flying charter flights down in the Southwest after the War but, with the Depression on and all ..." I let the thought trail off. Jordan Ross was set up as a good pilot with a clean record, now a little down on his luck, like plenty of people in North America.

"All right," Reynolds said, flipping the folder closed. "Well, Mr. Ross, we need a third officer on one of our new airships, the Hermes. She's a cargo ship, set for her maiden run in a couple weeks. We need someone who knows how to handle a plane and can manage a crew. Can you handle that?"

"I'm your man, Mr. Reynolds." The Imperial Air manager squinted in my direction for a moment and I maintained my friendliest smile. Then he nodded.

"All right, let's get you down to the airfield and checked out on a machine. If you're half as good a pilot as you say you are, you're hired." I stood and Reynolds did the same. "Let me be the first to welcome you on board with Imperial Air, Mr. Ross," he said, extending his hand. "I'm sure you'll enjoy working with us." I took the chubby hand and shook it vigorously.

"I'm sure I will, Mr. Reynolds, I'm sure I will."

Passing the tests the company required wasn't a problem. Once they were satisfied as to my flying qualifications, I was taken out to the Hermes where she was docked at the company's airfield. The zeppelin was a fine ship, her silvery form gleaming in the light of the early morning sun from where she was moored outside a hangar bay, heavy cables keeping the lighter-than-air ship tethered to the ground. She had an underslung gondola with several propellers mounted along the framework to give her thrust, with the flag of the Empire State, the sun rising behind the Empire State Building, emblazoned brightly on her side. As the cabbie brought me around to the parking area of the airfield, I stared out the window, the airship's sleek form growing larger and larger in my field of vision.

"Hello, beautiful," I muttered under my breath.

After paying the cabbie and making my way to the hangar, I inquired as to the whereabouts of Captain Simmons.

"The Captain and Mr. Bates are on board, Mr. Ross," the secretary told me with a smile. "They should be expecting you." I thanked her and made a mental note to see about getting her phone number later as I made my way out to the gantry and onto the Hermes.

The interior of the airship was modern, albeit somewhat plain, especially when compared to Imperial Air's luxury airships like the Luxor, which were more like flying hotels. The Hermes was more like a military ship, with few frills to interfere with the open steel beams and metal flooring of the gondola and the main body of the ship. I headed for the airship's bridge, where I found two men, my superior officers, going over a list of maintenance work.

Captain Reginald Simmons was a good ten or fifteen years older than me, and looked like he'd be at home on the deck of a sailing ship from a hundred years before that, holding a spyglass to his eye to scan the horizon. He was actually the shortest man in the room, although not by much and what he lacked in height he made up for in presence. He wore a full salt-and-pepper beard and his dark hair was streaked with gray at the temples. He had a sharp, hatchet-like profile and bushy brows that nearly met above his ice-blue eyes. He wore a captain's jacket and a peaked cap trimmed with gold braid.

Mitchell Bates, the first officer of the Hermes, was closer to my age with sandy-colored hair and hazel eyes that didn't miss a trick. He was about my height and his tanned and weathered skin spoke of a man who liked the outdoor life. The rumors I'd picked up around Imperial Air suggested he liked the indoor life almost as much; he was a regular patron of some of the speakeasies and similar establishment in Manhattan. Bates was also known to be a hard case on the job and several people warned me to stay on his good side, which was exactly what I had in mind... for the moment, anyway.

"Captain," I said, addressing myself solely to Simmons for the moment. "Jordan Ross, reporting for duty. Permission to come aboard?"

"Permission granted," the Captain said taking the hand I offered to shake it. "This is my first officer, Mr. Bates," he said and I extended me hand to Bates.

"A pleasure, sir," I said, keeping my face passive as Bates took my hand in his crushing grip and did his best to make me wince a bit. I didn't give him the satisfaction. It probably would have been wiser to knuckle under a little, but there was no way I was going to let someone get the better of me, and I figured "Jordan Ross" for the same type of guy. If he noticed, Bates must have approved, since he seemed happy enough to meet me.

"I hear you're a pretty good pilot, Ross," Bates said, looking me over.

"Then you heard wrong," I said, "I'm a great pilot."

That elicited a chuckle from the captain and the first officer. Bates clapped me on the shoulder in a friendly gesture.

"You flew with the 95th?" he asked and I nodded.

"So did I! Where were you assigned?"

Uh-oh, I should have checked out the affiliations of the officers on board the Hermes more carefully. Keeping my concern off my face, I didn't miss a beat, falling back on the story I concocted before even applying to Imperial Air.

"I worked mostly with the 94th Squadron along the Western Front," I said, "but I also spent some time in Russia."

"Damn shame about how that went," Bates said and I nodded agreement.

"Yeah, that's for sure." I thought of the friends I'd lost in the Revolution, and particularly of Natalia Fassenbiender, buried in a foreign country away from her family and everyone who ever knew her. "A damn shame."

"Well," Bates said, "we can catch up on war stories later over a drink. I'll show you around the ship and get you set up so you can get right to work."

"Thank you," I said. We both turned to the captain for his permission to withdraw and he acknowledged us with a wave of his hand.

"We can go over the rest of these later, Mitch," he told the first officer. "Mr. Ross, I'm looking forward to working with you."

"Likewise, Captain," I said.

Bates guided me from the bridge and took me on a tour of the airship, showing me the major compartments, particularly the engine room and the cargo bays, the walkways through the superstructure and the massive gasbags, filled with hydrogen that kept the zeppelin aloft. Naturally, Imperial Air would have used helium to lift their zeppelins, if they could, but helium was rare, very expensive, and difficult to import, so they made do with hydrogen, and posted signs everywhere prohibited smoking or any sort of open flames near the gas-envelopes.

"One spark in the wrong place," Bates said to me, "and this lady would go up like a bomb." I was certain to keep that in mind. It was something I wanted to avoid, especially when I happened to be on board.

I inquired about the route for the Hermes' maiden voyage and Bates told me we would be taking a run into the Industrial States of America, delivering some machine parts and equipment, along with a few passengers. Nothing too major, but a good shakedown cruise for the ship.

"What about pirates?" I asked. "The Red Skull Legion operates out of the ISA, and I've heard they'll attack just about any cargo ship that passes over ISA territory."

"We've got some protection," Bates said, "some planes flying escort all the way out to Chicago and back, and we've got a couple of machines stowed on board, just in case. You sound like you almost hope that pirates will attack," Bates said with a smile. "You looking to prove what a hotshot flyer you are?"

I returned the smile. "Any chance I get," I said, "but, hopefully, there won't be any trouble. I want things to go as smooth as possible."

***

Things quickly settled into a routine on board the Hermes as we prepared for the airship's maiden flight. As Mr. Reynolds said, I was placed in charge of hiring the additional crew needed to run the airship, including extra hands to take care of the cargo. The list of potential employees was huge, of course, and filled with people either over- or under-qualified, with unemployment so high. I didn't have much trouble picking out the right people for the job and filling out the rest of the crew roster in the space of a little over a week.

Training the new crew members fell to me, overseen by Mr. Bates, but things went smoothly enough in that department that Bates left me largely to my own devices, while he handled putting out the numerous other fires that sprang up regarding scheduling and maintenance. Despite all the problems, the Hermes was ready to go on schedule. I oversaw the loading of the cargo into the bays, including two new Hughes Devastators, sleek and dangerous-looking machines with curved paired wings and two .50-caliber machine guns mounted along the nose, forward of the cockpit.

The design of the Devastators could only have come from an imagination like that of Howard Hughes; I'd never seen any planes quite like them before. The two sets of wings had no support struts between them like an ordinary biplane, and they were closer together than the wings of a typical biplane were. The tail was flattened with no dorsal fin, just a pair of stubby side wings. They looked like a strange sort of flying fish, painted a blue-gray color that reminded me of scales: beautiful machines.

The departure of the Hermes was a minor news item for the Empire State press, which turned out a few reporters and photographers to get quotes and snap pictures of the zeppelin. Once the formalities were concluded, we cast off the moorings, fully inflated the gas envelopes, and the majestic airship lifted off, engines whirring to bring us around and put us on a course for the ISA.

We quickly reached an altitude of some 20,000 feet and the miles fell away beneath us as the Hermes passed over the Empire State. We would reach the ISA border, then head over the Great Lakes toward the Windy City. The most likely places for us to run into trouble were crossing the border and over the lakes, where air pirates might set up an ambush. That's why I figured the Hermes had to find trouble well before that happened.

I went down to the cargo hold to check in with one of the people I hired on as cargomaster. With his qualifications from the Navy, it had been easy to convince Imperial Air he was the best man for the job. He knew a lot about getting things done and taking care of inventory.

"Hey, Charlie, everything all set down here?" I asked him. He nodded in my direction.

"Sure thing, boss," he said. "We're ready."

"Good, you know what to do." I checked my watch and headed toward the engine room. The kid checking the pressure valves looked up from his work and grinned at me, happy as a clam among the machinery. The bulky sweater he was wearing was a good two-sizes too big for him, and he had a flat cap covering his curly blond locks. It wasn't easy convincing Bates to take the kid on, but he knew how to do the job and was a real whiz with machines.

"Hey, Mister, ah, Ross," he said, briefly groping for the name. "How's things?"

"Looking good, Simon," I replied, glancing toward the engineer on duty, who gave me a cut nod before returning to his work. "I'd say we're all set to go. Just keep an eye on things down here."

"You can count on me, sir," he said proudly.

I headed back to the bridge, glancing at my watch again; it was nearly time.

CHAPTER

20

PANDORA'S BOX

Captain Simmons and Mr. Bates were already on the bridge, the captain at the wheel of the airship while Bates kept an eye on the instruments and coordinated activity on board. He glanced up at me as I entered the room.

"Ross. Is everything shipshape?"

"Aye, sir," I said. "Everything's under control." I passed him the clipboard I was carrying, with the checklist carefully filled out. He glanced over it before hanging the list from one of the hooks on the back wall of the cabin.

"Good work," he replied. Just then, the radio crackled.

"Hermes, this is Escort One, we've got company, coming in from 4 o'clock, repeat, we've got company."

Bates moved to the window of the gondola while Captain Simmons picked up the radio mike.

"Roger that, Escort One. Can you identify them?"

"Negative, Hermes, no known markings or colors and they're coming in fast, but there's only two of them. I think we can handle it."

"Understood," the captain replied.

"Ross," the first officer said, turning toward me, "get down to the …" Bates trailed off when he saw the Colt pistol in my hand, leveled in his direction.

"What the hell? Ross, what are you doing?" Captain Simmons turned around at the sound of Bates' shock and likewise stared in surprise at the gun.

"What is the meaning of this?" he said, outrage clear in his voice and manner.

"I think the meaning is pretty clear, Captain," I said. "This is a skyjacking. Those planes coming in are mine, and so is this ship. Ah, I'd stay away from the intercom if I were you, Captain, Mr. Bates. I'd rather not have to shoot you, but I will if you give me no choice." Both men stood away from the controls, their hands kept carefully at their sides.

A knock sounded at the cabin door and I took two steps backward toward it, never taking my eyes off the captain and the first officer. I rapped on the doorframe twice and heard three quick raps in response. I reached down and slid the door open to admit two men dressed in work coveralls, one of them carrying a Tommy gun he'd hidden in a tool kit.

"My people are already taking control of the ship," I told the stunned Imperial Air officers. "Most of the crew I hired works for me, you see. We just have to make sure your escort doesn't cause any trouble and we'll be on our way. Charlie," I said to the guy with the Tommy gun, "keep them covered and keep them quiet. Don't cause Charlie any trouble, gentlemen, and he won't give you any." I clapped the other guy on the shoulder. "Let's go, Jack."

As we turned to head out the doorway, Captain Simmons spoke up. "Wait, who are you?" he said. "Why are you doing this?"

I glanced back toward him and smiled. "My real name is Nathan Zachary, Captain, and I'm doing this, well, because I'm a pirate, and this is what we do. Don't worry. If you don't cause any trouble, you won't be harmed."

Jack Mulligan and I made our way quickly down to the bay at the bottom of the airship's gondola, where the two Hughes Devastators waited in their cradles. My other people were already taking control of the key areas of the airship and making sure the remaining crew and passengers didn't give us any trouble. As much as I would have preferred to make sure everything on board was under control beforehand, there was no time. When we reached the bay, the sounds of machine gun fire could be heard over the constant thrumming of the zeppelin's engines.

Jack and I climbed into the cockpits of the Devastators. They were cramped, but certainly no worse than some of the machines I'd flown. I hit the controls to open the bay doors, and looked out to see the rolling green hills and fields thousands of feet below, a river cutting through them like a thin, blue ribbon. I fired up the Devastator's engine and it kicked over with a cough and roared to life. Jack did the same and I gave him a thumbs-up before pulling the canopy closed and hitting the hook release.

The plane rolled from the belly of the zeppelin and my stomach briefly considered staying behind in the hangar bay, but caught up with me quickly enough as the Devastator hit the open air. I pulled back on the stick, swooping up and out from under the zeppelin's shadow, with Jack in close formation behind me. Clicking on the radio and turning it to the right frequency, I called to my wingman first.

"Jack-o, you there? Come back."

"Right behind you, boss," he said. "Nice little machine Hughes has cooked up."

"Yeah, mighty nice of Imperial Air to provide 'em, I thought."

"Nice of you blokes to join the party!" said another voice over the radio.

"Wouldn't miss it, Eddie" I said. "Just make sure you leave some for us."

"Right-o, just don't waste any time," Eddie Lancourt replied.

"We're coming in," I said.

The Imperial Air security people were flying Devastators too virtually identical to the ones we were using, with the Empire State logo painted on the wings and fuselage. They had .50-caliber machine guns mounted along the nose and there were four planes, two flying forward of the Hermes and two flying to the aft. Our planes were distinctive for their bright red paint schemes. They were both British Sabers, a good ten years older than the Devastators they were going up against, armed with .30-caliber machine guns forward, and a good deal slower than the Hughes-made Devastator. No doubt the escort pilots figured they were up against some bush-league pirates from Appalachia or somewhere in the ISA, flying refitted crop-dusters or barnstormers. But then, that's exactly what they were supposed to think.

The forward escort planes had already moved back to help engage the newcomers, with the aft escorts breaking off to engage as well. If the escort pilots saw us at all, they probably assumed we were from the zeppelin, coming out to lend a hand. The two closest machines didn't change course at all as we approached and I settled one of them in my sights.

I squeezed the trigger and my machine guns chattered, sending a hail of bullets into the tail of the other Devastator, tracer rounds leaving trails of fire through the air. The .50-caliber rounds chewed up the other machine's tail, blowing one of the stubby wings off entirely, and sending the Devastator into a barrel roll as the pilot suddenly realized what was happening and tried to get out of the line of fire.

He was too late, of course, and his roll turned into a spiraling dive as he lost control of his machine. I watched as the Devastator barely managed to right itself long enough for the pilot to hit the silk several thousand feet below us. The white parachute spread out near the thin trail of smoke as the crippled plane fell to Earth.

At the same moment that I opened up on the first Devastator, Jack Mulligan did the same on the other, but a split-second later. That instant seemed to be enough to warn the reflexes of the other pilot (definitely someone who'd flown in wartime, I guessed). The second Devastator banked hard and Jack's fire hit its lower left wing instead of being dead on. There was some damage, but the heavy construction of the Devastator could clearly take a pounding. The escort pilot started to climb and bank around to come at the unexpected enemy behind him.

I dropped my machine down and banked toward him, gliding into a shallow dive. I pulled up a little more than halfway there and climbed sharply, bringing my plane up underneath the Devastator heading toward Jack, intent on getting him in its sights. I squeezed the trigger and sent a stream of lead up to intersect the incoming plane's angle, and the rounds punched through the Devastator's right wings, leaving several ragged holes. The attack threw the pilot's aim off and Jack avoided his fire, setting the Devastator in his own sights and letting loose with a volley that left the plane crippled as it started a long, slow dive toward the ground. I didn't see if the pilot jumped clear, but it looked like the cockpit had taken some damage, so it was likely that hitting the ground was the least of his concerns at this point.

"Gloryhound. I could have handled him, you know," Jack said over the radio.

"Sure," I replied. "I knew you had it under control."

"Yeah, I let ya get your licks in. Figgered you could use the practice," Jack said. "Thought you might be getting rusty."

With that we turned our attention toward the other two escort planes, engaged with the Sabers and proving the efficiency of Mr. Hughes' designs. The Devastators were much faster than the older Sabers, giving them the advantage in maneuverability and greater ceiling. They were using it to get above the other planes so they could swoop down on them, guns blazing. I could see signs of some damage to both planes, although it didn't look serious, yet. Eddie and Tom were good pilots, some of the best I knew, but their machines were outclassed.

Now, however, both Devastator pilots clearly saw their comrades shot down by the newcomers from the zeppelin and knew that we weren't there to help them. One of the Devastators broke off from pursing a Saber and turned its attentions toward us, opening up its throttle and coming at us at high speed.

I didn't radio Jack. There was no need. With a precision born of familiarity and practice, we banked off in opposite directions to avoid the heavy caliber rounds from the Devastator. Banking into a sharp turn, we came at the Devastator from behind. He climbed up into a *renversement*, coming back at us as we came at him.

The moment I came out of my turn, he was in my sights, and I opened fire. Rounds sparked off the leading edge of the Devastator's wings and across the fuselage. I pushed the stick down to slide under the oncoming plane. An instant later, Jack opened fire behind me, peppering the Devastator with a few hundred more rounds before he pulled back and soar up above the oncoming plane.

The Devastator flew in a straight line for a few hundred yards as smoke blossomed from its fuselage, followed by flames as one of the phosphorous tracer rounds found its way into a fuel tank. The plane started to drop, then exploded in a massive fireball as the fuel tank ignited like a bomb. I rode out the shockwave as burning bits of debris rained down over the area.

"Nice work," I told Jack.

I turned my attention to the last of the airship's escort. Already harried by the two Sabers, and now alone against four enemy machines, the remaining escort pilot decided on the better part of valor and began heading away from us at top speed, on a direct heading back towards Manhattan.

Jack's voice crackled over the radio. "These buckets should be fast enough to catch him, Cap'n, if we …"

"Negative," I said, "let him go. By the time the Empire State scrambles some pilots and machines and gets them out here, we'll be long gone. Besides," I said with a smile. "What's the use of pulling off something like this if you don't have someone to tell everyone about it? The papers all over the Empire State will be carrying this story on the front page.

"Fall into formation," I told the other pilots, "we'll escort this lady to our planned drop-off, then head west."

I hailed the airship, "This is Zachary to the Hermes, how's everything on board there, Charlie?"

A Brooklyn accented voice answered. "All set here, boss. Everything's under wraps and the kid says we've got no problems, no damage or nothin'. He really does know his stuff."

"Swell," I said. "All right, then, people, let's move out." We fell into formation around the majestic airship and altered our heading a bit toward the Pennsylvania district of the Empire State, where we would complete our business with the Empire Air shipping line, at least for now.

***

Our stopover in the field in Pennsylvania was necessarily brief, since Empire State pilots were probably scrambling to come after us at that moment. I went back aboard the zeppelin, where the crew and passengers were gathered in the main lounge area in the gondola. Most of them looked rather skittish, while Capt. Simmons and his first officer still looked outraged and apologetic about the seizure of their ship.

"No one will be hurt," I told the passengers and crew, "so long as you cooperate."

"What do you want from us?" Simmons asked.

"I've already got what I want, captain," I said. "This is about what you want." I swept my gaze over the assembled group of people. "If you want to go on being a part of the system that's tearing this country apart and fighting over the scraps, that's none of my business, and you're free to go. We'll let you off here and you can hoof it to the nearest town. However," I paused for a moment to let the implications sink in.

"However, if you want something else. If you want to be able to leave a life of struggling and slaving to make the bigwigs back home richer. If you want to take your life into your own hands and make something of it, live on your own terms and make yourselves rich doing it, then you can join up with us. We need good people, especially people who know the skies, because that's where our new home is.

"We may be pirates and outlaws, but we're free. We're going to live life to the fullest, spit in the eye of those that would hold us down, and surely hang because of it, as the pirates of old used to say. But if we do, then we die as free men and women and not tools of people who think they can control our lives and make us pawns in the power-games they're playing out. Who's with me?"

The crew I'd hired already stepped forward. Now several other members of the Hermes crew did the same. Simmons and Bates just glared at me, although I thought for a moment that Bates wanted to step forward, but his pride wouldn't let him.

I saw to it that everyone else was escorted a short distance away toward the nearest road. They could make their way to a town we spotted just a few miles from here. I paused for a moment and wondered if we were anywhere near that town in Pennsylvania that Captain Peterson had been from, Honesdale. I wondered what the people of that town thought of Peterson's sacrifice now, with the country he fought and died for nearly as much a memory as he was.

"Let's get underway!" I told the crew and we got the zeppelin ready to go. In short order, the Devastators were stowed in the hangar bay and the Sabers flew alongside us as the airship took to the skies again and we set a course westward.

Jack Mulligan, Charlie Stankowitz and I stood on the bridge of the airship, with me at the helm. I felt like the captain of a galleon, setting sail for unknown waters, out on the edges of the map that bore legends like "Here There Be Dragons."

"What do you think about expanding that bay to hold more planes?" I asked Charlie.

"We can do it, boss. A week or two's work and we could fit a whole Squadron in there."

"Good," I said. If we were going to use the zeppelin as a mobile headquarters, we were going to need to carry more planes. The sale of the cargo would go a long way toward paying for some of what we'd need. As for the rest, I was sure Fortune would provide.

"So," Charlie said. "What are we gonna call her?"

"I never liked the name Hermes," I said, "but the Greek mythology reminded me of a myth I read when I studied the classics at Oxford. Ever hear the story of Pandora's box?" Both men shook their heads.

"Pandora was created by the gods and given as a gift to a man they favored," I said. "But the gods also gave Pandora a locked box and told her never to open it. Pandora did her best to do as she was told, but eventually curiosity got the better of her. She opened up the box and out came all these terrible demons and plagues, that ended the Golden Age and brought suffering, disease, and war to mankind."

Jack snorted, "Kinda like all the politicos and robber barons did to America," he said. "Everything falling apart."

"Exactly, Jack-o. But do you know what the most important thing about Pandora's box was?"

"What's that?"

"Not everything escaped from it. Pandora managed to close the box and keep one thing from escaping, one thing that foiled the gods' plans to make life miserable for everyone. A little thing called Hope."

I patted the wheel as we followed a heading toward the setting sun.

"C'mon, Pandora," I said. "Let's find us all a new home."

BOOK

A GOLDEN OPPORTUNITY

I have discovered that, for good or ill, this motley collection of thieves, drunkards, dreamers, blackguards, bullies and scoundrels of every stripe are probably the freest, most vibrant men and women in the world today.
— Tamara Staples, *Behind the Crimson Veil*

CHAPTER 21

MESSAGE FROM A DEAD MAN

"When you get to the ground, tell 'em Nathan Zachary sent you!"

The Dixie J2 Fury went spiraling down trailing smoke from its smashed engine. I saw the pilot bail out, the white chute billowing out like a blossoming flower hundreds of feet below me. But I was already moving on to the next available target, as the other Furies buzzed around the ponderous Dixie zeppelin like angry hornets, hornets with a serious sting. The Furies carried some substantial armament: a pair of .30-caliber machine guns and a pair of .40-caliber machine guns mounted along the wings, plus the Goliath .70-caliber cannon that ran along the machine's underbelly, capable of punching big holes through just about anything, including us.

Still, we had the Dixie pilots outnumbered, especially after I downed one of their machines. There were six of us: Jack, Eddie, Buck, Tex, Big John, and me, and there were only four Furies left protecting the zep. We closed in on them and I think they must have known they didn't really have a chance. But they didn't give up, no sir. They decided to fight it out to the end, and you have to admire their courage, if not their good sense.

I came about, with Jack sticking close to my port wing, and opened up the throttle on my Devastator as I dived in toward the zeppelin again. One of the Furies climbed to meet us, guns blazing, trying to get enough of a climb to bring that monster cannon to bear. That's the thing with Furies, you need to take them from above if you can, and keep them from getting a chance to pound you with that Goliath. I kept heading straight for that Fury, waiting to see if the pilot would veer off. A near pass is one of the most dangerous maneuvers around, since it can seriously damage both planes, if you're not careful.

The pilot of the Fury wasn't looking to back down and neither was I. We headed straight for each other at what must have been 200 miles per hour. Then, at the last possible second, I pushed forward on the stick and dived down. The Fury fired its Goliath at me, but my maneuver caught the pilot by surprise and he hit the trigger just a second too late, like I figured. Those .70-caliber rounds passed through the air a good 100 feet away from where I was. I yanked the stick back and pulled up into a loop, while the Fury kept climbing, the pilot looking to get his bearings and figure out where I went. The silvery wall of the zeppelin flashed by in front of me as I climbed, then flipped. The gunners manning the zep's machine gun nests fired at me, but they never even came close.

Just after the top of the loop, I looked ahead and I could see the top of the Fury, less than a hundred yards below me, right in my sights. I squeezed the triggers and the .40-caliber guns on my wings shot four rows of glowing tracers at the Dixie machine. The rounds impacted on the Fury's wings, punching some nasty holes in them, and the Fury started to go from a climb to a dive as the pilot fought to keep her nose up. That's when Jack swooped in to finish it off. His shots took off a good part of the Fury's starboard wing and that was all she wrote—so to speak. The Fury went into a nosedive and the pilot hit the silk, probably still wondering what the hell happened.

"Fascinating, Mr. Zachary," Tamara Staples said in a dry tone of voice, indicating that she wasn't going to pronounce judgment on the veracity of my tale, "and then you took the zeppelin?"

I paused to take a sip from my drink, savoring the taste of the fine scotch before continuing.

"Well, the remaining Furies put up a bit more of a fight," I said, "but after we downed two more of them, the last one decided to give up the ghost and ran back home to tell them their cargo was now in the hands of the Fortune Hunters."

"That's an excellent story, Mr. Zachary," Tamara said, scribbling notes on the pad balanced on her knee. Her sitting position nicely showed off her shapely legs, clad in black nylon stockings.

"Please," I said, "Call me Nathan. May I call you Tamara? I'm happy to help you out. I just hope it's something you can use for your book."

"Well," she said with a smile, "if I used every story I've heard so far, I could fill a dozen books, I suspect. Still, I do have a few more questions."

"Of course," I said. "Would you like another drink?"

"No, thank you, I'm fine." I tossed back the remainder of my scotch and asked the waitress to bring me another, then turned my attention back to the lovely and talented Miss Staples.

It was Sky Haven, 1935, when the Free Colorado State was already well-established as a haven for, well, just about anybody. Colorado made no bones about its policy toward the outside world and it was common knowledge that cities like Denver and Boulder were havens for "pirates, blackguards, and scoundrels," as one of the articles I read put it. And Sky Haven was the real center of it all. The capitol of the Free State was still supposedly Denver, but everyone knew the real power lay in Sky Haven. It was built high atop a mountain, approachable only by the air, and even then only through a dangerous maze of canyons and passes, guarded by machine gun nests and some of the nastiest pirate gangs you've ever seen. Sky Haven was the place many pirates, including me, called home.

"I'm curious," Miss Staples said, continuing our interview. "Why 'Fortune Hunters'? In my experience, the name of a pirate band often has a meaning behind it."

I noticed how Tamara avoided calling us "gangs" like most everyone else, and politely avoided pointing it out.

"I suppose there is a meaning to it," I said, "or at least a reason for it. Some years ago, back during the war, Eddie Rickenbacker told me 'sometimes Fortune takes a hand and we never know what she will decide. Whatever

Fortune decides, she does so without consulting us.' I remember it to this day. He was talking about how senseless things happen in wartime, but it meant more than that to me. It said to me that we're each responsible for our own destiny. You have to be willing to go out and grab the bull by the horns, to track down your fortune and make it yours instead of sitting by and waiting for it to happen to you, letting other forces decide your life. That's the philosophy I live by, that all of us live by—we're fortune hunters."

Tamara scribbled rapidly on her pad before glancing up again.

"Speaking of your philosophy, you've made an impression with a number of people here in the Free State and elsewhere with your famous 'pirate's code.' Could you tell me more about that?"

"It's quite simple, really," I said. "A lot of people think that, because we have rejected conventional society and the laws of corrupt and illegal governments, that we live by no law at all. I suppose," I glanced around the bar where we sat, looking at the men and women drinking, talking, and laughing, "that some pirates believe that too, but not us. We live by a simple code that comes down to two rules.

"First," I said raising one finger, "no harm to non-combatants. We don't shoot at anyone who isn't pointing a gun at us already, and we don't put innocent people into the line of fire. And second"—I raised a second finger in the shape of a V—"we only take from the rich and the powerful, as the farmers and simple folk have enough trouble already. It's the governments and big businesses that need to be taken down a notch."

"So," Tamara said with a sly smile. "Do you view yourself as something of a latter-day Robin Hood?"

I smiled, "I think you've been watching too much of what's coming out of Hollywood, Tamara, although I guess I could see how folks might think of Sky Haven as Sherwood Forest, us as the Merry Men." I tipped my chair back and toyed with the idea a bit. "Paladin Blake as the Sheriff of Nottingham, perhaps?" I mused aloud, eliciting a giggle from Tamara, who covered her mouth with one hand. "President LaGuardia as Sir Guy of Gisbourne? No, I don't suppose that works very well, and I know Jack wouldn't care to change his callsign to "Little John," especially since we've already got Big John in the unit…"

A voice came from just behind me as Tamara laughed again. "Hey, boss, sorry to interrupt," said Tex, one of the pilots in my crew. I turned and looked over my shoulder, gesturing for her to come closer.

"No problem," I said, "we were just considering you for the role of Maid Marion, actually."

"Oh, is that so?" Tex said in a bemused Southern drawl, a smirk spreading across her face. She reached up and fluffed her long, curly blond hair in an exaggerated gesture. "Y'all think I would look good as a princess?" Tex was dressed in her usual worn blue jeans and a man's shirt under a beaten-up leather flying jacket, with leather cowboy boots on her feet and her gun belt hanging loosely around her waist. I tried to picture her in a gown of silk and satin, with one of those tall conical hats with its trailing veils, standing at the window of a castle, looking out and waiting for her Robin Hood to come save her.

"What're you all smilin' at?" Tex said to me with mischief in her eyes.

"I'm just trying to picture it," I said. "It paints an interesting image."

"Well don't get any ideas about swingin' in to rescue me, boss-man," she said playfully. "I've pulled your bacon out of the fire plenty of times." She turned to Tamara, who was sitting and listening to the exchange with a look of bemusement. "He ever tell you about the time in that bar in Tortuga…"

"Um, Tex?" I said. "Did you come over here for a reason?"

"Oh, right!" she said, successfully diverted from her tale. She reached into the pocket of her leather jacket, pulled out a folded piece of paper, and held it out to me. "The telegram office got this for you."

I took it from her hand with a raised eyebrow. Who'd be sending me a message Western Union, especially in Sky Haven? I unfolded the message to read it.

TO: NATHAN ZACHARY

AM BACK HOME STOP NEED SOME HELP DIGGING UP OUR OLD FRIEND G STOP IF YOU ARE INTERESTED MEET ME IN THE CAIRNGORM MOUNTAINS IN A WEEKS TIME STOP ANGUS MCMULLAN

A set of map coordinates followed at the end of the message. I let the hand holding the note drop to my lap as I stared off into space, not looking at anything in particular, but remembering.

"Well I'll be damned," I muttered, "Mad Angus McMullan."

"Who's it from?" Tamara asked, breaking me out of my recollections.

"Hmmm? Oh, a man I never thought I'd hear from again, that's for certain. Would you excuse me, Tamara? There's some business I need to take care of. Maybe we can finish this interview later on?"

"Of course," she said, flipping the notebook closed. "Can I contact you here?"

"Probably in a few weeks," I said. "I'll be unavailable for a while."

"All right then. Well, you can always reach me at my place in Boulder. We still have to do that portrait shot," she said, rising to shake my hand. Her grip was surprisingly firm. "It was a pleasure meeting you, Nathan."

"Likewise."

I watched Tamara Staples wind her way out of the bar before turning my attention back to the amused Tex, who stood there, watching me watching her with a smug look on her face.

"She's quite a reporter," I said and Tex nodded in agreement, a look of mock seriousness crossing her face.

"I bet she is."

"Get the crew together," I said, "and tell Sparks to get Pandora ready to cast off."

"Okay," Tex said. Her look of amusement was replaced by one of curiosity. "Mind tellin' me exactly where we're goin'?"

"Have you ever wanted to visit Scotland, Tex?" I asked.

***

A short while later we were all gathered on board Pandora to talk about the mysterious telegram and what it meant.

"Cor, bloody Angus McMullan," Eddie said, "After all these years. I don't believe it."

"He was a tough one," Jack said. "I always figured it would take a lot to kill him."

"So are y'all gonna explain who this Angus fella is or not?" Tex said, drawing our attention back to everyone else in the room. The other pilots of the squad were there; Tex, Buck, and Big John, along with Sparks, who was in charge of Pandora ever since we lost Charlie Stankowitz, nearly a year and a half previously.

Sparks, Simon, had grown up a lot from the dead-end kid I met on the streets of Brooklyn. He had an amazing head for machines of all kinds and an eagerness to learn everything he could. When he wasn't working on Pandora (the "old girl" as he called her) or one of the planes, he had his nose buried in a book or the latest issue of Air Action Weekly, keeping up to date on anything and everything new that came along. His new passion was radio and electronics, which earned him the nickname "Sparks." He kept the radios on Pandora and in our machines operating.

Tex and Buck made an unlikely pair. Not romantic, in fact, I'm sure the idea never even crossed their minds. Both of them were from the South, Tex from her namesake state of Texas and Buck from the Carolinas. Both of them lost family in the border wars, including Buck's mother and sisters. Buck adopted Tex like a sister not long after they met, and the two of them fought like only brother and sister could. Everybody knew they didn't mean it, it was just their way of showing how they felt about each other. When the chips were down, Buck would protect Tex with his life and I was sure she would do the same. They'd both proven themselves good pilots even before I found them and asked them to join the Hunters.

Big John was the newest member of the crew. As a Negro, he had a hard time growing up in the South, and eventually headed off on his own down to Texas and the southwest, working as an "Indian Fighter" with the Texas Rangers. But John soon figured out he had a lot more in common with the Injuns than the Cowboys, and quit the Rangers to head out to Free Colorado and find his fortune. He did when he found us and joined up. He was a good pilot, and tended to keep to himself. When he has something to say, it was usually something important.

All of them had a look of eager anticipation as I settled back in my seat and picked up the telegram from the table to glance at it again.

"Angus McMullan, Mad Angus as they used to call him," I said, "was a pilot for the British back in the War. Jack, Eddie, and I met him back in that German prison camp when we were all briefly 'guests' of the Kaiser.

"Of course, Angus wasn't exactly a prisoner of war. You see he and some friends of his decided army life wasn't their cup of tea, and they wanted to arrange for a comfortable retirement. So when they caught word of a British gold shipment going to Canada, and probably to the States after that, they arranged to hijack it."

"How much gold are we talking about here?" Buck asked eagerly.

"To hear Angus tell it, a small fortune," I said. "He and his friends hid the gold somewhere in Scotland. But after that, the Brits caught up with him and his friends. Most of them were shot down but Angus made it across the Channel, only to wander into German territory and get shot down. They took him prisoner and that's how we met up with him.

"When we escaped from Eisen, Angus' plane was shot down. Since we never heard anything about him after that, I always assumed he was dead, and the secret of his gold died with him. But, now it looks like he survived, and he's looking to recover the gold, only he needs some help to get to it."

"So we're going to go help him get it, just like that?" Jack said.

I shook my head. "Won't be that easy. If Angus wants our help, he's gonna have to pay for it. But you knew him, Jack, he's not stupid. He knows that a share of a fortune is better than nothing, and there probably aren't a lot of other people he can get to help him out, especially people who've got planes and a ship like the old girl here," I said, patting the bulkhead. "But if we're going to negotiate with Angus, we're going to have to meet him, and he wants to meet in only a few days. Simon, how's Pandora set for a trip across the Atlantic?"

"We'll need to lay in some more fuel to cover the whole distance," Sparks said, "but we should be able to get that right here. Old Man McCormick owes us for that last supply of parts and he'll sell us the gas. Otherwise we're all set. Pandora is shipshape and she can handle just about anything, as long as we don't run into a hurricane or something."

"Not bloody likely in the North Atlantic," Eddie said. He sighed. "It'll be good to see the islands again, even if it is Scotland and not England. When do we leave?"

"Right away," I said. "If we're going to make it in time. Sparks, talk to McCormick and get whatever we're going to need. The rest of you, make sure your machines are in the bay and ready to go. If you've got sweethearts to say goodbye to," I smiled, "make tonight count, because we're heading out first thing in the morning. And not a word about this to anyone, understand? The last thing we need is somebody trying to horn in on this opportunity. Got it?"

A chorus of "yes, sirs" and "got it, boss" ended the conversation.

"Then go to it!" I said, with a clap of my hands, and everyone started filtering out of the room, until it was just Jack and me left. He stood by the door, silently watching everyone go. Clearly there was something on his mind.

"What is it, Jack-o?" I asked.

"I dunno," he said with a shrug. "Don't you think it's kinda weird, ol' Angus McMullan contacting you out of the blue, after all these years, and asking for your help?"

"It is strange," I said, "but who knows what he's been up to for all this time? Besides, he hinted at the gold in his message; 'G. old friend,' 'gold friend', and he and I were the only ones who knew about that missing gold. He never even told any of you. It has to be him, and that means we've got a shot at a fortune. Just think about what that money could do for this outfit. Sparks won't admit it, but Pandora needs a lot of work, and we could get new machines to replace some of the clunkers we're flying that are four and five years out of date, maybe even hire on some more crew."

"I know, I know," Jack said gruffly, "it'd be great. Maybe I just don't think we've got that kind of luck."

"If I've learned anything in my life, it's that we make our own luck, Jack-o," I said. "Don't worry, everything'll work out. You'll see. This is a real golden opportunity, and I'm not going to pass it up."

When Jack left, I ran through the things I needed to do before we cast off. I decided I would give Tamara Staples a call and see about finishing our interview before she left for Boulder. There were a few questions I wanted to ask her, too. Hopefully, the answer was "yes."

CHAPTER

22

A FATEFUL MEETING

Cruise lines like Imperial Air and some of the new German zeppelins try to make the idea of a long, slow trip across the Atlantic Ocean seem like a grand, romantic sort of thing. That's true when you're on board one of those luxury liners, with nothing to do but while away the hours over cocktails, elegant dinners, and ballroom dancing, all while enjoying the view of flying high over the blue ocean waters through a clear blue sky or a night dappled with a thousand stars. But when you're on board a converted cargo zeppelin, with nothing to do but plot course corrections and coax stubborn machinery to perform well enough not to dump you in the drink, with the skies spending most of their time a leaden gray, and the nearest dancing is over a thousand miles behind you, it's no picnic, let me tell you.

Crossing the continent to get to the ocean was at least interesting (although Jack would call that an understatement). We had to make our way over the People's Collective, avoiding trouble with their aggressive air militia en route, skirt along the Industrial States of America via the Great Lakes, cut through the

Empire State, and then out into the broad expanse of the Atlantic. We could have gone through Dixie, but as the tale I told Miss Staples made clear, the Fortune Hunters were none too popular south of the Mason-Dixon at the time.

After playing hide and seek with the Dusters over the open fields of Kansas, avoiding a narrow brush with the Red Skull Legion, and putting paid to a couple of the Broadway Bombers in the Empire State, the trip settled into a long, dull expanse of water, broken up by occasional concerns about the weather. Although Eddie was right that there weren't any hurricanes to run into this far north, that didn't mean there weren't storms bad enough to cause problems for Pandora if we weren't careful.

"What do you think?" I asked Eddie as we were eating out of tins down in the galley, "Will be run into any trouble when we get to Scotland?"

"Probably not," he said, picking at his food. "God, this reminds me of what they used to feed us back in the Army," he said in disgust, putting down his fork.

"I think it's actually left over from then," I said with a laugh. "I'm sure looking forward to a real meal."

"Hey," Eddie said. "On our way back we should head south and stop over in Tortuga. Be a perfect place for a little R&R, especially if we have some of that gold to spend."

"Sure, and you can visit that little seniorita you meet up with last time."

"Not if her husband's still around!" Eddie said, and we both broke up laughing.

Buck came rushing around the doorway and stuck his head in.

"Hey boss," he said, "land ho! We're coming up past the northern coast of Ireland, Jack says it shouldn't be long now."

I tossed the remainder of my lunch into the trash and headed up to the Pandora's bridge, with Buck and Eddie not far behind me. Jack was on duty at the wheel, keeping us on course. Off to the south, we could make out the hazy coastline of the Emerald Isle as we cruised over the North Atlantic. The sky was clear compared to the rest of our journey, with only a few scattered white clouds, so the view was spectacular.

"We're almost there," Jack said, with a mixture of relief and trepidation in his voice. "Shouldn't be too long now, 'bout another couple hundred miles."

As Eddie predicted, there was no trouble as we made our way over the

Scottish countryside toward the mountains that rose up from the highlands to tower over the rolling green hills and countryside below. The Cairngorms were craggy, but smooth terrain compared to the Rockies in North America. Years of navigating around Free Colorado and Sky Haven made it a fairly easy matter to handle these mountain peaks. The trouble would be in finding a suitable place to put down a plane, but I suspected McMullan would have chosen a suitable spot for our meeting.

I was right. When we got closer to the coordinates he'd provided in his telegram, I could make out some kind of old manor house, nestled in a relatively flat plateau in the mountains. For the looks of it, the main part of the house dated back hundreds of years. It was a squat tower of gray stonework, pierced with arrow slits. The house itself was more modern, that is to say not more than a hundred years old, with dark beams and woodwork and heavy shutters to keep the mountain chill from the windows. There was a good-sized barn or similar building out behind the main structure, and the land immediately around them was level enough to land a plane, although it didn't offer much room for error. A thin trickle of smoke issued from the chimney of the house, indicating that someone was home.

"Nice digs," Jack said, looking the place over from his vantage next to me on the bridge. "How do you think a guy like Angus managed to get himself a place like that?"

"I don't know," I said. "Probably swindled somebody out of it, or maybe he got it cheap when someone went bust and had to sell off a few things. We'll find out soon enough."

"So, you're going down there?" Jack asked.

"Yep, and you're coming with me."

"Wouldn't have it any other way," Jack said dryly.

I told Sparks to maintain radio silence until he heard from us. Even if Angus had the equipment to receive us, we had no idea who else might be listening in. No sense in telling the whole country we were here and what we were looking for. Sooner or later, we'd have to go down for a face to face meeting, and I figured sooner was better than later.

We reversed the engines, bringing Pandora to an almost complete stop, using just enough power to keep her in roughly the same place against the mountain winds that tried to push her from side to side. Jack and I went down to the bay and climbed into the cockpits of our Devastators. I checked all the systems and made sure we were all go before giving Jack the thumbs up sign, closing the cockpit and firing up the engine. The Devastator roared to life and I released the docking hook, letting the machine roll out the open bay doors. Jack followed close behind.

We circled the brooding house, zeroing in on the open stretch of land between the house and the barn. There was still no sign of anyone outside. I brought the Devastator down toward the ground, giving myself as much room as I could to make a landing. It was a little bumpier than I would have liked, but I'd landed on far worse. My machine trundled down the open stretch of land, coming to a halt right between the two buildings. Jack touched down behind me and brought his machine up next to mine. I killed the engine and popped the canopy to climb out and take a look around.

The moment my feet touched the ground, the doors of the barn and the house burst open to disgorge about a dozen men, all armed with German-made submachine guns. Before Jack or I could climb back into our machines, much less consider taking off again, we were surrounded. The grim-eyed leader of the men barked at us in German not to move and to put our hands up.

"I just knew this was too good to be true," Jack muttered as he raised his hands into the air and I followed suit.

From the house came another figure that approached behind the knot of armed men on that side, and they parted to admit her into the circle of guns leveled in our direction. She wore khaki jodhpurs tucked into knee-high polished black boots. A pair of leather belts around her waist held a brace of knives, along with a German-made pistol holstered at her hip. The clothes did little to conceal a form at once feminine and also taut and athletic. She wore a leather bomber jacket over a white blouse that was open at the neck to reveal an expanse of creamy white flesh, leading up to a long, elegant neck and a face with classical features that could have been carved from marble. Long, golden hair was gathered in the back of her head in a carefully wrapped braid, with a few stray locks hanging in her face. The only thing that marred her beauty was the patch over her right eye, and the gleam of hatred from the remaining ice blue orb, directed particularly at me.

"Hello, Nathan," she said in a sultry tone, her English barely accented with German. "It's good to see you again." The sound of her voice brought back a flood of memories I'd been going over in my mind since receiving the telegram. I did my best to keep them from showing on my face.

"Hanna," I said. "It's good to see you, too, although I'd prefer it was under more pleasant circumstances."

"No less pleasant than our parting, darling," Hanna Ullen said bitterly, one hand coming up to brush against the cheek beneath the eye-patch. "I'm very happy to see you again. I'm sure you never expected to see me."

"No, that's true," I said.

"Why should you? After all, you left me for dead."

"You betrayed me."

"I remained loyal to my country."

"For all the good it did you. You lost the war. You could have come with me."

"But I didn't," Hanna said coldly. "I remained loyal and now my loyalty and patience have been rewarded; you've come back to me." Her smile sent a chill down my spine. "I'm sure we can find a way to show our gratitude to your friends."

I heard a familiar buzzing sound and looked up toward Pandora to see a group of four small planes escorting a larger cargo plane. They were coming up from behind the zeppelin, and I had no idea if my crew could even see them. I wanted more than anything to call out a warning of some kind, to get to the radio in my plane and call up to them. But I couldn't move. I could only stand and watch as the planes drew closer. They could see what was going on down here, but did they know what it meant? Did they know about the potential danger to them?

Hanna walked over to me, drawing the slim pistol from the holster at her hip. She leveled it at my heart and looked me in the eye.

"You can make matters for them a great deal easier if you simply call up to them and tell them to surrender," she said. "Otherwise, we cannot be responsible for any… accidents that might happen." I gritted my teeth and looked up at my zeppelin, with the enemy planes closing in fast. Hanna obviously wanted to take Pandora intact and figured if she could get us to surrender, so much the better. If I could warn them somehow, they might have a chance.

"All right," I said, "let me use the radio."

"No tricks, Nathan," Hanna said. "One wrong word and I will kill you, and then him," she nodded her chin toward Jack, "and your ship will still belong to us."

I climbed slowly up to the cockpit of my Devastator, with Hanna close behind me. I briefly contemplated making a grab for her gun or trying to use the Devastator's weapons, but it was useless. Even if I did manage to take down a few of the soldiers, there were more than enough of them to kill Jack, and holding Hanna as a hostage wouldn't get me very far if these pirates were as ruthless as they looked.

I clicked on the radio, tuned to the frequency we usually used and held the mike to my lips; one eye watching Hanna as she calmly kept her gun pointed in my direction.

"Zachary to Pandora, Zachary to Pandora, do you read? Over."

The speaker grille crackled and Sparks' voice came over the radio. "We read you, boss, what's going on down there? Over."

"Sparks, we've got a Jolly Roger situation," I said, "get the hell out of …" I saw stars as Hanna clubbed me upside the head with the butt of her pistol. She grabbed the microphone from my nerveless fingers as I stumbled and grabbed hold of the edge of the cockpit for support. Keeping her gun and her eye on me the entire time, she raised the mike to her lips.

"Boss, come back," Sparks said over the radio. "Are you there? Over."

"Listen carefully," Hanna said. "Your leader and his wingman are our prisoners. If you do not surrender to the boarders approaching your zeppelin and allow them to take control, we will kill them. If you surrender, then both you and your leader will remain unharmed. This is your only warning. " She replaced the mike into the cradle on the console, reached over and flicked the radio off before Sparks could reply.

She gestured for me to climb down and I did so, then the guards herded Jack and me toward the house. I glanced up to see boarders jumping from the cargo plane to the Pandora, but I couldn't tell if the crew was putting up a fight or not. There were no signs of Pandora launching any other planes, no sound of the machine guns nests opening fire. Then the guards forced me inside and I lost sight of what was happening.

The interior of the house felt sort of like a hunting lodge for gentlemen to get away from the city life and enjoy a bit of sport in the highlands of Scotland, perhaps some riding, shooting, and bird-watching, or the like. The main part of the small house contained a sitting room with a large flagstone hearth, complete with deer's head mounted above the mantle, a buck with an impressive spread of antlers. A fire burned in the fireplace and a figure sat in the shadows of a wing-backed chair. I felt a strong sense of déjà vu as Hanna strode over to take her place at the side of the chair, several of the guards remaining to cover us with their guns while the others headed back outside.

"*Herr* Zachary," the figure sitting in the chair said. "I am pleased you decided to accept my invitation, but I suspected a man of your reputation would be hard pressed to pass up a chance at such a fortune. A calculated gambit, but a reasonably safe one. You never could resist an opening in the game, even when it ended up placing you in check." He leaned forward a bit, coming into the light to reveal a face with noble, hawkish features. His hair was an iron gray, as was his neatly trimmed beard and moustache. There were crow's feet around the steely eyes and hard lines around his mouth, but I could still see the core of the proud officer I'd met nearly twenty years before.

"Heinrich Kisler," I said. He acknowledged the mention of his name with a brief incline of his head. "I'd heard you were dead."

"As one of your American writers once said, the rumors of my death have been greatly exaggerated," Kisler replied, rising from his chair and drawing himself to his full height. "Although there are certainly no few people on the Continent that would like to see me dead, I have thus far evaded the reaper's grasp."

"So this was all a set-up?" I asked. "The telegram from McMullan, just to get us to come here?"

"To get *you* to come here, to be more precise," Kisler said, moving over to the sideboard to pour a small glass of amber colored liquor from the crystal decanter there. "I doubted you would put in an appearance if you knew who'd really sent the message."

"I might have," I said honestly.

"But you would have come more prepared for trouble," Kisler said, "or more likely you'd have simply bombed this place, or given away my location to the authorities, neither of which I could have allowed. You would have come more prepared for trouble than if you were expecting to meet an 'old friend.' The deception was necessary to draw you here and to confirm that you possessed the information I need."

"What information is that?" I said. Kisler took a sip from his drink and a wry smile split his bearded face.

"Oh, come now, Nathan, let us not be coy. We are both privateers these days. I know your reputation well. You came to Scotland because you believed Angus McMullan was prepared to share his stolen gold with you in exchange for your help in recovering it. That was the tone I meant the message to have, but only if McMullan had in fact told you about the gold as he said he did."

"Then he's alive?"

"Alas, no," Kisler said, clutching one hand behind his back and he paced in front of the fireplace like a commander reviewing his troops. "When you escaped from Eisen all those years ago, I downed Angus McMullan's plane. It was badly damaged, but he managed to crash-land it, and he was injured in the process. German soldiers recovered him and I saw to it that he was interrogated. During the questioning, he offered me information about a hidden cache of British gold if I would release him. I learned from him how he and his former companions stole the gold and hid it somewhere in Scotland, but before I could learn the gold's exact location, McMullan's injuries worsened and he died.

"After the war, I gradually fell out of favor in Germany. In time, I decided to leave my native land and seek my fortunes abroad, much as you have done," he said gesturing in my direction. "I command a band of capable pilots and we have made a name for ourselves on the Continent as mercenaries and privateers, know as *Schwarze Adler*, the "Black Eagles". There are many opportunities in this world for men and women with the vision and the courage to seize them, as you know.

"Not long ago, stories of the exploits of your Fortune Hunters reached my attention. I learned that you were their leader, and that your band included other men you met during your time at Eisen. I pondered briefly if you might have recovered McMullan's gold yourself, using it to fund your organization, and so I began investigating the Fortune Hunters. I determined that your success was won solely through your own efforts, for which congratulations are in order, by the way."

"Thanks," I said dryly. "You don't know how much that means to me."

Kisler ignored the sarcasm in my tone and continued. "That meant the gold was still hidden, but I suspected you—or one of your men—might know something about it. Thus, the telegram intended to draw you here."

"Then you're in for a disappointment, Kisler," I said. "I don't know anything about any gold. Angus probably made the whole story up to try and pull one over on you."

"And yet you, and your entire crew, came all this way merely to assist a man you met in prison nearly twenty years ago? Without any hope of reward?" Kisler shook his head. "No, *Herr* Zachary, I do not think so. Plus, I already know that McMullan told you about the gold. When he tried to buy his freedom, he revealed to me that you were the only other soul he'd told, in order to assure that you would take him with you in your escape. So, you see, I know you have information that may be useful to me; check again, Herr Zachary. Now all that remains to be seen is whether or not you are willing to be reasonable in cooperating with me."

Just then the radio of the mantle crackled to life, a German voice coming over it. Kisler picked up the microphone and held a brief conversation in German with the speaker before replacing the mike and turning triumphantly toward me.

"Well," he said, "it seems that your crew is not entirely foolish. My men have secured your airship and your crew is in my custody. I believe that is check and mate. Now, are you willing to assist me in this endeavor, or shall I order my men to begin executing members of your crew, starting with him?" He jerked his chin toward Jack, who was standing stoically next to me.

"What's it to be, *Herr* Zachary?"

CHAPTER

23

THE SEARCH BEGINS

"I'll help you," I said, "but only under certain conditions."

"You're hardly in a position to bargain, Zachary," Kisler said. "Still, I will hear your conditions." He settled back down into his chair by the fire, crossing one booted foot over the other and sipping from his glass tumbler of liquor as he listened.

"If I help you, I want your word of honor, as a pilot and a gentleman, that I and my people will be released unharmed."

"Of course," Kisler said. "I am not a barbarian, *Herr* Zachary. You have my word that you and your people will be released once the gold is safely secured. Our business will be concluded."

"This is really between us, Kisler," I said. "My people aren't involved. Let Jack go back to the Pandora and escort them away from Scotland. Let them set course back to North America and I'll stay and help you."

Kisler looked at me for a moment, his expression unreadable, then his face split into a predatory grin and he chuckled. "No, I don't think so," he said. "I'm hardly about to part with my strongest pawn this early in the game. No, *Herr* Zachary, your ship and your people will remain under my care until we have secured the gold. Then you have my word that you and your people will be released."

There wasn't much else I could do. I nodded stiffly and Kisler smiled in triumph.

"Hanna," he said, turning his attention away from us. "Please escort our new guests to suitable accommodations and ensure they are comfortable while we take care of some logistical matters to get our search underway."

Hanna drew her pistol and gestured to one of the German guards, who broke from the pack to join her. She pointed toward the door opposite the hearth, leading into the tower portion of the manor house.

"After you," she said coldly, and Jack and I headed toward is, with Hanna and the guard following close behind.

"So, still working with Kisler, huh?" I said to Hanna. "And here I had you pegged for leader of this little band at first."

"Heinrich is a great man," she replied, "and a great leader. He has done well for us." The ground floor of the tower looked like it had been turned over into a kind of guard barracks of sorts, with cots and footlockers crammed into the room. It vaguely reminded me of the prisoner barracks at Castle Eisen, not a pleasant reminder at the moment. Hanna stepped forward and lifted a wooden trapdoor set into the floor. A set of stone steps slanted down into darkness. She gestured with her gun and Jack and I started heading down the steps.

Heinrich, eh? On a first-name basis with the boss-man now, Hanna? I thought. "Can't be that great," I said, "if you're hiding out here in Scotland."

"Hardly hiding, more like preparing for the largest haul we've ever taken, one that will set us up to expand our operations and strike terror into hearts all across this continent."

"Maybe even exert some influence with the new regime back home in Germany?" I said. The silent pause was noticeably long before Hanna replied.

"You had best concern yourself with remembering all that you can about McMullan's stories, Nathan," she said coldly, "and less about affairs that are none of your concern."

At the bottom of the stairs was another chamber, only slightly smaller han the bottom of the tower above. The walls were lined with fieldstone and he floor was covered in more of the same. There were a few simple bunks, a vashbasin, and very little else.

"This is where you'll wait until *Herr* Kisler wishes to speak with you gain," Hanna said.

"Throwing us into the dungeon? Really, Hanna, I think Kisler has seen a ew too many of the movies coming out of Hollywood these days."

She coldly ignored my attempts at humor and headed back up the stairs, ollowed by the guard training his submachine gun at us. When they reached he top of the stairs, she turned to look back down at us.

"If it were up to me," she said, "I would make sure that you rotted down here." They closed the wooden trap door behind them and I could hear the ound of it being barred. Then Jack and I were left in silence, with only the lickering glow of an oil lamp placed on a small table for light.

"You sure do have a way with the ladies, boss," Jack said, dropping down nto one of the cots. "So, now what do we do?"

I was already climbing up the stairs to check out the trap door. "We fig- ure a way out of this, that's what," I said. I tested the door and, sure enough, it vas solidly barred. "Well, we're not going out that way," I muttered, mostly to nyself.

Jack looked around the room from his vantage on the cot. "Doesn't look ike there are any other ways out of here," he said. "Unless you're real good at liggin'."

I settled onto the opposite cot and started thinking about our predica- nent, looking at it from different angles, none of them very encouraging.

"So," Jack spoke up after a few moments, "do you know were ol' Angus id the gold?"

"Not really," I said. "Angus told me a few things, clues maybe, but not *xactly where the gold was hidden. He was wily old bird. I think he made sure o tell me just enough to whet my appetite, to make me curious, and to make ure I took him with us when we got out of Eisen, like I wouldn't have done hat anyway. Sounds like he did the same thing to Kisler, strung him along with ints. But he didn't get a chance to use the leverage that bought him."

"Well, Kisler seems to think you know something."

"Depends on how much Angus told Kisler before he died. Doesn't sound like Kisler found out anything more than the fact that the gold existed and that it was hidden somewhere here in Scotland, but it's possible he's not telling us everything he knows. He didn't reveal that he knew that I knew something about the gold right off because he wanted to see what I'd do. Kisler's good at playing his cards close to his chest."

"Do you think he's serious about letting us go?" Jack said, "If he gets the gold?"

I shook my head. "I'm not willing to bet our lives on it. Back during the War, Kisler struck me as a man of his word. He thinks of himself as a gentleman, almost like a knight. But he's not stupid, either. He didn't get to be leader of a pirate band based solely on his charm and good word. If he thinks we're going to be a problem for him, I don't doubt that he'd kill all of us. If nothing else, Pandora is a real prize, and I'm not sure Kisler would just let us fly her away. And then there's Hanna …"

"Yeah," Jack said. "You see the way she looks at you? She really hates your guts, boss."

I nodded. "Even with Kisler's promise, I'm not sure Hanna wouldn't try to pull something. She wants revenge, that much is obvious. Maybe we can use that somehow, to drive a wedge between her and Kisler."

We talked a bit more about our impressions of the situation, wondering what Kisler and his men had done with the Pandora and her crew, despite his assurances that everything was under control and that no one would be harmed so long as he got what he wanted. Eventually, there was nothing more to do than sit and wait.

About an hour later, a pair of guards opened the trap door and gestured with their guns, explaining in broken English that I was to accompany them and Jack was to stay behind. Reluctantly, I climbed the stairs and followed the guards back out into the main room of the house, where Kisler, Hanna, and two more members of his crew waited, standing around a large dining table spread with maps of Scotland.

"Ah, *Herr* Zachary," Kisler said, like he was greeting an old friend he hadn't seen in weeks. "I trust you found our accommodations comfortable."

"One of the better dungeons I've been in," I said, brushing off the sleeve of my jacket and beating my hands across my thighs.

"*Gut*," Kisler said. He gestured toward the maps. "Now we can discuss the next step in this operation, locating the missing gold."

I stepped up to the table and took a look. The maps were good ones, survey maps of the entirety of Scotland and parts of England. There was one large map of the entire country and several smaller maps that provided additional details of particular sections.

"Now then," Kisler said, "what did Angus McMullan tell you about the location of the gold?"

"First, I want to talk to my crew," I replied, "and make sure they're safe."

"I have told you, *Herr* Zachary, you are in no position to bargain," Kisler said, his eyes narrowing dangerously.

"And you need the information I have. Is what I'm asking so unreasonable?"

Kisler stared at me for a moment before snapping his fingers, without taking his eyes off mine. One of the guards moved over to the radio and spoke quietly into the mike before Hanna guided me over to it, pistol in hand.

"Don't try anything clever like before," she said, "or, valuable or not, this time I will shoot you." I lifted the microphone to my lips, glancing into Hanna's cold gaze before I spoke.

"Zachary to Pandora, come in. Over." There was a long pause before anyone responded.

"Boss, is that you? Over." Sparks said from the speaker. The strain showed in his voice.

"Yeah, it's me, kid," I replied. "Jack and I are okay. How's the rest of the crew?"

"All right," Sparks said. "Buck got beat up a little but he's okay. They're keeping us locked up down in…" He paused and seemed to reconsider what he was saying before changing the subject. "What's going on, boss?"

"We're 'guests' of our host, Heinrich Kisler. Kisler wants to know the location of Angus McMullan's gold. If he gets that, he says he'll let us go. I want you and the rest of the crew to cooperate. Don't give Kisler's people any trouble, you hear? I'm going to get this sorted out and then we can get out of here. Over."

"Roger that, chief," Sparks said. "We'll sit tight here. Over."

"Good boy," I said. "Over and out." I released the switch on the mike and handed it back to the guard.

"You see?" Kisler said. "Your people are unharmed and are being fairly treated. Whether or not that continues to be the case is up to you." He turned his attention back to the map table. I walked back over to the table and looked at the maps.

"I don't know the location of the gold," I began. I held up a hand to cut off the expected protests. "But I do have a hint of where it might be. When Angus told me about hiding the gold shipment in Scotland, he said they hid the gold near a place where it would be 'well watched without being found'," I pointed out several on the map, "maybe in a building, or a cave or something like that."

"It could also be buried," Kisler interjected.

"Perhaps," I said, "but I doubt it. We're talking about a lot of gold and they didn't have much time to hide it. It would have taken a while to dig a good enough hole."

Kisler's brow furrowed as he looked over the maps. "What do you think McMullan meant by saying the gold would be 'well watched'?"

I shrugged. "I'm not sure."

"Perhaps he left the gold with friends or allies?" Hanna asked. I shook my head at almost the same time as Kisler.

"Couldn't be," I said. "First off, McMullan told me he was the only one who knew where the gold was hidden, which wouldn't be the case if he'd left it with someone else. Secondly, it's been over a decade. I tend to doubt anyone would watch a fortune in gold for that long without eventually deciding that McMullan and his chums weren't coming back for it. But there's no evidence anyone has spent the gold, as far as I know," I glanced at Kisler and he nodded slightly, confirming my suspicion that the German pirate had done some checking to see if the gold had turned up in the intervening years.

"Then what could be watching it," Hanna asked, eyeing me, "if it isn't a person?"

I snapped my fingers. "Something that's not a person," I said. "It's something else altogether, like a local legend." I grabbed the main map and started scanning it, looking for a particular place. When I found it, I turned the map toward Kisler and stabbed my finger down at a spot of blue.

"There," I said.

"Loch Ness?" Kisler said out loud. "Of course! The Monster!"

"Monster? What monster?" Hanna said with a puzzled look.

"A local legend," I supplied, "about some sort of sea-monster living in the loch. It's been sighted there on and off for years, so long that the locals have taken to call it 'Nessie', short for the Loch Ness Monster. I read something about it years ago but I never made the connection before."

"A reasonable theory," Kisler said, stroking his beard thoughtfully with one hand as he looked over the map. "Still, Loch Ness is by no means small, there are still dozens of miles of shoreline to consider where McMullan and his confederates could have concealed the gold."

"I have some ideas about that," I said. "They probably moved it by air, so they'd need a site where they could land, where they could hide the gold, and where they could take off from again." I traced my finger along the map of Loch Ness running from Inverness in the northeast down toward the southwest.

"What about here?" I said pointing to the small inlet midway along the Loch.

"Urquhart Bay," Kisler read. "Why there?"

"It's a small beach, rocky, but with enough level around it for a landing from the look of it. There's also this ruin nearby, Urquhart Castle. That means the area has been inhabited, meaning there might be some secret hideaways or bolt-holes nobody else knows about." Kisler looked at the map of Urquhart Bay for a long few moments, carefully tracing things out in his head. It seemed to me that he was looking for something, which made me think he still knew more than he was telling about the gold's location.

"Very well then," Kisler said, laying his hands flat on the table. "We'll put your theory to the test. He turned to Ullen.

"Hanna, make preparations to get underway. We'll take *Herr* Zachary's zeppelin so we can all travel together in comfort," he said with a smile, "and keep an eye on our guests."

CHAPTER

24

LOST TREASURES

Kisler allowed Jack and I to fly our Devastators up to Pandora. He was assured we wouldn't try causing any trouble with the rest of the Fortune Hunters under the watchful eyes (and guns) of his men, and he was right. Kisler already had enough people on Pandora to make sure there was no trouble, so all we could do for now was go along with him. I'll admit, I was also curious about Angus McMullan's gold. Were his stories true or just tall tales told by a pirate to ingratiate himself with me and to possibly buy himself some leniency from Kisler? Was the gold anywhere near where we suspected, or was this just a wild goose chase?

After securing our machines in the hangar bay, the German pirates escorted us to the bridge, where Kisler and Hanna waited, having gone ahead of us, to ensure there weren't any problems. I took the helm of the airship and we plotted a course to take us from the Cairngorm Mountains to Urquhart Bay. It wasn't all that far, so we would be there shortly, even at Pandora's relatively sedate speed.

Once everything was under control, Kisler ordered Jack placed with the rest of the prisoners and me confined to my cabin. Once the guard closed the door behind me, I slumped down on my bunk and started thinking of ways to get us all out of this mess. Part of me hoped it was all a con, that Kisler would come up with nothing to show for his effort. But, as much as the idea amused me, it didn't bode well for us if that was the case. If he got the gold, Kisler might be inclined to keep his word and let us go. If he didn't, then he'd probably decide that the Pandora and everything aboard was a good enough haul for this expedition and decide to quit while he was ahead, ensuring his claim by disposing of the former occupants. That is to say, us.

As a plan was forming in my mind, the cabin door opened and I was immediately on my feet, ready for one of the pirates, or possibly Kisler, come down to gloat. Hanna Ullen stepped inside the cabin, with the guard close behind her.

"What do you want?" I asked.

"To talk."

I glanced over her shoulder at the Black Eagle behind her and she turned to him. "Leave us," she said in German and he withdrew, closing the door behind him. Hanna took a couple more steps into the room while I stood my ground.

"What do you want to talk about?" I said. "I thought we said everything that needed to be said back at Kisler's little hideaway. Must be quite a romantic spot for you two."

"You sound jealous, Nathan," she said with a hint of a smile. "But Heinrich and I aren't lovers. Our relationship is strictly business. He has been my teacher and mentor for a long time."

"And you're very loyal to him," I said, with a touch of bitterness.

"Yes, I am," she said, looking away from me. It didn't sound quite sincere to me. Hanna seemed torn, like she wanted to say something, but wasn't certain.

"But?" I said. She turned to face me, her hair hanging loose, like golden wheat. Her good eye brimming with tears.

"But he's not you," she said quietly.

I'll admit, I was taken aback a bit. Was this the same woman who said she wanted me dead only a short while before?

"What we had together, Nathan, was … very special," she continued.

"I've never forgotten it. It could be that way again."

"What are you asking?" I said. Hanna stepped forward, placing a warm hand on the side of my face, resting another on my shoulder.

"You could join us!" she said. "Ask Heinrich to let you join our band. He respects you already, and he knows you're a good pilot. I'm sure he would agree."

"And then what?" I asked. "Be Kisler's flunky? Is that what you want for me, Hanna? Is that good enough for you, to work for somebody else, to give them everything, and for what? You're still nothing but a student to him! Even less than that, a pawn!"

"That's not true!" Hanna said, turning away from me. "Heinrich respects me, more than most, more than you did!"

"Now who's twisting the truth?" I asked, pressing harder. "I always respected you, Hanna. You were the one that betrayed me, remember? I was always honest with you about who I was, how I felt, and what I was doing. You're the one that lied to me, pretended to be something you weren't, and set me up like a chump so Kisler could play mind-games with me."

Hanna turned toward me like I'd struck her, mouth open for a moment and working to find the words. "I ... I was loyal ..." she began.

"Sure, loyal to your country and your mentor," I said, rolling right over her. "But you expected me to betray my country when the time came; what about your loyalty to me, Hanna? Did you care about me at all, or was that just an act, too?"

"I did care, Nathan," she said quietly, a tear escaping her eye to roll down her cheek, "more than I ever dared to tell you, more than I ever told anyone. I felt so torn when, when you asked me to go with you. I pretended it didn't matter to me, tried to concentrate on my duty. Then, when you were gone, I tried to forget about you. When you left, I cursed you at first but then I suppose I realized I couldn't expect of you what I wasn't willing to do myself.

"When I heard you were alive, and leader of the Fortune Hunters, I hated you at first, for surviving, for succeeding ... and for leaving me. I tried to focus on that, hating you, but from the moment I saw you again I ..." With a sob, she turned away from me holding her face in her hands. I came up to her and put my hands gently on her shoulders.

"Hanna, I …" she turned suddenly and threw herself into my arms and I found myself on the receiving end of the most passionate kiss I've ever known. Her mouth was hungry for mine, and we both tried to put the past to rest with that one kiss. For a moment, we were like teenagers again, enjoying that first young love, but it couldn't last. I broke the kiss and Hanna opened her eye and looked up at me. She pulled away, touching one hand self-consciously to the patch over her other eye.

"You must think me hideous," she said.

"No," I said, "I think you are the most beautiful woman I've ever seen, then or now." Hanna actually blushed a bit, color rising in her cheeks.

"Hanna, I can't leave the Fortune Hunters," I said bluntly, "and I won't work for Kisler."

"I know. I suppose I knew that even before I came to see you."

"But there is another option," I began. Hanna looked me in the eye, knowing what I was about to say. "You could come with me, like you wanted to back then, like I wanted you to."

"Leave Heinrich?" she said almost to herself. For the first time, I heard her say it like it was something other than a terrible, unthinkable idea.

"You could do it," I said. "Make the decision you could have, should have, made years ago. Come with me."

She shook her head. "It's too late for that now. I can no more betray my mentor now than I could then," she started for the door.

"It's only too late if you do nothing, Hanna," I said, bringing her up short. "It's only too late if you let it be too late." She knocked on the door and the guard came to open it.

"Think about what I said," I said to her back. She paused for a moment before stepping through the door. The door clanged shut behind her, leaving me alone with my thoughts again, and with a lot more to think about this time.

***

The Pandora approached Loch Ness not long after that, a shimmering mirror running along a deep mountain valley. The hour was growing late when we arrived, so Kisler wasted no time in going down to have a look around. He appeared at the door of my cabin to tell me we'd arrived and that I would be going down to the bay with him and Hanna.

"Why me?" I asked.

"Because you've proven so insightful thus far, *Herr* Zachary," the German air pirate said with a sardonic smile, "because you may have other insights into McMullan's mind and where his gold is hidden, and because I prefer to have you where I can watch you."

So I found myself escorted down to the hangar bay where Hanna was already waiting. She avoided looking at me as we suited up and prepared to depart. Kisler and Hanna flew their own machines, while I took my Devastator. We suited up in silence then Kisler boarded his machine and launched from the bay. I was next, followed by Hanna. Before I closed the cockpit of my Devastator, I glanced back at Hanna and caught her eye for a moment before she resolutely looked away from me. No help there, I thought glumly as I fired up the engine and released the docking hook, launching my machine out into the air over the loch.

We circled the area before landing a short distance from the castle on an open stretch of land. Kisler estimated it would be some time before the authorities even noticed our presence, much less sent anyone to investigate, but he wanted to be airborne when and if that happened. The British air force was limite to mostly old machines left over from the War, with some newer ones purchased from manufacturers in North America. It was unlikely they'd muster any kind of aerial response before it was far too late.

I climbed down from the cockpit of my machine under the watchful eyes of Kisler and Hanna. Kisler took a piece of paper from inside his flight jacket and unfolded it, turning slowly to look at the surrounding landscape and back to the paper.

"What's that?" I asked, taking a step closer. Kisler turned my way and smiled his knowing smile.

"A map," he said. "It was drawn according to McMullan's descriptions of the whereabouts of his treasure before he expired. Unfortunately, he never provided any specifics as to where exactly the map described, just general features and landmarks that could have been anywhere, but look," he said showing me the map. "You see this inlet? It looks much like that area of the bay over there. Here are the ruins of the castle and here is stretch of beach," he pointed to the features on the map. "This must be the place."

"If you had a map," I asked, "why didn't you just find this place yourself?"

"Zachary, do you have any idea how many ruins and old castles there are in Scotland? Searching them all would have taken forever and likely alerted the authorities as to our whereabouts and what we were after. No, far simpler to go straight to the source that might know something more."

And provide you with transportation to carry your booty, I thought to myself, to say nothing of an opportunity for revenge. This was starting to look less and less like a simple business arrangement. Despite his words to the contrary, I didn't think Kisler was interested in just the gold, or that I was merely a means to that end. He also wanted revenge against the men who'd embarrassed him and put a black mark on his honor by escaping from Eisen. And now he had three of the four remaining survivors in his hands.

Kisler led the way across the heath to where it dropped off steeply, leading down toward the bay itself. A stiff wind blew in from the Loch as we stood atop the grassy overlook, looking down at the narrow beach below.

"Down there," Kisler said, "pointing toward the beach." He turned toward me and gave a courtly bow. "After you, *Herr* Zachary."

"Oh no, ladies first," I said turning toward Hanna. She pressed her lips into a tight line and strode past me, clambering carefully down the rocky slope toward the beach. Kisler drew his pistol from its holster and leveled it at me.

"Now then, *Herr* Zachary," he said, "after you." I followed Hanna down to the slope to the beach, with Kisler not far behind me, although too far for me to try anything should I be so inclined.

We paced along the beach, with Kisler consulting the map as we went, checking it against landmarks and such.

"There," he said, "that rock," pointing toward a narrow standing stone that stuck up from the beach about ten feet from the waterline. It was barely waist-high and years of weather had worn its exposed surface smooth.

"Twenty-four paces from here due west," Kisler said, almost to himself. "If you would, *Herr* Zachary?" He emphasized his request with a wave of his pistol. I stood at the rock and oriented myself from the sun, then took twenty-four paces almost due west, toward the rocky cliff face. I came to a stop right in front of the cliff itself, a tumbled mass of rocks in front of me.

Brushing away some of the gravel and smaller stones, I could see they covered a larger, flat stone that didn't look to me like it had fallen there. As Kisler and Hanna approached, I found a narrow crack behind the stone and managed to slip my hands into it. I gave it a hard tug and felt the stone move.

"There's something back here," I said, pulling harder. Hanna came over to help me, although Kisler only continued to watch from a short distance away. Together we pulled on the stone and it came away from the cliff. We had to scramble back as the stone toppled over onto the beach with a thud, revealing a dark cave mouth behind it.

The cave was shallow and went back only about eight or nine feet, with an entrance just large enough for me to enter if I stooped down quite a bit. Inside was a boxy object covered with an olive-drab canvas showing signs of mildew and water-damage. With a glance at Kisler, I stooped down and clambered into the cave to pull aside the canvas. Beneath it was a wooden crate with the markings of the British Royal Army. Hanna passed me a small crowbar that I used to pop open the lid.

The sunlight slanting through the cave mouth gleamed on neatly stacked bars of gold; each of them stamped with the Royal Seal of England. The gold Angus McMullan and his confederates stole from the British Army twenty years before. There was a small fortune there and I confess I was somewhat mesmerized by the sight of it, such that Kisler's voice startled me when he finally spoke.

"Hanna, call up to the ship and have them send down some additional men," he said. "We should get out prize loaded on board as quickly as possible." His voice carried a note of triumph and pure greed as he contemplated the gold. "Then we can bring this matter to a conclusion," he said, glancing over at me and smiling a smile that sent a chill down my spine.

CHAPTER

25

A LAST CHANCE

Kisler's men assisted in hauling the crate partway out of the cave. Kisler decided it would take too long to lever the crate up the cliff face, and there was no time to get a boat down to the beach to carry it. So he had his men divide up the gold into canvas sacks and carry them up to the waiting planes above, to be loaded into the cargo areas. Naturally, he did not place temptation in my path by loading any of the gold onto my Devastator. The operation was conducted quickly and, before it was concluded, Kisler sent Hanna and I back to the Pandora, her to oversee getting the airship underway and me to be put back under guard until Kisler's business was concluded.

We climbed back up to the heath where the airplanes waited, with me in the lead and Hanna following close behind and keeping me covered with her pistol. When we reached the machines, I turned around slowly, resting a hand on the side of my Devastator.

"So," I said, "it looks like you're a rich woman, assuming Kisler decides to share any of his haul."

"He divides what we take fairly," she said flatly, "putting some aside to handle our expenses."

"Well I'm sure your share will be enough to treat yourself to a nice vacation or something," I said mockingly. When I saw her mouth tighten, I thought I'd gone too far, but Hanna only gestured toward the plane with her gun.

"Get in," she said. "I'll follow you up and no tricks. Remember, we still have your crew and your ship, and there's nothing you can do about that without risking both." Didn't I know it! I climbed up into the cockpit of the Devastator and watched Hanna make her way over to her machine, parked not far behind mine, laden with some of the gold in its cargo space.

I took off first, followed by Hanna. I probably could have made a run for it—there was a time when I would have without a second thought. I figured I could out-fly Hanna, especially with her plane carrying the extra weight but, even if I did manage to evade her, my Devastator's ammo bins were empty and I only had so much fuel. Where would I go? And what about the crew I'd be leaving behind? I was responsible for getting them into this situation, so it was up to me to try and get them out of it, somehow.

We docked our planes in Pandora's bay, with Kisler's people scurrying about, preparing to load up the remainder of the gold and get underway. I was escorted back to my cabin and left there, under guard. I waited a few minutes to make sure there wasn't any activity out in the gangway before I made my way over to the narrow air vent mounted on the wall above my bunk. It was much too small for anything bigger than a cat to fit through, but I had something else in mind. They'd searched my cabin fairly thoroughly before locking me in here, but I was hoping they'd missed the one thing that might give me a shot at getting my ship back.

First, I needed something I could use to get the screws holding the grate in place off. I settled for a metal slat from my bunk, which I broke off as quietly as possible. Then I set to work. I'd gotten the first two screws off, when I head footsteps coming from outside the door. I quickly dropped down onto my bunk, stuffing the slat under my pillow and the screws into my pocket.

The door opened to admit Hanna, who closed it behind her. There was a moment of silence as we just looked at each other.

"Were you serious," she asked quietly, "when you asked me to join you?"

"I've never been more serious in my life," I said, feeling a touch of hope. It died as Hanna drew the pistol at her side and leveled it at me, slowly walking toward me.

"Heinrich has just come back on board. He's ordered that you and your people be disposed of," she said. "He's not willing to delay moving the gold out of the country and your ship offers the best opportunity to do that. He seems to think you might object."

"He's right," I said eyeing the gun, if only I'd had a few more minutes. "So much for Kisler's word of honor."

"He's changed," Hanna admitted. She was standing right next to me, the barrel of the gun inches away from my chest. I might be able to grab it, wrestle it away. "Losing the war, becoming a mercenary, he's not the same man."

"I don't suppose any of us is the same any more," I said.

"No," she said. "He sent me to take care of matters." She looked me in the eye, and then she lowered the gun and threw herself into my arms, kissing me passionately. I found myself kissing her back, my hands going around her body, pulling her tighter into my embrace. The kiss seemed to last forever before she broke it.

"But I can't do it," she said. "I can't kill you in cold blood, and I can't let Heinrich do it, either. I was taught better than that." She looked down and her chin trembled before she set her jaw firmly and looked me in the eye. "If your offer is still open, then I accept."

"The offer's still good." Provided I can trust you, I thought. It was entirely possible this was some kind of trap, Kisler's twisted way of getting me to break our agreement first and give him the upper hand, so he could dispose of us with a clear conscience or something. It was just the kind of chess-game he loved to play. Still, my best bet was to go along, and keep an eye on Hanna along the way. Fool me once, shame on you, fool me twice, shame on me.

"Good," she said. "We can work out the … details later. For now, we have to do something. It won't be long before Heinrich will expect to hear from me. The rest of the crew is getting the ship ready to get underway. The remainder of the squadron is on its way here from the mountains. Heinrich is planning to leave as soon as they arrive. He wants you and your crew eliminated, and your bodies thrown in the Loch before they get here."

"How long before they arrive?" I asked.

"Not long, less than half an hour."

"All right," I said, "the first thing is where's my crew being held?"

"They're together in the cargo hold. There are two guards outside and at least three inside."

"That makes things a little easier," I said hopping back up on my bunk.

"What are you doing?" Hanna asked as I retrieved the metal slat from under the pilot and went back to work on the remaining screws.

"Evening the odds a little more," I said. I pulled the grate free and dropped it onto the bed, reached into the vent and pulled out the Colt .45 and the small box of ammo I kept there in case of emergencies. I loaded it and dumped the extra rounds into the pockets of my jacket.

"Ready?" I asked Hanna with a smile. She returned it. "Let's go."

We moved over by the door. I flattened myself against the wall beside it.

"Guard!" Hanna called out and a moment later the door opened as the guard outside the cabin rushed in to see Hanna standing in an apparently empty room.

His eyes flashed to the missing vent grille and I could practically hear the gears turning as, for a split second, he wondered how I could have possibly managed to crawl out through a foot-wide grille with Hanna Ullen in the room with me the whole time. Then the gears ground to a halt and he thought to look behind him, but not before my right fist connected with his jaw. The pirate dropped like a sack of potatoes to the deck and Hanna and I wasted no time in securing him in the room and reliving him of his rifle, which I picked up, tucking the Colt into the waistband of my pants.

"Give me that," Hanna said.

"What?"

"Give me the rifle," she repeated, holding out her hand for it. "Nathan, we haven't time to argue. If we're seen in the corridors we can pretend you are still a prisoner and I am taking you to the cargo bay to deal with you and your crew all at once, but no one will believe that if they see you are armed! Keep your pistol underneath your jacket and give me the rifle. Please, you have to trust me."

I started to say "why should I?" but thought the better of it and instead just handled her the rifle.

"*Danke*," she said. "I know you have no reason to trust me, but thank you. I promise I will be worthy of your faith in me, this time."

I nodded and soon we were on our way. We didn't encounter any of the other pirates in the gangways, since they were probably busy getting Pandora ready to get underway. It felt to me like we were still at station keeping, but there was no way to tell how long that would last. The rest of Kisler's squadron could arrive at any moment.

We arrived outside the cargo bay and, as Hanna said, there were two guards outside, keeping watch. They came immediately to attention when they saw us. I walked in front, arms on top of my head, while Hanna walked behind, occasionally prodding me in the back with her rifle.

"Move, swine!" she told me in German.

"*Fräulein* Ullen!" one of the guards said.

"*Herr* Kisler has sent me to take care of the prisoners," she said before they could ask any questions. "They're all to be disposed off, along with this one," she turned a contemptuous glance in my direction.

"*Ja, Fräulein*!" the guard replied, turning to open the door. When he unlocked it, I stepped aside and Hanna shot the other guard at almost point-blank range. He never even saw it coming, and crumpled to the ground, leaving a smear of blood on the bulkhead behind him.

The other pirate turned at the sound of the gunshot and met my fist as it connected with his jaw. The right-hook spun him around and left him slumped against the wall, out cold. I grabbed his rifle and kicked the unlocked door open.

The guards inside the cargo bay were responding to the gunshot, Hanna and I cut down the first two as they moved toward the door, their bodies dropping to the floor. We spun into the room to see the third guard level his rifle at us. Jack Mulligan jumped up and knocked the barrel up, throwing off the pirate's aim and sending his shot wild. The guard hit Jack in the stomach with the butt of his rifle, knocking the wind out of him and doubling him over but, when he turned back toward us, he saw two guns leveled in his direction.

"Drop it!" I barked in German and the pirate, apparently no fool, complied. Buck picked up his gun while Jack straightened up. He gave the pirate a wicked grin before clocking him in the jaw with an uppercut that left him flat out on the floor.

"That's for shootin' at my friend!" he said, as he turned back toward us. His eyes narrowed when he spotted Hanna, then he and the rest of the crew quickly gathered around us. I passed the other pirate's weapons out to them as Jack continued to glare.

"What's she doin' here?" he asked. "Come to sell us out again, lady?"

"Not now, Jack. Hanna's with us and anyone who has a problem with that can take it up with me." Jack and I stared at each other for a few long seconds before he shrugged and hefted a rifle.

"You're the boss," he said.

"Okay," I sighed, "The first thing we need to do is regain control of the ship. Jack, you and Sparks take a couple people and go down to engineering. Tex, Buck, you see about securing the machine guns near the nacelles, we're gonna need them real soon now. Hanna and I are going to the bridge to take care of things there. Check in with me there using the intercom when you've got your section secured. Understood?" Everyone nodded. "All right, then people, let's do it!"

We broke up, everyone heading off to their assigned tasks. I tucked my pistol back into my waistband and lead Hanna to the bridge, where I could still pretend to be her prisoner, if need be. We didn't pass anyone in the gangway and there were only two people on the bridge when we arrived, Kisler and one of his men. The air pirate turned toward us as we stepped onto the bridge with a quizzical look on his face.

"Hanna, why did you bring him here?" he began, "I thought I told you ..." Kisler's eyes widened as he realized what was happening, but a second too late.

I ducked to the side and Hanna shot the other pirate before he could even reach for his gun. He went down in a heap and I drew my pistol and leveled it at Kisler as he put his hand on his own gun.

"Don't bother," I said, and Kisler slowly moved his hand away from the butt of the pistol, looking from me to Hanna and back.

"So, *Herr* Zachary," he said, "it seems you have me in check."

"Check and mate, pal. This is over."

"Hardly that," Kisler said. "The rest of my squadron will be here in minutes, and they'll be expecting a communication from me. When they don't get it, they'll attack and take this ship."

"Not if you're on board," I said. Kisler shook his head.

"My men are loyal, Zachary, not stupid. Well, most of them," he said, glaring at Hanna, who quailed a bit under the penetrating stare. "I'm very disappointed in you, Hanna. I thought you understood, I thought almost twenty years of service and companionship meant something to you. But now I see I was wrong."

"Heinrich …" Hanna began, but Kisler simply ignored her and kept talking.

"As I said, my men are not fools. If they cannot reach me, then they will still take this ship, regardless of the cost. After all, if I am dead, then they can claim this ship and the gold. I can think of one or two of my lieutenants that would welcome the opportunity, in fact."

"That's what you get from associating with cutthroats, Kisler," I said, "sooner or later one of them stabs you in the back."

"Yes," Kisler said slowly, directing another look at Hanna. "It's a lesson I suspect you will also learn in the fullness of time, Zachary. Associating with less honorable men—and women—is a hazard of the life we have chosen. It can't be avoided."

"Enough chatter," I said. "Step away from the controls. I'd like to introduce you to our new brig. If you surrender and convince your men to do the same, I promise you'll be released unharmed and, unlike you, I keep my promises."

"Yes, I'm sure you do," Kisler muttered. He glanced past me, out the windows of the gondola, and I thought I heard something above the hum of Pandora's engines.

"Nathan, look out!" Hanna said and I spun to see the pirate she'd shot raising a pistol toward me, clutching at the bleeding wound in his side. I raised my gun at the same time and that's when Kisler made his move. Not toward me, but toward Hanna. The pirate and I fired at the same time as I heard a repeat from Hanna's rifle. The pirate missed, but I didn't and he slumped back to the floor with a fatal bullet hole in his chest. The rifle shot shattered one of the windows on the bridge, letting a chill wind blow in with a shower of glass and the roar of the engines. Then there was a clatter as something fell to the floor.

I turned to see Kisler had wrested the rifle from Hanna's grasp, it lay on the floor nearly. He held her tightly with one arm around her throat, using her as a human shield, the barrel of his pistol pressed against her exposed throat.

"Drop your gun now, Zachary," he said. "Or she dies."

"You're bluffing," I said.

"I think you should know by now that I never bluff in matters of life and death," Kisler said. I looked him in the eye. He was right.

I dropped the gun.

"*Ser gut*," Kisler said. "Now kick it away." I did as he said.

A voice crackled over the intercom. "Boss, this is Sparks, boss are you there? Over." There was a pause. "We've taken the engineering area and we've got the rest of the Germans rounded up, except for a few that put up a fight. I think Tex and Buck are all set with the machine gun nets, too. Do you copy? Over."

"You hear that, Kisler?" I said. "It's over. My people have re-taken Pandora and yours are under guard or dead. Give it up, you've lost."

"No yet," Kisler said. "I am leaving. If you or any of your people try to stop me, Hanna dies," he pressed his gun harder against her neck for emphasis. "The game is not over yet, Zachary." He backed out of the room, dragging Hanna with him. She gave me a last, pleading look before they disappeared into the gangway. I immediately pounced on the intercom.

"Sparks, Sparks this is Zachary. Over."

"Boss? Gosh, I was afraid you were hurt or something, are you okay? Over."

"Yeah, yeah, I'm fine, but Kisler is loose and he has Hanna as a hostage. Tell everyone to steer clear of him. I think he's headed for the hangar bay. Don't try to stop him, let me deal with him. Over."

"Are you sure?" Sparks asked, "Jack says he could give you a hand. Over."

"No!" I said, "Kisler's mine. Over and out." I went over and picked up my gun, then headed out into the gangway, carefully looking to see if there was any sign of Kisler before stepping out and heading down toward the hangar bay.

CHAPTER 26

FIGHT IN THE SKIES!

The corridors of the Pandora were strangely empty and silent as I made my way down to the hangar bay, alert for any more signs of trouble from Kisler or his men. My crew followed orders and stayed out of the way, and it looked like they'd taken care of all the other Black Eagle pirates on board. Now only their leader was left to deal with, and he was my problem.

When I reached the hangar bay I saw the door was open. I flattened myself against the wall and listened. I could hear the sound of someone moving and it sounded like someone else struggling and being dragged along.

"I'm sorry, Hanna my dear, but this is as far as you can accompany me," I heard Kisler say in German. "It's a pity you decided to side with Zachary against me. I could have made you a rich woman, perhaps even given you command one day. Now all you'll have is an unmarked grave." I heard the sound of someone being roughly thrown to the floor, then the sound of the hangar bay doors opening.

"Go to hell!" Hanna shouted over the sound of the rushing wind.

"After you, my dear," Kisler said. I spun around the corner, leveling my pistol into the room.

I didn't hear the other pilot in the room with them, one of Kisler's men standing near the door. He brought the heavy crescent wrench he wielded down on my wrist hard and I dropped my gun, which the German pilot kicked away. It slid across the floor and out the open bay doors to tumble through the air down toward the waters of Loch Ness.

Kisler dropped down to the floor from the ladder of his Messerschmitt. Hanna was sprawled out on the floor nearby, where he'd pushed her. "Well, *Herr* Zachary," he said, "so glad you could join us. This gives me the opportunity to say good-bye properly." He took a few steps closer and raised his gun toward me. His mistake was ignoring Hanna. She tackled him around the waist grabbing for his gun, which clattered to the floor and skittered away.

I immediately turned toward the other pilot and gave him a right cross to the jaw that staggered him back, but he was a big guy, several inches taller than I was, with a nasty looking scar running along his right cheek and close-cropped blond hair. He grinned savagely and came at me with the wrench. I ducked under a swing that probably would have taken my head off and punched him in the gut. It felt like hitting a brick wall, but it still knocked the wind out of him, somewhat. He kept on coming and I danced back a few steps to avoid him.

He swung the wrench again and I ducked, the metal striking sparks from the wall of the bay. Hanna wrestled with Kisler, but it was clear he outmatched her in both size and experience. A jab from me broke the German bruiser's nose, sending blood flowing freely down over his mouth and chin, but it only seemed to make him madder. He charged at me, swinging his makeshift weapon, which caught me in the ribs and picked me up off my feet. I stumbled back a few steps and fell, perilously close to the open bay doors. I glanced back and I could see the dark waters of the Loch thousands of feet below us. I pushed myself up on one arm as the German came in, sensing weakness and raising his wrench to club me in the head.

I grabbed the edge of the open doors with one hand to steady myself, planted my foot in his belly, and grabbed the front of his shirt with my other hand, using his momentum to throw him up and over me. The pirate lost his balance, pinwheeling his arms and legs for a moment in the air above me, the wrench dropping forgotten to slide off the open door and out the bay before the pilot followed it. He hit the door with a bone-jarring "thud," hands scrabbling to try and find something to grip on the smooth metal surface. Then with a cry, he slid down the door and dropped off into the open air.

Happy landings, I thought. I picked myself up and went to help Hanna as Kisler threw her off of him and rolled to his feet. Our eyes both fell on his pistol at the same moment and we ran for it, but Kisler was closer. He scooped up the gun and leveled it at me, bringing me up short near Hanna.

"A valiant effort, Zachary," Kisler panted, moving in an arc toward his plane, keeping the gun trained on me the entire time. "You've cost me a great deal. But that is nothing compared to what I will have once my men and I have re-taken this airship. It will be all the easier once I've removed the vaunted leader of the Fortune Hunters from the picture. Cut off the head, and the body will soon die." He smiled tightly and cocked the pistol. "You've been a worthy adversary, but the game is over. Farewell, Zachary."

"No!" Hanna screamed and slammed into me as the gun went off. We went down onto the floor in a heap, her weight pinning me down, and I felt something hot and sticky spreading across my shirt. From outside the bay I could hear the sounds of people approaching, their steps ringing on the deck plates.

"Hanna, no!" I said. Kisler bolted for his plane as I rolled Hanna off me onto the floor. I heard him pull the canopy closed and fire up his engine as I saw the bright red stain spreading across Hanna's side beneath her flight jacket, pooling on the hard metal floor beneath her.

I cradled her head and her eyelid fluttered, her ice blue eye looking up into mine.

"Hanna, why?" I asked.

"I couldn't let you die," she said simply. "I'm too loyal ... to the man I love."

"I love you," I said, looking down on her.

"Ah," she gasped, "If only I'd said those words then, then everything might have been different."

"It will be different," I said. "You'll be all right." I did what I could to try and staunch the bleeding. I heard a metallic "chunk" and glanced over my shoulder to see Kisler's machine released from the docking hook to slide out of the bay and take to the air. A second later, Jack Mulligan and several other members of my crew came into the bay, weapons at the ready.

"Boss!" Jack yelled rushing over to me. He took one look at Hanna and all the blood, and his face went dark. He knelt down next to me as I worked to save her life.

"Hold on, Hanna," I said, "just hold on."

"It's all right," she said softly, barely audible above the sound of the wind and the Pandora's engines. "I'm glad I got to say the words, and that I was able to live up to your trust, this time. Oh!" she gasped loudly and her head rolled back, her mouth going wide. "It feels, it feels … like flying," she whispered. Then her mouth went slack and her eye closed as her breath went out with a sigh. I grabbed her chin in my hand and called to her.

"Hanna? Hanna!" I said. Jack put his hands on my shoulders.

"She's gone, Cap'n," he said. I looked at her still face for a moment, so strangely peaceful. Then I slowly stood up, turned, and started walking toward the Devastator, loading up its ammo bins.

"What are you doing?" Jack asked.

"I have an appointment with Kisler," I said, "and I plan to keep it. He's probably meeting up with the rest of his squadron and you can be sure they're going to come back here." I glanced over at where Hanna lay. "Take care of her," I said, "then get every pilot that can stand to their plane and into the air, got it?"

"Yes, sir," Jack said.

I finished loading up the Devastator's guns, then I climbed into the cockpit, ignoring the sticky feeling of Hanna's blood on my shirt as I strapped myself in and checked to make sure all the systems were go. I slammed the canopy closed, fired up the engine, and launched out of the bay and into the clear sky. The sun was setting over the Loch, turning the sky fiery red, orange, and pink with a deepening indigo high above. I thought of Hanna's last words—"it feels like flying"—and scanned the sky for any other planes.

You and me, Kisler, I thought. You're not going to get away this time.

In the distance I spotted a cluster of planes heading toward the Pandora. I turned toward them and opened up the throttle on my Devastator, heading for them. My radio crackled and I heard Jack's voice.

"We're right behind you, boss," he said. I glanced back to see five more planes heading out from the airship. Jack, Eddie, Buck, Tex, and Big John were coming into formation behind me as the enemy planes approached. I spoke into the radio.

"All right, everybody, break off into pairs, standard formation. And keep away from Kisler, he's mine." I got an affirmative and we headed in. Kisler's Black Eagle squadron got closer and closer, until I could clearly make out their black and gray colors, with red markings. I carefully counted down the range from a thousand yards, five hundred yards. When they were within three hundred yards I jammed down on the triggers, firing my Devastator's 40-cals, sending a stream of tracers cutting through the dark sky at them. The rest of the Fortune Hunters did the same.

The enemy planes broke and veered off in different directions to avoid our fire, staying together in pairs as they banked around to engage us. Things turned into a dogfight quickly as we all watched our tails and tried to get the enemy in our sights. A Messerschmitt screamed in at me from above and I threw my plane into a dive, dodging machine gun fire.

"I've got one on my tail!" I said.

"I'm on him, boss," said Jack, as he came in at the pirate plane, guns blazing. The enemy was forced to veer off rather than pursue me, giving me a chance to loop up and get above him. I settled my sights on the enemy plane and squeezed the trigger, then watched as my rounds chewed into his tail, igniting a plume of smoke from it. The Messerschmitt faltered in the air and started to drop into a dive.

"Thanks, Jack," I said.

"I could use a little help over here," said another voice over the radio. It was Eddie Lancourt. I searched the skies looking for Eddie's plane and spotted it trying to shake one of the Messerschmitts. It looked like Big John was busy with one of his own and couldn't help.

"Try and lose him, Eddie, we're on our way," I said, then banked toward that side of the fight, knowing Jack would stick close with me.

Eddie did his best staying ahead of the German pilot, but he stuck to him like glue and Eddie's fanciest flying couldn't seem to shake him. I watched Eddie's machine climb and dive, loop and roll, but the enemy stayed on his tail, peppering him with bullets. Whoever was piloting it had to be one of the best pilots I'd ... I realized then who had to be at the controls: Kisler! Eddie veered to the left just as another barrage from the German's 40-cals chopped the end of his right wing to pieces, sending his machine into a spin.

"I'm hit!" Eddie said over the radio, as he clearly struggled to keep his machine under control.

"C'mon, c'mon," I muttered as I tried to get the enemy plane into my sights. "Eddie, hit the silk!" I said into the radio, "get out of there!"

"I can handle it!" he said, "I can ..." another volley of fire from the Messerschmitt slammed into Eddie's plane and flames burst from the engine as it fell into a steep dive.

"Eddie? Eddie, bail out! Bail out!" I said. There was no sign that he heard me as his plane fell in a long, slow arc down toward the dark waters of the Loch below, burning like a shooting star.

"Eddie!" I said, but there was nothing I could do. I watched the plane hit the water and explode in a red-orange ball of fire and smoke. Then I had to turn my attention to my own problems as Kisler's plane banked around and headed into a loop designed to get up above me. I climbed to intercept him, guns blazing, hoping to cut across his loop and damage him. But there was no sign that I hit him as he looped around. I veered to the side to avoid his return fire, the world spinning around me as I maneuvered.

As I righted my Devastator, I could see Kisler just below me, coming out of his loop and leveling out. He presented a tempting target, which was why I looked to six o'clock and spotted the other Black Eagle plane coming in at me, probably Kisler's wingman. I rolled to avoid the volley of fire directed my way and banked around to get behind and under the incoming plane. As I did I could hear more machine gun fire from above as Jack swooped in and peppered the Messerschmitt with 40-cal rounds, letting me deal with Kisler. I silently thanked Jack and focused back on the Black Ace's plane.

That's when I noticed that the fight had taken us a good distance from Pandora and that Kisler's heading wasn't toward the airship, but away from it. That made no sense. Why would Kisler be heading away from the airship, unless ...

I grabbed the radio and broadcast to the rest of the Fortune Hunters.

"Head back to Pandora! They're trying to draw us away from her! Everyone who doesn't have a dance partner, head back now!"

"What about you, boss? Over." Tex said.

"Don't worry about the rest of us," I said, "just go!"

Tex, Buck, and Big John broke off from the fight and headed back toward Pandora at top speed, leaving Jack and me to deal with Kisler and his wingman. I climbed as Kisler started into another loop. I caught him near the top of it and dropped in behind him, following him through the loop and coming out on his tail. I let loose a volley of gunfire as Kisler dodged from side to side, trying to stay out of my sights. The radio crackled and I heard Kisler speaking to me.

"You're too late," he said. "More of my men should already be boarding your ship. If you want to put an end to this, I can be reasonable." I grabbed the mike like it was Kisler's throat.

"Reasonable like you were to Hanna?" I said.

"We're both better off without her," Kisler said. "She couldn't be trusted. She betrayed us both. If you agree to surrender, I can still ensure you and your crew are not harmed, and that you are properly compensated."

"Wrong gambit to play, Kisler," I said. "This isn't about money anymore." I fired off another burst in his direction, but Kisler's machine rolled onto its side to avoid it, then started banking around. He executed a *renversement* and headed straight at me! As the distance closed between us, I wanted to open fire, but I forced myself to wait until the last possible moment, waiting to see if he'd veer off. He didn't. The distance between us dwindled rapidly. I suddenly slammed the stick forward, throwing my Devastator into a dive, like I'd lost my nerve and was trying to get out of the way. Then I immediately pulled up on the nose, letting the air slap against my wings and my tail like a brake, pointing my nose upward. As the Messerschmitt passed almost directly above me, I squeezed the triggers on my guns.

Forty-cal slugs tore up into the fuselage of Kisler's plane, shredding armor and punching holes along its length. The black and gray plane began spilling smoke from its engine as its forward power died and it started to drop. I continued to climb and banked around to watch it go down, keying open the microphone.

"When you get to the ground, you bastard, tell them Nathan Zachary sent you!" I said.

Even then Kisler had the last laugh on me. One of the magnesium tracers must have caught close enough to the gas tank that the Messerschmitt only fell a few hundred feet before it exploded in an orange-fireball, raining debris down over the area. My plane bucked against the shockwave, but I managed to keep her under control as I veered around back toward Pandora. I keyed open the radio again to the frequency the mercenaries were using.

"Black Eagles," I said, "this is Nathan Zachary, commander of the Fortune Hunters. Your commander—and his first officer—are dead. You can't win. Break off your attack and give yourselves up now and I promise there will be no further reprisals against you, and you and your comrades will be freed. If you keep fighting us, then I promise we'll gun you down to the last man. It's your choice."

Seeing Kisler destroyed, and five planes closing in on Pandora without any escort for the larger Black Eagle cargo plane, the fight went out of them. The Eagles surrendered and we kept control of the airship, directing the German mercenaries to follow us back to Kisler's landing site in the mountains (escorted by our own Devastators to ensure they didn't make a break for it). We'd won the day and Angus McMullan's gold; although the real treasure—a chance to change some of the mistakes of the past, and the life of a trusted friend and comrade—was lost.

CHAPTER

27

ABSENT FRIENDS

"Ashes to ashes, dust to dust." The minister's words flowed over me as I looked down at the two open graves. Only one of them would actually contain a body. We weren't able to retrieve Eddie Lancourt from where his plane had crashed into the Loch, so this burial was symbolic only. Hanna Ullen rested inside the other coffin, lowered down into the ground. I looked down and thought about the friend and comrade I'd lost and the woman I thought I'd found again, only to have her taken away from me.

I'd kept my word, and let the rest of the Black Eagles go. Hopefully they knew enough not to cause us any further trouble. We kept the gold, of course, stowed in Pandora's hold. None of the Eagles were willing to voice an objection once their leader was dead and they surrendered. We took Hanna's body to a small Scottish village near the mountains. The vicar of their church was more than willing to allow us to bury her and Eddie in their small graveyard, especially after a small gift of gold taken from our haul was made to the church's poor box.

"Amen," the vicar said, concluding his service. The rest of us echoed him, looking sober in the face of our own mortality. All eyes turned toward me and I stepped forward to say a few words, recalling what Rickenbacker told me during the War.

"It doesn't make much sense," I said. "Although we do our best, learn all the tricks in the book, sometimes Fortune takes a hand and we never know what she'll decide. Is it life or death? Do we make it back today, or crash and burn?" I lifted my eyes from the graves to meet each and every one of my people.

"Whatever Fortune decides," I said. "She does it without consulting us. That's why we have to live each day as if it were our last, make each second count. That's why we make our own fortunes in this world, so they aren't made for us. Eddie Lancourt believed in that, and Hanna Ullen learned it in the end. They were valiant comrades who embodied the spirit of our unit, and we salute them."

I raised my hand in salute toward the two silent gravestones and the rest of the squadron did the same. Then they slowly broke up and headed back toward the field where we'd left our planes, to go back to the Pandora and resume their duties. I stood and looked at those two gravestones for a long while.

"Boss?" Jack asked, laying a hand on my shoulder. "You ready to head back?"

"Yeah, yeah," I said.

"I'm ... I'm sorry about Hanna," he said awkwardly. I patted him on the shoulder.

"Yeah, I know."

"Sparks says ol' Pandora took a pretty good pounding from the raid 'n' all," Jack said. "He thinks we should put in for repairs somewhere once we're back on the other side of the Atlantic."

I nodded. "I was thinking about Tortuga," I said. Jack's face brightened a bit.

"Really?"

"Yeah, I think we could all use a break, and we've certainly got the money for it," I grinned. Tortuga was famous throughout the world as a haven for air pirates and mercenaries, a place where anything could be had for the right price. We'd visited before on several occasions. "Besides," I continued,

"Eddie wanted to go there after this caper was over with. I think it'd be only fair for us to go and raise a glass to his memory."

"And Hanna's?" Jack asked.

"Yeah, and Hanna's. We can get some repairs there and maybe even hire on some more crew and dig up some other things. We've got the money, we might as well spend it on something."

Jack laughed, "Boss, Sparks already has a list as long as my arm!" he said. "You'd better catch up with him before he has all of that money spent!"

I smiled. Leave it to Simon to only think about spending a fortune on new toys for him to play with. "We'll have to make sure he takes some shore leave this time," I said, turning to walk slowly away from the graves as the gravedigger began filling them in with shovels of dirt. "The kid takes things way too seriously. There are a couple of ladies I'd like to introduce him to down in Tortuga. He's got to learn to get out there and live a little."

"Sure thing, boss," Jack said, walking beside me.

"Life's too damn short, Jack," I said. That's why we make our own fortunes in this world, so they aren't made for us.

So we headed back to the Pandora, to see what else Fortune had in store.

ABOUT THE AUTHOR

Steve Kenson is known to fans of the Shadowrun® and BattleTech® universes for novels like *Crossroads* and *Ghost of Winter*, as well as his work on various roleplaying games. *Pirate's Gold* is his first novel set in the world of Crimson Skies™. Steve lives with his partner in Merrimack, NH. In addition to roleplaying games and history, his interests include reading (particularly science-fiction, fantasy, and comic books) and working with young people. He's happy to hear from readers, who can contact him at talonmail@aol.com.

PUT AN AIRFORCE ON YOUR DESK!

Want to own the planes flown by Nathan Zachary and the Black Swan but can't afford the real thing? Then give these completely accurate solid-cast models a test-flight. Each model is a highly detailed replica of the fighters flown by the aces of Crimson Skies.

Models come unassembled and unpainted. Available from fine game and hobby stores, or order direct from FASA by visiting **www.fasa.com**